PRAISE FOR

Finnegan Begins Again

"Finnegan's adventures, from his last assignment in Kandahar, Afghanistan, and having to leave the Army and find a "real" job to his managing a key Army procurement program, are hilarious and improbable—but maybe not as improbable as you may think. It's a great treatment of a difficult time in any veteran's transition to civilian life. Ultimately, Finnegan faces the federal bureaucracy mountain. He may not be able to move the mountain, but his climb is uproariously funny."

—Robert Flowers, Lieutenant General, US Army (Ret.)

"Brian Osterndorf's tale of Finnegan's retirement from the Army and starting anew is hilarious. Every retired soldier will see him or herself in this story. His tongue-in-cheek description of the defense acquisition system is masterful, as are the creative 'solutions' Finnegan and Tiger Corp come up with. You are really going to enjoy this, and the acquisition community may learn a thing or two."

—M. Stephen Rhoades, Brigadier General, US Army (Ret.)

"*Finnegan Begins Again* is fiction, but ever so true. Every active or retired member of the military will fully relate to Finnegan's experiences. And if you think military acquisition is dull and dry, read *Finnegan Begins Again*, and you'll find some of the funniest and wildest ideas ever. Thoroughly enjoyable, a laugh on every page."

—Dana Robertson, Colonel, US Army (Ret.)

MORE CRITICAL ACCLAIM

"I've read lots of books, and this is certainly one of them. Some books are great; some are even classics. This one is short. Just not short enough."

—Bill E., Cofounder, Old Farts Beer Drinking Club

"Wait, where is that piece of paper you gave me? Ok, here it is: 'A rollicking good story, with memorable characters, a real page burner!' Oh, that's a 't.' I can't read your damned writing. 'A literary tour de force. If you just copy this and put your name on it, I'll buy the next round of beer.' Did you want me to say that part? You're a cheap SOB and probably won't buy anyway."

—Bill B., Cofounder, Old Farts Beer Drinking Club

"A book? Really? Well, ain't that something."

—Joe, junior but well-qualified member, Old Farts Beer Drinking Club

"This is the best book I've ever read. But I don't remember the other one real well, so it might only be the second best."

—Dana R., retired old curmudgeon in New Hampshire

"You may be a WINNER. Our records indicate that you are among the few winners of the Irish Sweepstakes. Contact the Bank of England through this link to claim your winnings. A&73@ph!)scamme+#/"

—Honorable Panin Thias, Barrister

I decided not to include the Very Critical Acclaim.

Finnegan Begins Again

by Brian Osterndorf

© Copyright 2024 Brian Osterndorf

ISBN 979-8-88824-192-9

All rights reserved. No part of this publication may be reproduced, stored in a retrieval system, or transmitted in any form or by any means—electronic, mechanical, photocopy, recording, or any other—except for brief quotations in printed reviews, without the prior written permission of the author.

This is a work of fiction. All the characters in this book are fictitious, and any resemblance to actual persons, living or dead, is purely coincidental. The names, incidents, dialogue, and opinions expressed are products of the author's imagination and are not to be construed as real.

Published by

3705 Shore Drive
Virginia Beach, VA 23455
800-435-4811
www.koehlerbooks.com

FINNEGAN BEGINS AGAIN

A Sometimes-True Novel

COL. BRIAN OSTERNDORF
US Army (Ret.)

VIRGINIA BEACH
CAPE CHARLES

I DON'T REALLY HAVE ANYONE that I can dedicate this book to. My wife politely—and adamantly—declined, and my daughters said they would change their names. They subsequently did anyway.

But, I wrote it on a Dell™ laptop, using Microsoft Word™. Inspiration was provided by Jack Daniels™. I drove my Toyota™ to deliver a free copy to a couple of my cheap friends after I gassed up at the local Texaco™ station. I sent the manuscript to my agent via FedEx™. So, if any of these companies do endorsement deals, let's get together.

Table of Contents

Preface 4
Part I: army 7
Chapter 1: Apple and Others Let Me Down 8
Chapter 2: A Most Undistinguished Career 13
Chapter 3: Kandahar Swan Song 25
Chapter 4: A Memorable Weekend 41
Chapter 5: Camo'd Up to Buttoned Down 52
Part II: Limbo 77
Chapter 6: Interlude 78
Part III: Army 89
Chapter 7: Opening Battle 90
Chapter 8: Sweet Home 99
Chapter 9: Getting Down to Business 118
Chapter 10: The Business I'm Getting Down To Is Funky 129
Chapter 11: You Say Toe-May-Toe, I Say—
Wait, What Did You Say? 153
Chapter 12: Playing Golf with the Devil 165
Chapter 13: Surprise! 171

Chapter 14: The Attack Commences ... 190

Chapter 15: Did You Know That Blueprints Aren't Really Blue? ... 205

Chapter 16: I Wear a White Hat 'Cause the
　　　Good Guys Always Win ... 219

Epilogue ... 237

Author's Notes, Excuses, and Alibis ... 245

About the Author ... 251

PREFACE

EXCEPT FOR THE TRUE PARTS, this is a work of fiction.

All the characters, including Finnegan, are figments of my imagination, so don't call me, and don't have your lawyers call me. None of them are you. But the characters and the fiction are just the vehicles I use to convey the bigger parts of the story—the parts that not many people know that much about. Even those who think they do. And for those parts, every word is true. About 90 percent of the combinations of the words are true, and so are the vast majority of the sentences. Some of the paragraphs and pages you might have doubts about, but I am entitled to some artistic license because that's what authors do. Besides, I am "truthier" than the network and cable news, and if that's a low bar, it's at least a standard with which you are familiar.

This is a story about the Army. The first part is about the little "a" army, the army that is deployed doing God's work and wears a bayonet to work. The rest of the story is about the big "A" Army, the Army that recruits, trains, and supplies the army and develops and procures the weapons and other systems the army needs to win. Historically, if we develop and procure more weapons that are bigger, faster, and more lethal than those of the bad guy, we win. Lately, some untrained, illiterate, and unwashed buttheads (as Finnegan would call them) haven't read the rules or are just flat-out cheating. Somewhat quickly, the little "a" army noticed and began adapting. Little "a" then turned to big "A" and said it didn't need bigger, faster, and more lethal; it needed more aware and more survivable. Since big "A" is about as nimble as an elephant on roller skates, things became, euphemistically speaking, interesting.

I am retired now, but when I wasn't, I lived a small part of this story. At the time, it was like a knife fight: very personal, not very funny, and it required a great deal of my attention. But now that I have put my knives away, I can afford a different, kinder, and gentler perspective, and I can see that this part of my life was exciting, maddening, frustrating, and damn funny. And I can tell this story now without worrying, too much, about knife-wielding attackers lurking in the shadows. Also, like a lot of (surviving and relatively unwounded) knife-fighters, I started to miss the action and got bored. Writing seemed like a good way to recapture at least the maddening and frustrating part.

And I have an ulterior motive. We ask a lot of our soldiers, and they always respond. But sometimes, like everybody else, bad things can happen to them and their families. It's tougher for soldiers to deal with these problems because they don't get paid a lot and because it's hard for them to approach their leaders and admit they need help. That's why Army Emergency Relief is such a great organization—it's "Soldiers Helping Soldiers." I will donate half of my net proceeds from this book to AER, so if you bought it off the discount shelf, rush right back to the store and demand to pay full price. Or, if you are real clever and want to "soldier up" directly, go to www.armyemergencyrelief.org to learn about AER and donate directly. Because there are some things thirty push-ups and an enthusiastic "Whoo-Aah!" just can't fix.

Be forewarned. I am going to throw a lot of technical jargon at you because, well, it's the Army. I considered including a glossary at the end, but I was afraid I might put Google out of business. Besides, if you can't turn to your neighborhood megagiant information technology monopoly in your time of need, what do you expect me to do for you? Good luck.

PART I
army

CHAPTER 1

Apple and Others Let Me Down

I SLAMMED DOWN THE PHONE. At least I would have if it hadn't been a brand new iPhone that doesn't come with a handset that you can slam into the receiver. But if it did, it would be more useful than any of the million other things Apple puts on its phone. I did jab the red button—real hard—but it wasn't very satisfying, and I doubt the guy at the other end of the call even knew how pissed off I was. If Apple ever comes up with an app that replicates the telephone slam, I would pay big bucks for it. Well, at least ten bucks. I figure I would be using it a lot.

He had answered on the second ring, even though he didn't know who was calling. If he had known it was me, he would have waited until the fifth ring just to let me know he was really busy. It was the same self-confident voice, with just a hint of cultivated snobbery that intimated "Major General James J. Strack, US Army (Retired), West Point Class of 1984, Harvard's Kennedy School of Government, Commander of Men, and Water Walker." But the, "Hi, this is Jim," threw me. I mean, I knew he had a first name, but I had never heard him use it. Even his wife referred to him as "the general." I said hello, and then it was the familiar response with just a very small hint of humility that tells you: "Hey, I'm just a grunt like you."

"Griff, buddy, how're they hanging?"

"Well, they haven't been shot off yet. Thanks for asking."

"You still in Kandahar?"

Not a lucky guess, considering he was the reason I had been in Kandahar. For the third time. In fact, those three tours followed two tours in Iraq, so I had a full house in the poker game nobody wins. About eighteen months earlier, with one more assignment to go before mandatory Army retirement at the ripe old age of forty-four, I was looking for something comfortable that could ease me into an equally comfortable but better-paying civilian job. Jim and I were never really close, but I had worked for him a couple of times, and I guess if I were to call anyone a mentor, it would be him. Turns out I would be calling him a lot of other things.

At the time, Jim had one of those Pentagon jobs reserved for the fast movers. As a result, he attracted lots of other fast movers who wanted to latch on to his trajectory. So I set an appointment to meet with him and brought up the idea of being one of them. Jim put on his tap shoes and began kicking up his heels to some lively tune only he could hear. Turns out, the Pentagon wasn't the place for me; I was a soldier, not a desk jockey, and the Army *really* needed me at the tip of the spear. Et cetera. At least, that was his opinion. Sounded like a woof ticket to me. Sure enough, that fishing line was baited.

"You know, the Army takes care of those that do the hard jobs."

In my right mind, I would never fall for that. After all, I had been doing the hard jobs for twenty-two years, and the Army hadn't done squat for me. At best, they ignored me. More often, they sent me right back to another hard job in another crappy place.

But after twenty-two years, I needed coattails to latch on to, and I never had the good sense to cultivate any of the better-dressed fast movers. So Jim was it, and a few minutes later, I was calling to give the assignments officer the good news. And a week later, Jim retired and went to work the next day for one of the giant government contractors that occasionally make headlines and make gazillions the rest of the time. And that's how it feels when your parachute doesn't open. And the reason for this call.

"Nope, Tampa. Got back two days ago."

"Welcome back, buddy. If you're ever in DC, stop by, and we'll get together."

I decided to jump in with both feet and maybe catch him off guard.

"I was hoping we could talk about me doing something with you. I'm hanging it up and looking for what's next."

Well, somewhere that music started playing again. His ole buck-and-wing went on for about ten minutes, and after about sixteen reasons, excuses, and wherefores, the music must have stopped because Jim concluded with: "So you see how it is." And he wasn't even out of breath.

I was wrong. He wasn't through.

"But hey, I got an idea. You know Duke Earl and Sticks Stapleton?"

No, I didn't, but I knew who they were. Retired major generals who now run the big logistics support programs for the Army. You see, the Army doesn't build, maintain, or operate their infrastructure in war zones; they hire contractors to do that. So all the Army has to do is live there and bitch about it. And the contractors have to do all that work and rake in their gazillions. Oh, and they also have to find and hire the cooks, electricians, dozer operators, laundry specialists, and hundreds of other people needed. Foreign nationals are big favorites since they come cheap, and speaking English isn't a job requirement; it's not even a desired skill. Neither are technical abilities, as far as I can tell. But the site manager is an American, or sometimes an Aussie, because the Army likes to know that when they are bitching at their contractors, somebody actually understands them. And then ignores them. I have outstanding qualifications for that.

"Sure," I said, "we got a standing tee time out at Congressional every Saturday morning. Want to join us?"

I keep confusing sarcasm with subtlety, but I figured either would get the message through. I wasn't interested in establishing permanent residency in Shitcanistan or any other garden spot the Army felt they just had to visit, although a couple of years before, I had been considering exactly that. Good pay and, well, uh—real good pay. But toward the end of my second tour in Kandahar, I started to pick up one of those uncool nicknames, like "Stinky" or "Four-Eyes" or "Booger Breath." Not like "Duke" or "Sticks." Mine was "Mortar Magnet."

I started to notice, as did quite a few others, because it's not like they're a secret, that mortar attacks were increasing and that I was always real close to ground zero. Notwithstanding the nickname's cute alliteration, it really started to bug the hell out of me. Unfortunately, I lost close personal friends. Not that anything bad happened to them; they just decided they didn't want to be close. Same with close personal acquaintances and close personal strangers. The frequency and intensity of the attacks picked up during the last tour, and I was starting to take things personally. My new workout routine was the sprint-like-hell dash and dive-into-a-ditch drill, and I was doing two or three reps a day. Great cardio exercise, as my heart rate was about five hundred beats per second, but the long-term health benefits weren't real apparent.

One day, as I was cowering in a nearby, but never close enough, ditch, it occurred to me that the attacks had started about the time X2 and I decided to divorce. I'll tell you more about X1 and X2 later, and trust me, you can wait. Since X2 is a ruthless and revengeful rhymes-with-witch, I began to suspect that somehow she had hired the local Two Men and a Truck and a Mortar franchise, which, unlike its several competitors, guarantees satisfaction. I know it sounds like paranoia, but when there are loud explosions and flying shrapnel way too near, one's conspiratorial idea juices start to flow. Along with one's bodily waste juices. And there were way too many opportunities to consider the topic.

By the way, you probably have noticed that when there are periodic peaks and lulls in attacks on American troops in Afghanistan, the news networks trot out retired senior military officers to assess their meaning. Invariably, ISIS or the Taliban is "staging a strategic pause to signal an intent to resume peace negotiations" or "escalating their offensive operations to gain and consolidate territory prior to the resumption of peace negotiations" or some variation on that theme. Not even close. I'm pretty sure that these cycles coincided exactly with when I was in or out of the country. And from my vantage point, nose deep—and trying to get ear deep—in some muddy ditch, my theory seemed far more plausible than theirs.

Toward the end of my tour, I got several offers to stay on as a contractor, presented during late-night sessions featuring top-shelf booze. The idea was to loosen me up and show me that the no drinking or fraternization or dope smoking, etc. rules that applied to the Army didn't really apply to contractors, *wink, wink, nod, nod,* and so this is a really cool place to be a contractor. Apparently, if they were able to hire me, they could leave, so the Mortar Magnet matter was never discussed. But it was pretty prominent in my decision-making process, so I politely declined all offers—after we finished off all the booze. But as the well-mannered guest I try to be, I did suggest that my mind wasn't completely made up if they wanted to get together again. And all of the flights from Kandahar back to Tampa were completely painless.

I guess Jim got the message.

"Well, Griff, buddy, keep in touch, and if something comes up, I'll be sure to let you know."

"Hey Jim, thanks . . . And screw you too."

He didn't hear that last part because I had already smashed my hypothetical handset into its theoretical receiver. Come on, Apple. How hard can this be?

CHAPTER 2

A Most Undistinguished Career

I GUESS IT'S TIME TO INTRODUCE MYSELF. Sir or ma'am, I'm Lieutenant Colonel (US Army, Retired) Griffin R. Finnegan.

I am what the military community calls an Army brat. My dad is a retired sergeant first class who drove Army trucks—until his chronic hemorrhoids and several promotions pushed him over to supervising other soldiers who drove Army trucks. Upon reaching twenty years of service, he promptly retired to Fort Leonard Wood, Missouri, and as a civilian, started teaching soldiers to drive Army trucks. If you have never heard of Fort Leonard Wood, you might have heard of Fort Lost in the Woods, which is what it is more commonly called. Frankly, that's a great disservice to a very distinguished Army general, not the nickname, but the fact that the Army chose to name this godforsaken post after him. On the other hand, just about all of the Army posts are godforsaken, so maybe neither he nor I should take offense.

FLW is in the middle of northern Missouri, about halfway between St. Louis and Kansas City on I-44, and if you are partial to hunting and fishing, this is your place. Otherwise, it definitely is not. The nearest town is St. Robert, which is a typical GI town, except much, much smaller. We lived in Waynesville, just a few miles away, because my mom didn't want to raise a family in a town full of sleazy bars, strip joints, and tattoo parlors. And that included raising my dad. I ended up being an only child, except for Dad, so I was the beneficiary of all of her admonitions about avoiding those kinds of places. It must have worked somewhat since I don't have any tattoos.

And yes, my mother is a saint. With one small vice. She is hooked on playing the lottery. All the games, all the time, and she is the world's most unlucky player, having never won even a single time in twenty-five years. Which just convinces her that she is due. My dad and I used to joke—but only just a little—that the lottery's Mega-Jackpots would only be Slightly Greater Than Average-Jackpots if she didn't play.

The Army's Engineer School is located in FLW since they can blow things up and nobody cares, and some basic training units are stationed there, as well as the Army's truck driving school. Several years ago, the Defense Department decided to combine the truck training for all the services there, a decision for which my dad takes full but dubious credit. The logic is that FLW is the ideal place for lots of inexperienced young knuckleheads to learn to drive heavy trucks because no one would care how many wrecks they might have or how much damage they might do since that's what the locals do for fun anyway. In a stroke of genius, the Army also moved the Military Police School to FLW so budding Army cops can learn to write lots of tickets. And to top that off, the Army then moved the Chemical Warfare School from the backwoods of Alabama to FLW because, well, you get the idea.

My prospects, growing up, weren't that great. First of all, I was saddled with the name Griffin. In north-central Missouri, that was different, so it wasn't cool. I could keep calling myself Griff, but when the teachers called on Griffin, all my efforts were for naught. You may ask why I don't use my middle name, and that's a fair question. My middle name is RoyBean. So you may withdraw your question. My mother is a huge Paul Newman fan, and a particular Paul Newman movie came out about the time I was born. I don't know what Paul did wrong in *Cool Hand Luke* or *Hud* or any other movie with a cooler name, but RoyBean is what I was stuck with.

My parents weren't poor, but college was too much of a stretch unless my mother actually hit the jackpot. So, no. And I was a pretty average student unless you consider what that average is for St. Robert and Waynesville, Missouri, and if you do, well, then I wasn't. So a scholarship didn't seem likely, which really didn't faze me that much because I had a better plan anyway.

I could play baseball. Shortstop, second base, pitcher, and I was a really good hitter. Made the high school wrap-up articles in the local papers most weeks; well, at least a guy named Greg Finnegan did. I could never find any reporter in the stands before, during, or after the games, so I guess Coach just sent a report to the papers. I am pretty sure he knew my name, although I never could tell; with his mouth full of chewing tobacco, "Finnegan" generally came out "Frang," or something like that. And he was pretty drunk after the game (actually by about the fifth inning), so no telling what his report called me. I have to give credit to whoever did put the printed item together for getting as close as he did. But Coach was a pretty good coach.

My junior year in high school, a couple of scouts were interested enough to come out and watch me play. I don't think they worked for any particular team, just a couple of "birddogs," who would look at local players and if they thought they had found a gem, would call any of the major league teams that would take their calls. I had a pretty good game: a double and two singles, and I handled all of my fielding chances cleanly. Afterward, I hustled to the parking lot to flag the scouts down just as they were about to pull away.

Turns out they weren't too impressed. One scout said I was too small, but on the flip side, I was also too slow. The other scout said my hands were too small, which is inside-baseball lingo that meant that I would never develop into a really deft fielder. I offered to wear an extra-large fielder's glove, but he just shook his head. What I should have said is: "Wait just a few years, and I'll be injecting so many steroids into these hands, I'll be able to shake your hand up to your elbow." But we didn't know about steroids then, so as their car squealed out of the parking lot, my plans for major league stardom seemed to scatter just like the gravel that kicked up. And hit me in the forehead. You can still see the scar.

So I scratched my plan. But that doesn't mean I was going to jump and do what my dad wanted—become an Army truck driver. We had some pretty spirited but cerebral arguments on the subject (Yes. No. Yes! No!), but I had medical science on my side, so I eventually won out. I told him that hemorrhoids are hereditary, and I am pretty sure I am genetically disposed, so I would be risking my life, and I really couldn't retire at seventeen and become a driving instructor. But from those arguments, a new plan started to develop that would give us each just a little of what we wanted.

Like I said, we weren't exactly poor white trash, despite what the neighbors said as they walked by the several junk cars on our lawn. Just after I was born, my dad bought a 120-acre parcel of prime hunting land just outside the FLW boundary. My mom was none too pleased, but my dad said it was "an investment for the boy." By which he meant himself, but when I was old enough, I would tag along and carry his extra rifle. Well, well, well. Seems that a particular congressman from the 8th District was partial to hunting and was looking for a place outside his own district (we live in the 5th District) to bring his beer-drinking buddies and menace deer, wild turkeys, and hikers without the story making a splash in his own district if things got a little out of hand. So he had been paying $120 a weekend to use the property for the entire time my dad owned it. Now, if you think you see where this is going and that we actually had a sizeable stash that my dad had responsibly socked away, you're way off. That money went to present and future lawn ornament junk cars. But did I mention that the congressman was a trustee of the University of Missouri-Rolla? So now if you think you know where this is headed, you are likely right.

And that's how I ended up with a partial Army ROTC and a partial baseball scholarship for UMO-Rolla. Go Miners. The two partials didn't make a whole, but with the couple of jobs I was able to hold down (I don't claim that I kept the men's sports locker rooms spotless, but you didn't gag when you walked in, so I earned my pay) and my parents continuing to send me my allowance, I was able to pay for tuition, the dormitory and dining hall plan, half or so of the books I was supposed to buy, and enough beer to keep my more generous friends from ditching me completely.

Miraculously, four years later, I had a BS in Engineering degree, a commission as a second lieutenant in the US Army, and a fiancée (the future X1). Not just a commission, but a regular army commission, not a reserve commission. It was a big deal since it meant that the Army was pretty much stuck with me for at least the next four years. And for a whole year, the congressman hunted for free. Logically, with an engineering degree, I would be commissioned in the Corps of Engineers, unless you reckon that a 2.1 GPA might just chip away a little of that logic. Which it did. So I was sporting the crossed rifles of an infantryman on my uniform lapels. I hate to think what a 2.0 GPA would have done to me . . . probably air defense artillery.

My first assignment was to Korea, unaccompanied, so my fiancée was able to continue her studies at UMO-Rolla. I wasn't assigned to the cushy places in Korea, like Seoul and Pusan, but the DMZ (that's Demilitarized Zone, but this is the last time I am going to give you these easy answers). Part of the time, I parked out in one of the two guard posts (GP Collier and GP Oulette) that overlooked Panmunjom, where periodic peace discussions and bitch sessions were held (remember, after the Korean War, we really only made a truce with North Korea and it's not like it counted for anything). The GPs also overlooked likely North Korean attack avenues through the DMZ and into South Korea. A GP consists of a concrete bunker/observation post, lots of ditches to hide in while the North shelled you, and most importantly, a telephone that linked directly back to a battalion command operations center. Since we didn't yet have the technology to encrypt our communications, we had to resort to an elaborate code to alert them that the North was attacking. The code words were: "Oh, SHIT!" If the next part of the transmission was in Korean, the operations center had what we call "confirmation" and would begin implementing an elaborate plan for the defense of South Korea.

The plan started with a staged withdrawal of US and South Korean forces from the DMZ across the Imjin River on the only bridge in our sector. The *You've got to be kidding me*ly named "Freedom Bridge." And if I didn't happen to be in one of the GPs when the attack started (if I was, I had about twenty seconds to live), my platoon and I were to hold the northern approach to the bridge, pass friendly troops through, and identify to the nervous engineer lieutenant who was supposed to blow up the bridge, when the last friendlies (i.e., me) had passed. There were just a few minor flaws that nagged at me.

A. I didn't know who the last friendlies (other than me) were supposed to be.
B. The North Koreans weren't read in on the plan and probably were going to try and cut the line.
C. The engineer lieutenant, who I had never met, likely wasn't too sure just how friendly I was; if I didn't get my ass over the bridge now, the last friendly unit was going to be the one that had just already crossed.

But I needn't have worried. Higher headquarters had anticipated that the fog of war was going to hang heavily along the Imjin River banks and had positioned just about every artillery unit in South Korea about five miles south of the bridge with orders to fire just about every artillery round in South Korea at the bridge. Since the artillery units would have no earthly idea of when or if friendlies had crossed, they would fire when they damned well pleased, blowing friendlies, unfriendlies, the uncommitted, the bridge, and any water buffalo wandering by all to hell. Welcome to the Army, 2nd Lt. Finnegan.

For the next twenty-one years, I got to hop around to various Army bases across the country and in Germany. I really liked the ones in Germany because, try as they might, the Army couldn't find really ugly spots to base American soldiers, and if some of the spots were a bit below standards (German, not American), they were still real close to very pretty German towns with very pretty German women and very pretty breweries. The rest of the assignments, it was ugly American bases next to ugly American towns with Miller beer cases from the PX. And it took a lot of those to make the women pretty.

Somewhere along the line (about 1993, give or take a year or two), X1 and I got married. She had decided to continue her studies, and her single focus on master's and then doctorate degrees kept her from committing wholly to marriage, or so she claimed. That focus emerged during or shortly after her junior year spring break trip to Cancun and a day trip tour of the ancient Mayan ruins in Chichen Itza. So while her spring break buddies didn't think much of one of the new wonders of the world, X1 was inspired. That inspiration was based on the simple premise that since nobody knew how those now-extinct Mayans lived, what they did, or where they went, she could make lots of things up, and nobody could prove her wrong. A second simple premise was that Chichen Itza is really close to Cancun—and a long way from Army bases—and margaritas are absolutely wonderful. So for the next four years, in none too rapid succession, she produced a master's degree thesis and a doctoral dissertation about "Patterns of Something or Other of the Ancient Mayans" (the *something or other* part is a real word, but I can never remember what it is). The task must have been difficult because it required multiple trips to Cancun, and on one of those occasions, a trip to Chichen Itza to take the pictures she included in her papers. The pictures consisted exclusively of her posing in a bikini in front of old ruins. In one of the pictures, the old ruin was her dissertation advisor.

Apparently, *all* of her efforts comprised satisfactory academic rigor, and she became Dr. X1. At which point she discovered that none of the great universities, fair to middling colleges, or anyone else was at all interested in establishing a department of Mayan studies. X1 thought this was extremely unfair in that there were departments to study every other race, creed, ethnicity, religion, language, or favorite boy band, but apparently academia draws the line at extinct cultures on the completely reasonable grounds that student recruitment would be difficult. So marrying me became the consolation prize, and I said, "I do," she said, "I don't know what else to do," the justice of the peace said, "Close enough," and we embarked on married life in the Army. After five years of inflicting the complete spectrum of military operations on one another, from low-intensity conflict to nuclear war, we divorced.

At which point, X1 got her second great inspiration and developed the now world-famous Ancient Mayan Diet, authoring several books that sold very well because she was a doctor and instantly credible. After the opening two sentences, the book just seemed to write itself: "Have you ever seen a fat ancient Mayan? Well, have you?" Seems that the world was just waiting for a coconut and leafy plant-based diet favored (because there was nothing else around) by an extinct culture where everybody died by age forty and whose tallest member topped out at about five feet, two inches. Amazingly, the diet works extremely well, especially if you run up and down the 365 steps of the Chichen Itza stone temple every day. I have to give her credit; X1 did walk the walk. On the back page of every one of her books is a picture of her in Coco Loco, one of the Cancun bars, holding a coconut. With a straw and a tiny umbrella sticking out. For a brief time, she gained international fame as the one who, taking a page out of Jimmy Buffet's book, coined the phrase: "Hey, it's Cinco de Mayo somewhere." Nobody knew what that meant except her and her bartender, but it sounded so cool it became everyone's go-to phrase until Paris Hilton said something equally forgettable a couple of weeks later. I really do wish her well. Paris, not X1.

Of course, there were also my obligatory, "by invitation only," all-expense paid trips to Panama (Operation Just Cause—dirty, stinky, hot and humid), Iraq (Operation Desert Storm—dirty, surprisingly cold in January and February, followed by hot and then really hot because the Army thought I should stay until June), Somalia (Operation Restore Hope—dirty, stinky, hot, humid), and Bosnia (Operation Joint Endeavour—dirty, stinky, cold, and the only one in which I didn't live in a tent. I didn't exactly get an upgrade since I lived in the basement beneath the bombed-out 1984 Olympic swimming pool in Sarajevo; nobody had bothered to empty the pool, so my suite came with a perpetually wet floor and soggy sleeping bag). In Bosnia, I developed my frothing-at-the-mouth hatred of the media when I saw some CNN commentator (we had a dayroom where we could watch week-old American TV news) say something witty about how the first casualty of war is truth. Other than the fact that he didn't invent the phrase—it probably started after Og threw a rock at Ug, who then hit Og with a stick—he couldn't have been more wrong. The first casualties of war are windows since there didn't seem to be a single one still intact in all of Sarajevo. Truth had died many years earlier.

I still get really pissed off at journalists who try to analyze military operations, but to me, come off as stupid, invariably wrong, and utterly sanctimonious. The world would be a much better place if that type of analysis was left to retired military professionals, who also don't know what's going on, are just as invariably wrong but look far less stupid saying it.

I did miss out on Operation Iraqi Freedom—or Iraq War II, the sequel, if you don't keep up with operational names. For some reason that still baffles a lot of people, the Army selected me to attend the Command and General Staff College (CGSC) in Fort Leavenworth, Kansas. Ft. Leavenworth, not to be confused with Fort Leonard Wood, is an old, remote cavalry post notably famous for its Buffalo Soldiers, the famed all-Black (except for its leaders) 10th Cavalry Regiment. The Army has done a real good job of preserving some of the historical flavor and all of the remoteness of the original base.

Normally, this year-long study of how to be a good Army staff officer—planning, writing orders, doing studies, presenting PowerPoint slides—would have been too innocuous to include in this litany of my military achievements. Leavenworth isn't that dirty, hot or cold, or stinky, and I didn't live in a tent. I didn't wear a bayonet to work. And there weren't any artillery battalions waiting to blow me up if I didn't beat the North Koreans in the 100-meter bridge dash.

But two important things happened that year. First, I was introduced to the fact that there is a big "A" Army. CGSC is like that nondenominational megachurch in that it takes in captains and majors from all over the Army, preaches at them, baptizes them, blesses them, and then sends them forth to do God's work, each in their own way. And we got to all sit around and listen to how everyone in the flock (or Army) was important, and couldn't you please tell us all about it. Of course, I didn't give a shit, not even a small turd. Much to my subsequent regret. So I graduated with my accustomed bottom-third of the class ranking, earning such laudatory instructor comments as: "Major Finnegan is the student I would most like to be with in the trenches, and then leave there when I moved on," and "Major Finnegan has surpassed the zenith of his potential," which sounds good if you don't read it twice.

And then I met X2. She was a West Point graduate and military police officer, with previous assignments at West Point (because you know how rowdy those cadets can get), the Pentagon (because you know how rowdy those generals can get), and Fort Bragg (well, yeah, those guys can get pretty rowdy). In between, she had managed to get a master's degree in criminal justice and was well on her way to getting her law degree before being tagged to teach social sciences at West Point. She paid attention in class, always did the homework, and was the favorite to be the honor graduate. And she took an interest in me, or at least returned my interest in her, so she had her faults too.

I was fresh from my divorce from X1, so you would think that I would know better. Actually, I have no idea why you would think that now that you are pretty familiar with my life up to this point. Maybe it's because X2 looks so much like X1. Both are tall, blonde, and mean, so maybe I go for a certain type. But there are subtle differences:

X1 is tall, naturally blonde, and her meanness comes from a bottle.

X2 is tall, her blondeness comes from a bottle, and she is naturally mean.

Maybe I did miss just one little hint. About halfway through the course, the Army notified students of what their subsequent assignment would be. Mine was no mystery—head to Central Command Headquarters for subsequent reassignment TBD (Oh, come on. You have to know this one). Some may have held out hope that it would be a relatively pleasant assignment in Qatar or UAE, but this smelled very much like either Iraq or Afghanistan, and of course it was. On the other hand, X2 got orders to Eighth Army Headquarters in Yongsan, Korea, a relatively plush assignment in the Land of the Morning Calm. This news made her absolutely batshit crazy, as she had pulled strings and called in favors to line up an assignment with Third Army Headquarters in Atlanta. After calling her assignment officer and determining that (a) he had not made a mistake and (b) he was of dubious parentage, she marched right over to the Ft. Leavenworth personnel office and submitted her resignation, effective immediately. We expected this to be just a bit problematic since the Army usually requires a little more notice, and upon accepting an assignment to CGSC, an officer acknowledges a commitment of at least two more years of service. To our great surprise, the Army quickly accepted the resignation.

Yep, definitely missed that hint.

About that same time, X1 finally signed and sent me our divorce papers. She demonstrated that she had mastered Spanish by including a paragraph they don't teach in school. Not appreciating my bilingual skills, she'd thoughtfully included the English translation on the back of the page. My unaided translation was real close.

Two weeks later, X2 and I got married. I said, "I do," she said, "Oh, what the hell," the justice of the peace said, "Close enough," and we promptly began our reenactment of Ali vs. Frazier 2. That was the one without the cool nickname (i.e., not Bout 1's "Fight of the Century" or Bout 3's "Thrilla in Manila"). Our version starred her as Smokin' Joe and me as Ali. And in Ali-Frazier 2, Frazier knocked out Ali. So by the time I got to Tampa, she was already enrolled in the University of Kansas Law School, and any hope of reconciliation, or even a cessation of hostilities, had vanished.

Like X1, X2 proved to be remarkably resilient and recovered quickly after our divorce. She graduated Cum Laude, passed the Kansas bar, and is now a senior partner in a personal injury law firm with clients in Kansas and Missouri, where she zealously chases ambulances carrying patients allegedly injured by out-of-control Army truck drivers based in Fort Leonard Wood. And somewhere in her office, amongst all her law books, is a ragged copy of the Afghanistan Yellow Pages with one page that shows signs of very heavy use.

CHAPTER 3

Kandahar Swan Song

THIS WAS MY THIRD ASSIGNMENT TO TAMPA, nominally. The first time, after CGSC, I hung around about a year; there was a place on the Central Command staff for a CGSC graduate that was eager but not too aggressive. After that year of what should have been a three-year assignment, the chief of staff and I decided that I would be more valuable—and less of a pain in his ass—in Afghanistan.

Actually, he decided, and I didn't get a vote.

The next two times, the residing chief of staff was able to arrive at the same decision quicker, sight unseen. So, to begin my last tour in the Army, I was bussed to the out-processing station and was POMmed. (Okay, this is a tough one, so I'll cut you some slack—processed for overseas movement.) This is a fairly short process made infinitely longer because there are about a thousand soldiers in line and two clerks to conduct the process. When it was finally my turn, I turned over my medical records to show that I had undergone my annual physical within the last six months, checked the box to affirm I wasn't pregnant, updated my Serviceman's Group Life Insurance information and upped the amount to the max (thus keeping Mom in lottery money for a year while she mourns my untimely demise), and presented my half-filled yellow shot booklet to the medic. And when he started writing down all the shots I needed, I gave him the other two filled ones. He smirked, I smirked, and he moved me to the final station, where a clerk double-checked everything that had already been checked. And twenty-four hours later, I was up, up, and away.

I clambered down the ramp of the large C-5A transport plane, costumed in a desert camouflage uniform with the sleeves rolled down, a helmet, a large rucksack, a gas mask (really?), and a big shit-eating grin. After sharing the nine-hour flight with twenty others, several large pallet loads of equipment and materiel, and an unhappy flight crew of National Guardsmen, we touched down in Kandahar. I don't know why the flight crew was so unhappy; they would overnight in VIP accommodations reserved for flight crews and fly home tomorrow morning. The rest of us would begin serving our one-year sentence.

Can't figure out why I was happy? Me neither, but I just was. Maybe it was the contentment of being in a familiar place, but I doubt it because this place sucks. As I shuffled to the rear of the plane, where they had just lowered the cargo ramp, I was already beginning to sweat; the temperature on the tarmac was a cozy ninety-five degrees, which in fact was almost welcome after nearly freezing to death in the unheated cargo hold. I grabbed my duffle bag and started dragging it to the inspection station.

And it hit me. I was where I wanted to be. I had come full cycle.

I wasn't a ROAD warrior; I had seen too many of my contemporaries with their sights on completing twenty years and then checking out, "retire on active duty." They were the slugs that barely passed the physical fitness and weight limit tests, never quite finished assignments on time, looked sloppy in their uniform, and generally sat around with a permanent "I don't give a damn" attitude. I was going to leave on my own terms. Somewhere, Frank Sinatra was singing "My Way," and I started humming along.

Full cycle. Korea to Kandahar. Then: Unheated Quonset hut, lousy food, bad guys crawling all around, one year to go before I could get back to civilization. Now: Uncooled tent, lousy food, bad guys crawling all around, one year to go before I could get back to civilization. I guess the thing about a full cycle is that if you start out in a crappy place, that's where you end up.

Man, this is going to be a depressing chapter.

The destination of my duffle bag drag was the inspection station tent, where MPs would go through all of your things to look for contraband. Because in a country full of guns, bombs, and about 90 percent of the world's opium production, there is no room for booze, dirty magazines, funny-looking pills, or Cuban cigars. One doesn't have to memorize the list of contraband items since it is posted on a big sign at the tent entrance. With a smaller sign that says: *Violators will be prosecuted.* And that prompts someone in every group to ask: "What are they going to do, send me to Afghanistan?" I'm sure the MPs never get tired of that one.

I passed inspection with flying colors because Cuban cigars rewrapped in Honduran cigar wrappers don't even raise an eyebrow. Since this was my third time through, I pretty much knew what I could get away with. Even Fidel can't tell the difference between a Honduran and a Cuban cigar without the wrapper. But an MP that opens your cough medicine bottle and sniffs can tell the difference between Robitussin and Jack Daniels. However, he can't tell the difference between a bottle full of Robitussin and a bottle full of mostly Smirnoff and a little Robitussin. Especially when I am coughing in his face. Pardon me.

Anyway, I call my syrupy vodka cocktail an "Amnesty Box" after the big metal box positioned at the entrance of the inspection station, where newbies and West Pointers can slink up and deposit contraband before being searched. The second-, third-, and and-counting-timers, and the devious, don't make deposits, and as the years of our Afghan Adventure mounted, amnesty boxes were less and less filled. But filled enough to keep the MPs from bitching about the place far less than the rest of us.

Most of the soldiers will then wait for their units to come by with a truck and drive them to the in-processing station. Lieutenant colonels have enough status that the unit will send over a Humvee, and the driver will load the bags and drive him to the in-processing station, where he'll be first in line. Unless he is still sitting on a bench at the inspection station ninety minutes later. I didn't mind; I was already on the clock.

So I got a chance to look around and see what had changed. Nothing. Kandahar base sits in a large desert-like plateau beneath a bunch of hills that look like thousands of years ago a giant took a series of craps and didn't bother flushing. Over the years, the crap hills somewhat hardened and got covered with a bunch of dirt, but no vegetation ever grew. Must be something he ate. Somewhere down the road lies the city of Kandahar, the capital of Kandahar Province, in the southeastern part of Afghanistan, so Mr. Kandahar must have been a pretty important guy way back when. I frankly don't think the whole province has much going for it, but the Taliban seem to like it, so we set up a base here just to find out what the attraction is. Still looking.

Kandahar is about the worst place in Afghanistan, but there are lots of close runners-up. Wherever the Marines and Special Forces are don't count because those are the kind of places they like. The first best-worst place to be is the big, sprawling base at Bagram, located just about twenty-five miles north of Kabul, the capital city. Bagram isn't just big; it's huge with two extra-long runways, warehouses, paved streets, real buildings, reliable power and internet, latrines and showers that work, and ice cream in the mess hall. It houses between ten and fifteen thousand soldiers, airmen, and contractors and is the logistical hub for US forces in Afghanistan. It was originally built by the Soviets, but relatively speaking, it appears to be operated by Disney, and all of us kiddies really wanted to be stationed there. Sometimes, even when you wish upon a star, your dreams really do kick you in the nuts, and so for me, it was Kandahar 3, Bagram 0.

Once, when I was assigned to CENTCOM HQ, they sent me to Kabul to assess force protection at the several small US bases there. These bases may not be operated by Disney, but I had several thrilling rides from the airport to those bases and back again.

Apparently I was tall enough to ride but not so tall as to go without parental supervision; in this case, Mom and Dad were played by a couple of burly majors decked out from head to toe in Kevlar and sporting some really cool automatic weapons while the make-believe pumpkin-carriage was an armored Humvee, heavily armored in the front, lightly armored in the back, where I sat. The two majors kept up a running commentary as we sped through Kabul, never stopping at intersections and never giving other vehicles and pedestrians an even break. Kabul has paved roads; that is, the pavement is about three feet long between thousands of the world's largest potholes. My instructions were to watch from four to eight on the imaginary clock surrounding the vehicle, or our back third. The Humvee frame blocked from four to five and from seven to eight, and I felt that I was letting the fellas down, but since they didn't give me a weapon, there wasn't much I could do for them anyway but yell, "Look out!" Apparently, what we were looking out for were buttheads who might try to run up and shoot us, bomb us, or sell us a rug, and the accepted response (within the Rules of Engagement) was for the majors to blast away should anyone approach too closely. I guess the results of this policy were positive, at least for the Americans, so the shooters, bombers, and small businessmen kept their distance.

As a result of being super-vigilant, I didn't get a chance to see much of Kabul except to note that it looked like any other third-world city that had been ravaged by war for decades and considered bombing the most effective means of urban renewal. There were several two- or three-story buildings, but some of them might have been garbage piles. It was hard to tell the difference. Somebody should start a nongovernmental organization, Sanitation Workers Without Borders. Other than that, Kabul is probably the most civilized place in Afghanistan, so my congratulations to the local chamber of commerce; keep up the good work.

In my then sixteen years in the Army, I had been given orders that ran the gamut from ridiculous to absurd to insane, but the majors seemed like they wanted to expand the spectrum and invent their own category. In the event that we were attacked, and they became "hors de combat," I was to make sure that I destroyed the radio. I guess we didn't want the Taliban to be able to listen in on our conversations because they might be able to make more sense of them than we could. I gave the majors a thumbs-up and kept my eyes open for a restaurant so I could use the radio to call for lamb kebob takeout and invite any attackers to lunch. Preferably a restaurant that delivers via helicopter gunship.

The force protection inspections went well, and after a couple of days, the rides between the bases became only mildly exciting. After a week, the majors dropped me back at Kabul International for the day-and-a-half trip back to Tampa, where I submitted a very positive report, concluding that there wasn't a need for follow-up inspections for at least two years.

But here I was, back in Kandahar for another tour in Afghanistan. My ride finally arrived, and after apologizing in a way I didn't find particularly sincere, drove me to the in-processing tent. I slid into the end of the line, right next to the two large containers of toothpaste, toothbrushes, deodorant, socks, toilet paper packets, shaving cream, peanut butter, and a whole bunch of other goodies that a grateful nation had sent to "any soldier." So I stuffed my pockets with about four months' worth, including sanitary napkins, which are pretty efficient earmuffs at bedtime. There were lots of cards and pictures from cute kids too, so thanks, Kaylee and Hunter of Mrs. Thornburgh's 3rd Grade Class in Dubuque, and I was thinking of you too.

Processing consisted of basically rechecking my assignment orders and providing an emergency point of contact name. After some thought, I gave them X2's name and address, thinking that after she got the news of my passing, and the week-long celebration that followed, she might cancel the mortar contract, and I would become a posthumous hero, saving dozens of lives.

A clerk gave me the news that I had been assigned to base

headquarters, working in the operations division. I asked the name of the chief of the division (J3 in military parlance), and I didn't know him, which at least partially explains why I was assigned there.

My official title was force protection officer, which was just ambiguous enough to get away without having to do very much. On the flip side, it was just ambiguous enough to get assigned all the shit jobs that didn't fit with any other section and that nobody else wanted. I guess they thought they were dealing with a real rube because I mostly just responded that I was working on a special project for the general. Since there were about five generals hanging around doing Lord knows what, and the J3 wasn't real anxious to start quizzing all of them about what they were doing with Finnegan, I skated through pretty easily.

The real part of my job, that is, the part that didn't consist of dodging work, was to "plan, implement, and monitor" all the things we were doing, or needed to do, to keep the bad guys out and the good guys in. So I would ride around looking for holes in the fences, watch the guards at the gate admit and search the trucks that came in and out of the base, turn on and test various sirens in the middle of the night, and generally be a nuisance to everyone else trying to do their jobs.

There were a couple of neat things about my job. For one, I was in charge of the radar section that would detect and track incoming bad guy artillery and mortar rounds; the radars could rapidly back-calculate the trajectory and thus determine the firing location of incoming rounds. And then we could either return fire or send out helicopter gunships. This was music to my ears, which I hoped I would now be able to keep out of the foot-deep mud in the ditches I had gotten used to diving into. As the world's most advanced technological fighting force, you would expect the radar system to work extremely well. And it did. If the radar operator was awake and paying attention, the time it took to detect, calculate, and locate the mortar location was only just slightly longer than the mortar round flight time plus the time it took two men to load a mortar into a truck and skedaddle without a trace.

The J3 interpreted *force protection* pretty loosely, so he lumped oversight of the new arrival inspection station into my job description, which meant I was also in charge of the MPs there. For about six months I was successfully able to ignore any of those duties, until there was a spate of soldiers getting caught with booze, funny cigarettes, and dirty magazines in their tents. This made the commanding general unhappy, who vented to the deputy commanding general, who took the chief of staff to task, who blasted the J3, who, eschewing the precedent of aimed, pinpoint fire, nuked the whole section, including and especially me. And this made everybody from the general on down to me very unhappy. But after twenty-one-and-a-half years in the Army, and with an engineering degree that enabled me to figure out which direction shit flowed, I lit into the fat turd of a MP major who was downhill from me. Besides, I suspected him of hoarding all the confiscated dirty magazines, if for no other reason than he looked like that type. In the Army, the shit flows downhill, but somehow, the solution to the problem is supposed to come from the guy at the bottom, notwithstanding the fact that he is probably clueless, while the bosses at the top have all the smarts and experience. So, not wanting to upset honored tradition, I let the MP major sweat for a couple of days and then snuck into the inspection station tent after midnight and replaced the existing *Violators Will Be Prosecuted* sign with one that said *Violators Will Have Their Tour Of Duty In Kandahar Extended By One Year*. Within a week, the amnesty box was overflowing, and two more were added. There weren't any more illicit contraband incidents, and everyone was happy, especially the MPs whose own caches were replenished.

The most fun times were at the end of the month because that's when the circus came to town: dogs, ponies, dancing bears, and congressional delegations or CO-DELs. CO-DELs were popular at the end of the month, not because the congressmen gave a hoot about which days they visited, but because that's when their military escorts recommended they visit. You see, the military provides a monthly combat pay allowance for those deployed to a designated combat zone, and Tampa, where the escorts usually come from, isn't so designated. Which just means that Congress hasn't been counting the bodies in Tampa grocery stores on double-coupon days. So, the military escorts can most easily collect two months of combat pay by visiting a designated combat zone on the last day of one month and the first day of the next. Most everybody hates the CO-DELs, except the top generals who get to cozy up with congressmen who ultimately approve their promotions and me. I think they're highly entertaining, or at least they break up the monotony a bit.

Upon arriving, the delegation and entourage are given a base tour, followed by a PowerPoint briefing on why we are here, what we are doing, and why God is so happy with our efforts. Followed by lunch. As a group, the congressmen will insist on no special status or treatment; they will stand in the chow line just like the rest of us. Of course, the mess sergeant has been holding the line out of sight behind the mess hall, and the congressmen fall in behind about three or four people in line instead of the usual couple hundred. And then they wait just a bit while their thick steak is cooked to order. The rest of us will get a steak-like piece of meat that has been sitting in the steam table tray for two to four hours, but hey, it's better than the usual fare. The congressmen then will be ushered to special tables where they will lunch with soldiers from their congressional districts or states. These soldiers are hand-picked because (a) they are the most junior and therefore least likely to cause trouble and (b) can be expected to offer up nothing more than name, rank, and hometown and under no circumstances complain about all the things the Army is supposed to be providing but isn't.

After lunch, there are more briefings, including on topics the congressmen might have expressed an interest in to their escorts. If that interest had anything remotely to do with force protection, I got to be the circus ringmaster for a while and herded figurative dogs, ponies, and dancing bears through their acts while dressed as chart after chart of statistics and while my buddies were making obscene gestures at the back of the room. The women were the worst.

Every time the briefings finally came to a merciful end, the congressmen would thank us and tell us how proud they were of us. Since I am pretty good at reading the nonverbal part of the message, I know they were really saying: "If I have to sit through one more briefing, I'll get PTSD." And the briefers would thank the congressmen for visiting and for all the support they were providing us in Congress and hope that the congressmen weren't equally good at reading nonverbal messaging.

And then they would be trundled off to their waiting planes and fly to Bagram, where they would get another tour, more briefings, be treated to steak *and* lobster, and put to bed in visiting VIP quarters. The mint on the pillow is always a nice touch.

Since my duties weren't usually overwhelming (or even whelming), I had plenty of time to think about things, especially at night. My most frequent musings were about which equally unappealing entrée I would have for dinner or which equally distant latrine I would run to in the middle of the night when I inevitably chose wrong. But sometimes my thoughts ran really deep, like when I considered what the hell the US was doing in Afghanistan in the first place.

Understand that the Army doesn't encourage its grunts to have these types of deep thoughts; deep thinking is reserved for the water walkers and graduates of the Army's Deep Thoughts and Advanced Strategy School. The honor graduates are the ones who smoke pipes and have never had an assignment outside of Washington, DC.

Although my thoughts are decidedly shallow, I do have the advantage of having been in places where the consequences of the much more deeply thought-out strategies are real apparent. So it occurred to me that our strategy is completely wrong. I don't mean to disparage the Army's large-butted pipe smokers, but if after twenty years, you have already come to the same conclusion, it's hardly my fault. Back in 2001, when all the terrorists decided to play hide-and-seek in Afghanistan, we covered our eyes, counted to ten, and decided to play too. Since, once the Soviets left, there was nothing worth blowing up in Afghanistan, the terrorists would have had to travel to someplace else to do their thing. And that's when we could nab them; just look for the guys wearing the traditional *pakol* hat and carrying an AK-47 under their clothes. It's guaranteed to work everywhere *but* Afghanistan, where this particular Taliban clothing line is extremely popular and available in men's, women's and, unfortunately, kids' sizes with three-day free delivery. Thank you, Amazon.

Instead, we invaded Afghanistan, set up lots of bases, schemed to drive the terrorists *out* of Afghanistan, and suddenly the buttheads had lots of things to blow up right in their own backyards. I don't want to sell our deep thinkers short because they had probably already figured this out; their grand strategy is to put a few of our nation's finest at great risk and keep the buttheads distracted, thereby greatly reducing the risks for everyone else. So how's that working out? Not so grand because terrorists have learned how to multitask and become nuisances just about everywhere else in the Middle East. And once in a while, they open up international offices. I bet my old chum Jim Buddy and his Pentagon Pals never thought about things that way and are probably regretting they didn't give me a big Pentagon office to slap all these deeply shallow thoughts into a PowerPoint briefing. Well, thank you, Mr. President, and yes, yes, I did think of this all by myself. In the meantime, I kept marking Xes on my short-timer calendar.

About the time there were only three un-X'd months left, I began to feel guilty about not having done anything yet to find something to do after I retired. A month later, the guilt reached the point where I felt like I needed to do something about it. And then, a month later, I actually did something about it. The steady march of progress.

I had no idea what I wanted to do, where I wanted to live, or who might want to hire me. The second question seemed like it might be the easiest to figure out; I didn't particularly like anywhere I'd ever been, so there was a whole lot left over, and I made the decision that location would not be a factor in my job search—except for places where there were Army bases. Anyplace the Army thought was so God-awful that it deserved a base was a place I didn't want to be. Feeling a grand sense of accomplishment, I knocked off thinking any more about it for a week.

When the guilt started in on me again, I searched various job websites to see if anything just jumped out at me and screamed: "Griff, this is for you." Internet service wasn't very good even when it worked, which it mostly didn't. It didn't really make much difference if I was trying to use the internet in the evening or two o'clock in the morning; I'd get about twenty minutes of slow downloads before the system would crap out, and I'd lose everything. The websites weren't screaming anything at me, but I was sure letting them have it.

A big problem with these websites is that you can't search on anything like "job for Griff" or "retiring lieutenant colonel willing to work for food" and come up with anything useful, although the latter search got me a lot of emails willing to help me enhance my manhood. You have to have some kind of a starting point, and I began to regret my decision to not settle on a location. That got me more depressed, and I didn't get over that for another couple of days.

So I took another approach and started working on a résumé. The first step was to figure out what a résumé looked like, and there are only about a thousand different formats floating around the web. I looked at several different examples, hoping to find one that looked like I could slip in the things I had been doing for twenty-two years (that is, the good parts), and found a résumé of an engineer colonel that looked pretty impressive. We didn't have much in common, but I liked the way he could fit his job history, accomplishments, and education into two pages and make it look like there was a whole lot of good stuff left out. I figured I could get to two pages, but I would have to use a larger font and not leave anything out. Which might work in my favor since I didn't know what prospective employers were looking for anyway, and my extra duties as vermin control officer while I was in Korea just might be my ticket.

I finished my résumé the next day and was pretty pleased, although spell-check didn't think too highly of my acronyms, punctuation, and some of the places I had been. Thankfully, there is no computer feature that checks content, or I might just have given up altogether. But I polished a bit here and tweaked a bit there and toned down my accomplishments from having won Desert Storm single-handedly to acknowledging that a few others may have helped a bit and ultimately dumped the vermin control part because it put me one line over onto a third page.

Finally, X's filled up my short-timer calendar, and I awoke early and sat outside in the predawn, smoking the last Havana that I had been saving. It was pretty dried out, and the tobacco leaf kept flaking off on my tongue; best smoke I've ever had. The butt was down to about an eighth of an inch, so I kicked out a shallow grave and rendered full military honors (minus the three-gun salute) at its burial. I grabbed my half-full duffle bag, slung it over my shoulder, and started to saunter to the marshaling area, where we fortunate few were about to leave.

The first mortar round was closer than usual—about the closest it had been all year. The nearest ditch was about two hundred yards away, and I set a new personal best record for the dash and dive. It was a three-round affair; my cigar butt had gotten full military honors after all. Somebody should write a book about all the weird things that come into peoples' minds when they are being shelled. My theory is that the weirdness of the thoughts correlates inversely with how messed up that person's mind is once the shelling stops. I sure hope I'm right because that means I'm going to be just fine.

After a minute, I stood up and then collapsed back into the ditch, laughing uncontrollably, and if forced to admit it, I was blubbering like a baby too. I must have been quite the spectacle because a number of ditchmates kept staring, although none seemed inclined to come over to see if I'd been hit. I hadn't; this was sheer relief. I had made it through the year unscathed. For almost three months, there hadn't been more than one mortar attack per day, and the bastards had missed. Laughing, crying, whatever, I stood up and breathed deeply and then heard the "whump, whump, whump" again. This time, the rounds were falling much farther away, at the other side of the base. The buttheads had upped their game: two attacks in a row and on the same day. This could be a bad omen. Or, this could be X2 getting a 10 percent discount on her bill for a referral.

When the excitement was over, I did my customary check; I was intact, but there was a four-inch-long rip in my right trouser leg. I briefly thought about changing uniforms but decided against it. After twenty-two years, this is what I had to show for . . . for . . . for whatever it was I was showing, and everyone else deserved to see it. I headed to the out-processing station, picked up my orders, and caught a ride to the airfield.

Prior to boarding, we all had to go through the inspection station again, so I got into another line. One more thing the Army does real well is form lines. If every day of my Army career was like today, I figured I must have been in at least thirty thousand lines. Somehow, as large as that number is, it seems low. The turd MP major fell in behind me.

There is a different set of contraband articles going the other way: explosives, ammunition, captured weapons, classified information, and a lot more. It didn't really make any difference to me; the plane wasn't going to leave until everybody got through. I had long since run out of vodka, and my last Cuban was now reposing peacefully. So I dumped my duffle bag out on the inspection table, and out fell about a half dozen dirty magazines. I just stood there, frozen. The regular contraband rules still applied; circumstantially, if they were in someone's possession upon leaving, they had to have been in that someone's possession while still in Afghanistan. I didn't have to be Perry Mason to realize that the giggling major behind me had enacted his revenge.

A new MP major appeared at the inspection table, took a quick look and suggested that I might prefer going to the end of the line and trying again. I still just stood there, dumbfounded, but she nodded toward the rear, and I finally got it. The turd was just about doubled over with laughter, so I gathered up my stuff, turned around, and jabbed him in the ribs, causing him to double up all the way but didn't interrupt the laughter. The new MP major escorted me to a new line, which conveniently formed right in front of the amnesty box, and the magazines flew in.

She also pulled out a roll of duct tape and told me to roll up my torn trouser leg. "No way you're getting on the plane looking like that. The officer in charge will boot you off. Let me fix it."

I conceded the point, but only because yesterday I had literally turned in my pistol and figuratively turned in the means of gentle persuasion I would have used to convince the OIC that he could make me an exception to the rule.

Repairs were made, and I got to the inspection table hoping there weren't any more surprises. There was, but it wasn't unpleasant. The female MP major elbowed the MP inspector aside and told him to take a break, and while thoroughly going through all my items, and thankfully not finding any more contraband, she slipped a dark plastic water bottle into the duffle bag as I was cramming my stuff back in.

"A little something to calm you down and keep you from committing murder. We're not all like that asshole, so think kindly of MPs." And she winked.

By this time, I had been high and low so many times already that I was dizzy, and I kind of hoped that the water bottle was full of Dramamine tablets.

"Yeah, thanks," was the best that I could manage.

Because of all the extra-curricular activities, I was the last to board, and the better seats had all been taken. There are only bad, worse, and worst seats to begin with, but the absolute worst is the one next to the "bathroom." The bathroom consisted of two vertical tubes that stick out the bottom of the plane. One tube is dick high, and the other is shorter, with a large funnel-type plate over the top for all other purposes. But you can't sit on the plate; it is a "squat tube." Completing the designer look is a box of paper towels and two cases of water, all behind a gray shower curtain. Shortly after take-off, the following was certain:

A. Every woman, upon drawing back the curtain, would find it necessary to let all the passengers and crew know just how unacceptable the arrangement was. A couple would believe that all of the people in the part of Asia that we were flying over were similarly entitled to know.
B. Everyone would line up for an opportunity to piss on Afghanistan.
C. About half of the women and most of the men would miss the tubes, and, well, the steel aircraft deck wasn't absorbent, so about halfway through the flight, the proximate passengers would be enacting emergency flood control measures.

Rank has its privileges, so I found the MP major and rousted him out of his seat. He had an idea about stomping my toes as he went by but missed, mainly because my toes were in the boot that was just then making solid contact with his ankle. He limped away but pulled rank on some captain, and for the next fifteen minutes we all played musical chairs while the copilot yelled that we wouldn't leave until everyone was seated. And eventually we were, but not all happily.

The mystery water bottle contained a very fine Kentucky bourbon. I'm partial to Jack, but being broadminded, I could see myself becoming more geographically diverse in my tastes—by one state, anyway.

The flight may have been the worst in recorded aviation history. I wouldn't know. My last conscious thoughts were kindly ones about MPs. Great Americans, just like I've always said.

CHAPTER 4

A Memorable Weekend

THE HEADQUARTERS OF THE US CENTRAL COMMAND is on MacDill Air Force Base. MacDill Air Force Base is in Tampa, Florida. Let that sink in for a bit. Notice that I didn't say, "Godforsaken MacDill" or "Lost-In-The-Woods" Air Force Base. And it's a very nice base, with nice new buildings, excellent housing for its officers and airmen, and a beautiful golf course.

The Army and Air Force have two distinct attitudes about operating and maintaining their bases. The Army's attitude is that they spend so much on tanks and soldiers and training that they can't afford to spend anything on their stateside bases. The Air Force approach is that they spend so much on airplanes and weapons systems and airmen that nobody cares how much they spend on stateside bases. I don't think the Air Force is very military, but I can't say they aren't smart.

Before landing, the plane crew chief had warned us that we had been on a long flight (no shit?), were jet-lagged, etc. and that we shouldn't try to overdo it our first night back. Naturally, most of the soldiers heard only the "overdo it" part and considered it an order. Since we arrived about 0900 on an August Friday, on about the hottest day of the year, the Army arrivals coordinator told me and the other separating soldiers that we would have the weekend off and we were to report to the Army personnel office at 0800 on Monday morning.

Being a little older and a little wiser and having already overdone it thanks to my water bottle, I was content to catch a ride to the VIP Transient Quarters and check in. August in Tampa is a guarantee that there is, literally, room in the inn. The Air Force stocks its VIP quarters with decent booze, not top-shelf, but decent, so I opened the drawer to where it is normally kept and found a sign instead. *Due to recent DOD regulations, this facility will no longer provide alcoholic spirits to our guests.* Disappointment gave way to gratitude as I next opened the refrigerator and found two six-packs (minus two cans) that must have been left behind by a previous guest. I knocked the inventory down to eight and thought about what to do next.

Since I had most of the day and wanted to adjust to the new time zone, I put on a semi-clean uniform and walked over to the PX, bought a pair of shorts and a couple of T-shirts, and rented a car. Next stop was the Verizon concession booth, and after an hour, I walked away with a new phone and the cheapest plan they had, leaving behind the booth attendant who couldn't believe I wasn't on three or four social media sites and didn't want to be. I didn't bother changing and instead drove to the storage facility where I had rented a unit and piled all of my worldly possessions. Thankfully, as every storage unit in Tampa has to be, it was climate-controlled and after checking in at the front desk, I parked in front of the unit, unlocked it, and lifted the roll-up door.

I've eaten my own cooking, the X's cooking for the few months they felt like doing any, and Army MREs, and I've been to places that fall just a bit short of meeting basic sanitation standards, so I have a stronger constitution than most. The facility attendant, who followed me to the storage unit, was not similarly advantaged and started puking all over the back of my trousers and boots. Well, that was the tipping point for me, and I proceeded to do the same all over the front of my trousers and boots. In his subsequent haste to depart the premises, he slipped on the now well-lubricated concrete floor, executing a near-perfect takeout slide that put us both rolling around on the floor.

Forensic evidence suggested that in the past few weeks a large cat had somehow gotten into the unit and subsequently forgot how he had done so, making his exit a bit problematic, and before he died, he deposited a couple of large piles of cat shit. Coincidentally, about the same time, the block of storage units, of which mine was a part, had lost power for the better part of a week. In Tampa. In July. Besides the stink, the black mold on the walls was a good indication that the whole Finnegan estate had taken a spectacular fall. I expected a hazmat team at any moment.

The attendant was long gone, and after a while, my stomach settled down to the point I was able to assess the damage. The few items of furniture I had were so moldy one couldn't even determine the original colors. Clothes just fell apart in my hands. Every boy needs a hobby, and mine was a fairly sizeable LP collection of rock, jazz, and country classics; the records were so badly warped they looked like parabolas instead of disks, and the covers were slimy green paper. Other items were just plain unrecognizable.

I picked up my golf bag and it fell apart, with clubs and balls falling to the floor. Somebody watching the facility security video is just busting a gut watching a puke-covered, screaming maniac chasing down golf balls rolling down the street. The only other survivor was a sealed plastic bag in which I had hidden my Army dress blues hanging bag. Inside was an old pair of shit-kicker boots that looked like the shit had been kicking back, but they were my faithful old boots, and even those that don't like me acknowledge that I am loyal to old friends. X2 had sworn to throw them away if she ever saw them again. She didn't have anything in particular against boots; she had the same attitude about most things I owned. Inside the boots was a bonus. I found my wadded-up Grateful Dead T-shirt, which also had been on X2's hit list. So I threw the dozen golf clubs and about fifteen loose golf balls, along with the boots and T-shirt into the trunk and headed back to the facility office.

The attendant looked like he had mostly recovered but was still sweating heavily.

"Hey man, we was going to contact you but knowed you was out of the country, and we didn't have no way to get to hold of you."

My file was on his desk, and I beat him to it. Inside, stapled to the contract, was my contact information through the CENTCOM duty desk, as well as a letter addressed to me with a yellow Post-it note saying: *Put on stamp and send.*

"Oh man, I guess there ain't nothing more to say. Your contract says we'll pay you ten cent per pound for damage an' I figure they is about five-hundred pound."

Calmly, as I was wiping the puke from my pants legs on the office furniture, I suggested he contact the manager.

"Hey now, you quit that. I'm the manager."

"Good. Now we can negotiate. I figure that there are two thousand pounds, and in the interest of good customer relations and to keep me from wiping my boots off on your ass, you would want to pay me a quarter a pound."

I could see the brain wheels turning. I was two feet away, there was a low counter that I could go over or around in about two seconds, and he could see that my boots were very much in need of a good cleaning.

"Okay, I'll send you a check for two hundred dollars."

I narrowed the distance between us to about three inches.

"That's *five* hundred dollars, and I'll take the check now. You don't seem to be very good at mailing things."

The wheels were turning again, but it was taking more time than a crisp "yes, sir" would have required.

"You know, now that I think about it, it probably was closer to five thousand pounds, and a dollar a pound seems much more fair to me."

That got the wheels going much faster and he reached into a drawer and pulled out his checkbook.

"While you're making out my check, give me a piece of paper and a pen, and we'll make a little agreement about what will happen should you try to cancel the check when I walk out."

"No, sir. Wouldn't do that. We has us an arrangement."

"Yes, we do. And since we are now such good friends, I'll let you come with me to my bank while I cash this check, but if you are too busy, just sign this paper saying you'll pay me five thousand dollars if I have to come back due to a change in our *arrangement*."

And with that, a check, and a signed statement, I headed to my car with all my worldly possessions rolling around in the trunk.

"Say, you can jus' throw all your stuff into the dumpster at the end of the street."

"Nope, I can't do that. It's not mine; you just bought it all. And I wouldn't touch it if I were you. The EPA is on its way over and will have to examine the scene, and they'd probably arrest you if you moved anything and spread the contagion. I've gotta get to the hospital now because I think we inhaled enough of that toxic mold to do some serious harm. I figure we have about twenty minutes to get a shot of Vagisil, or we're goners. Remember, that's Vagisil. It will save your life!"

I squealed the tires as I drove off, keeping my eyes on the rearview mirror, and just before turning the corner and heading out of sight, I could see him running toward his car.

By this time, the jet lag, the puke-covered uniform, and the excitement of finding all that I had owned in the world completely ruined had just about done me in. I headed back to the transient quarters, downed a couple of beers, and turned on the TV with the idea of making it until at least nine o'clock and thus be pretty much back on a normal sleep cycle. I got all the way to 6:30, and the last thing I remember was the weather girl with the big smile whipping through charts showing "what a fabulous day it will be tomorrow."

The pouring rain woke me up around five in the morning. Same news set, different weather person explaining—with the requisite charts—that today was going to be a complete washout. I remember the days when the weather was presented by a good-looking girl in a tight dress who would invariably refer to either a high or a low-pressure system and Stradivarius clouds or whatever and point to a map that had either a big smiling sun or a frowning rain cloud plastered on it. Today, the weather is presented by degreed meteorologists, who look, frankly, like someone who would study meteorology in college, and they have all kinds of devices and gadgets that zoom in, out, over, and under, changing screens just before you can register what it is they had been pointing at. And they still never get it right. Well, that's what you think when you wake up in a foul mood. The least they could do was apologize for ruining my day.

So I had to put Plan B into effect. As soon as I figured out what that would be. Since my wardrobe consisted of about six pairs of battle dress uniforms, including the puke-covered one I had thrown in the corner, a Grateful Dead T-shirt, what I had just picked up in the PX, and an old pair of boots, I decided to spend a rainy day outfitting myself in what I imagined the well-dressed business executive would have in his closet. But since I hadn't been peeking into any successful businessman's closet lately, I turned the matter over to Google. I hadn't realized that the entire US business community was now comprised of twenty-three-year-old males with hair buns, wearing too-tight, too-short suits without ties and standing around with their hands in their pockets. The good news was that the job market competition didn't seem too formidable.

Google also helpfully gave a nearby address for fine men's fashions, and shortly after it opened, I pulled into one of several open parking spots on the street. I don't normally associate fine men's clothing stores as being between a strip joint and a tattoo parlor, but there was plenty of parking at nine o'clock, so I went in. The store clerk seemed pretty surprised that anyone would walk into the store at that ungodly hour. At least he did after I shook him awake.

"Yo, wassup?"

"I'm looking for a couple of business suits."

He registered his skepticism in the usual way. "No shit?"

At this point, I was beginning to share his skepticism. The place didn't quite have that middle-aged businessman look about it unless that business was pimping.

"Man, you don't look like no playa. You look like a cop." But since his hands stayed in sight, I didn't dash for the door.

"Man, I'm not, and now that we both have figured out I'm in the wrong place, where should a nonplaya like me be?"

He directed me across town to the old White guys' store, the name of which he couldn't remember but said I couldn't miss it because there would be a bunch of old White guys hanging out. Which he thought was pretty funny, so we both laughed at that for a bit. His laugh was a little more enthusiastic than mine. I suggested that maybe it was Brooks Brothers, and he started laughing again because "Ain't no brothers hanging there," and I started laughing too because that was funny.

And twenty minutes later, I found the old White guys hanging out at the old White guys' store and bought a black suit, a blue blazer, a couple of dress shirts, ties, and dress trousers and headed back to MacDill. I hung up my new wardrobe in the closet and then headed back to the same part of town because I realized that I had forgotten dress shoes. I added black wingtips and a pair of casual shoes to my wardrobe and headed back to MacDill again and upon arriving, I promptly turned back around, but this time only as far as the neighborhood Walmart for a belt, socks, underwear, toiletries, and another tie just because I thought Tabasco bottles on a tie was pretty funny. I also stopped at my favorite cigar store, where I found out that Cuban cigars were now legal. And more expensive now than when they were illegal. Looks like the Cubans have discovered capitalism. I passed on the Cubans and bought a box of Dominican Macanudo Churchills because, as I am sure somebody has already said, "Life is too short for bad booze or cheap cigars." My corollary is that the difference between very good and insanely expensive only matters if you can tell the difference. This reminded me that my next stop needed to be the liquor store for a fifth of Jack Daniels Old No.

7 because I haven't tasted anything better at any price.

My last stop for the day was the MacDill commissary because I had about a week of out-processing ahead, and eating out alone three times a day wasn't going to be fun. The military commissary is the GI grocery store, and what it lacks in frills, certain brands, and about a quarter of what you are looking for, it makes up for in price.

It takes a brave man to try and shop at the commissary on a Saturday. Retirees shop every day, active duty can only find time on the weekends, and every single National Guardsman or Reservist who is supposed to be training that weekend is in the commissary instead. Or the dispensary, food court, bowling alley, gym, or any other place except where they should be. And nobody can figure out why Reserve component readiness sucks. Anyway, store managers take the maximum capacity signs down on Saturdays, and most of the cashiers call in sick. The aisles are about one-and-a-half shopping carts wide, so it really doesn't matter much if retirees park in the middle and read the ingredient labels on every item they may or may not put in their cart, even if they had read them two days before. I parked my cart as unobtrusively as I could, went to the meat counter and got five steaks, put them in the cart, picked up five potatoes for baking, remembered the garlic salt (I think that may be a first for me), got a dozen eggs, and because it was on my mind, a bottle of Tabasco. It took me two hours to get through the checkout line, and I was exhausted; you have to give it to the retirees and their stamina. And in one week, I would be one of them.

After cooking the steak (and setting off the smoke alarm, which I promptly disabled), the baked potato, and saying something appropriately sacrosanct as I opened the bottle of Jack, I enjoyed dinner while rewatching the Duke classic *Red River* on the Western channel. I conked out about eight o'clock, but not before checking the weather channel and seeing that the rain was likely to continue all of Sunday. I fell asleep pretty confident that tomorrow would be a nice day.

And it was; beautiful sunshine and the return of the high heat and humidity that makes Tampa such a lovely place in August. This suited me just fine because today was a golf day, and the heat and humidity would keep most sane golfers away. Which is only about 50 percent but enough to make a difference. The optimum time to show up to a golf course on a Sunday morning is about ten thirty because the regulars that play every day at six thirty have cleared out and the churchgoers haven't yet shown up. I arrived at the MacDill course around nine thirty, bought a new bag, shoes, and two dozen golf balls and took my paper bag of the old golf balls rattling around in my trunk out to the practice range. The results weren't promising, and I half suspected that I should have bought a new set of clubs too, but the other half of my suspicions remained rooted in the basic premise that crappy swings are club independent.

I had made a cardboard sign that read: *JUST BACK FROM A-STAN. LEAVE ME ALONE* and fastened it to the front of my golf cart. The starter, I suspect more out of empathy than intimidation, waved me ahead of the foursome that had a ten thirty tee time, and I pulled up to the first tee. Two drives (and one mulligan) later, I was somewhere in the left rough and thinking that two dozen golf balls might not be enough. I looked just long enough to find a ball that wasn't mine, hacked my way into the fairway, and proceeded to put some distance between me and the following foursome.

There is just something about golf that always picked me up. Hitting a golf ball three hundred yards is great stress relief. Or 240-ish yards. And even better when I hit them straight-ish. All in all, after a year of not playing, it wasn't a bad day. I had a spectacular shot on the twelfth hole where I drove the ball onto the green and made the putt (second try) for an eagle. Unfortunately, I was actually playing the eighth hole and duck-hooked my drive onto the twelfth green. I recorded the eagle on my scorecard anyway. Now, for those who have played the North Course at MacDill, you may be thinking that I would have had to slice, not hook, my ball on the eighth hole to pull off such a feat. However, you fail to consider that I am left-handed, which probably explains a lot of the things you have been wondering about me.

Several years ago, I personally invented a variation of the ancient and honorable rules of golf whereby I and anybody I was playing with would take a swig of Jack after each shot, gimme putts excepted. That way, low score wins, high score wins, and everybody goes home happy. God, I love golf.

The perfect day was marred by one slight mishap. As you know, on very hot and humid days, it's important to keep oneself properly hydrated, and believe it or not, half a bottle of Jack doesn't fill the bill. Consequently, while pulling up to the eighteenth green, I got a bad cramp in my right leg, causing me to straighten it and put weight on it, which is normally a good move unless one is driving a golf cart and the foot of the cramping leg is on the accelerator. On a positive note, I was going fast enough to make it all the way through the sand trap without getting stuck, but on the flip side, the cart stalled on the green. And just in case nobody noticed that some idiot had just driven a cart onto the green right in front of the clubhouse, they probably didn't miss said idiot flopping around on the green while trying to get the cramp out. In short order, a couple of golfers came over and rolled the cart off the green, got me to my feet, and handed me my clubs.

"Don't worry, buddy, happens more than you think. Welcome back."

I mustered a weak grin and limped to my car. I got about a mile when I realized that my half bottle of Jack was missing. Son of a bitch.

Somehow, I got home, and three gallons of water, two more cramps, and a hot shower later, I finally faced up to doing something about my future. I grudgingly admitted to myself that I had been screwing off and that it was totally unreasonable to think that something would just fall into my lap this week. I spent an hour reviewing job sites and another hour editing my résumé several times before deciding the edits didn't make it any better and taking a selfie that I pasted into my résumé. And that didn't help my résumé either unless a picture taken at about chin level and pointing upward of a face on which sunscreen had been haphazardly applied and then had been in the sun for five hours is just what you are looking for. So, upon reconsidering, I figured that hoping something would fall into my lap was a perfectly reasonable course of action, whipped up some scrambled eggs with Tabasco, and went to bed. I didn't even give a shit about the weather tomorrow.

CHAPTER 5

Camo'd Up to Buttoned Down

I ARRIVED AT THE ARMY PERSONNEL CENTER promptly at seven thirty for my eight o'clock appointment because in the Army, if you are on time, you're late. Which meant I only had an hour and a half to wait. Apparently, Monday morning is admin time for the administrators, followed by a safety briefing. Really. I guess word processors count as heavy equipment because you never know when one will back over you without sounding its backup horn. The rest of the admin time was devoted to writing each other up for Purple Hearts because the coffee was too strong that morning.

Administratively, retiring meant filling out a bunch of forms, being briefed that your Serviceman's Group Life Insurance would cease on the actual date of retirement, and receiving your retired military identification card. The retired ID card is blue and looks just like the classic green ID card for active duty personnel, except nobody has that anymore as it has been replaced by a Common Access Card (CAC), which has a computer chip in it. At this point, there is nothing the chip can access, but the rumor was that it contained vital information like your blood type. The old card also had blood type printed right on it, which could be read directly in an emergency without trying to find a card reader. I presume that no one could figure out why retirees would need a chip, so we remain predigital.

With my retirement ID card, I got a list of the benefits I would continue to receive, which mostly didn't matter to me. I am not much of a shopper, so commissary and PX benefits don't float my boat, and there were a couple of benefits I didn't use while on active duty and saw no reason to use while retired. So the retirement ID basically would allow me to get on to a nearby military base and renew the ID before it expired.

However, there are two very valuable benefits. First, all of the military bases have golf courses, and many have two full courses. They aren't among the top 100 courses in the world, but the only membership requirement is a military ID, and greens fees are generally only a couple of bucks. Check!

The very best thing about continuing to receive military benefits is the Class VI store. Let me explain. The Army categorizes the things it provides by classes: Class I, Class II, etc. Generally, no one cares about the classes of supply and just orders chow, bullets, spare parts, etc. The exception is Class VI, which is technically "personal demand items," but everyone knows it is just booze. The Class VI store is the military liquor store. And as much as soldiers complain about the Army, and every aspect of the Army, and all the people in the Army, no one has ever complained about the Class VI store. The shelves are stocked with wine, beer, and spirits from around the world, from the very best to the very passable, all at significant discounts and without tax. Although I had no desire to live anywhere near a military base, a road trip with a pickup, a couple thousand dollars, and a military ID card a couple of times a year was definitely part of the plan. And don't discount the secondary benefits. The Class VI store is the military equivalent of a state 529 College Tuition Savings Plan. Over the years, soldiers, provided they "invested" enough, would be able to save for at least one and probably more college tuitions. Many the time I would be near enough to military family housing to hear the familiar: "Hey hon, how about stopping by the fridge and bringing me another cold credit hour?"

Back at the personnel office, a clerk went over my military record and prepared the DD Form 214, which is the official record of discharge. The DD 214 contained all my vital service information, like the date of entry into active service and the computations of how much total time I had served, which would be important in calculating my retired pension and VA benefits. The Army is now transitioning to a different system that reduces pensions but allows soldiers to invest in a 401K instead. Luckily, that didn't affect me, and if it had, I would have been pissed off. It's not that I don't understand and appreciate 401Ks; it's just that when things start to go to hell in Shitcanistan, the stock market invariably tanks, putting the soldier's financial future in jeopardy at the same time the Army is preparing to send him there and put his breathing present in jeopardy.

The DD214 also contains a record of all the awards and decorations I had received over my twenty-two years, and it suitably impressed the administrative clerk who wanted to start a conversation about it while she was entering the data, which means that the first two attempts at completing the form were full of mistakes. The most important part of the DD214, as far as I was concerned, was the calculation of days of accrued leave, which are vacation days I had earned but not used. The Army gives you a choice of taking the lump sum payout of the value of those accrued days or going on "terminal leave" and being paid as if I were still on active duty while in a vacation status. I had the clerk verify that the Army couldn't recall me and send me to Afghanistan for a couple of weeks while I was on terminal leave and then had her call over her supervisor to confirm her verification. I was about to call over the supervisor's supervisor just to be sure, but the clerk had already marked my terminal leave choice and gave the DD214 to me for signature. And then gave me fifty copies to provide to whoever might need to know that I had been honorably discharged. Which so far has been nobody, including the waitresses at Denny's who give out free breakfasts on Veteran's Day.

The next stop was the finance office, where I decided to be on my best behavior (such as it is) because pissing those people off could really get me screwed over. We went over my terminal leave options again, and I just smiled and took the leave rather than the payout option without pressing for a validated, confirmed verification. I gave them my bank account information for direct deposit, indicating that it was the same one that I had been using for the last twenty-two years, but was very pleasant in making that point so the clerk didn't seem too put out. The calculation of my monthly retirement pay (pension) got a little sticky.

Normally, a military retiree, under the old system, received 50 percent of their active duty pay after twenty years and then an additional 5 percent for every full year after that. Or in my case, 60 percent. Or in my case, not 60 percent.

A family court judge decides a divorce case, which means I'd had the pleasure two different times. As a rule, these judges are partial to military wives who give up careers to share their husband's military life and thus, the reasoning goes, are entitled to hefty compensation. That's a polite way of saying the military husband gets royally screwed.

The first time, with X1, the judge heard both of our sides and then asked X1 if she was a real doctor, by which he meant, "Are you a medical doctor, in which case you gave up a lucrative practice for the benefit of your husband?" And X1 answered "Yes," by which she meant "No." I objected, but the judge reminded me that this was an administrative hearing and that I couldn't object. So the judge awarded her one-half of my retirement pay for the five years we were together.

I was smarter the second time and brought my divorce attorney to the hearing. X2 presented her case, which was that basically, she had given up her promising military career and was thus entitled to half of my military pay for the ten years she gave up, plus half for the two years we were together. My lawyer, well-schooled in the difference between administrative and nonadministrative hearings, kept interjecting with the apparently more proper legal term: "That's bullshit!" This had the same basic effect as objecting because the judge just told X2 to continue her presentation. And awarded her what she asked for.

After the hearing, my lawyer tried to get away, but I was too quick and cornered him in the court lobby. I guess he was worried that I would be upset, but I wasn't since at that point, retirement pay didn't seem real to me. I did have a couple of questions, and when he figured out he would live through my interview, he was quite forthcoming.

"I don't get it. Why didn't she ask for alimony or something?"

"Well, she makes a hell of a lot more than you do. The judge wouldn't go for alimony."

"Oh, yeah. But why retirement pay? That's years away, and why does everybody think I'll stick around the Army until I can retire anyway?"

I guess that seemed to him to be the equivalent of a *Why is the grass green, and why is the sky blue?* line of questioning.

"I don't know you as well as she does, but I can't figure out what else you would do. And it looks like she figures the same."

"Well, if you're so damn smart, how come she won?"

"She may be that much more damned smart than me, but I don't think so. This was a highly unusual outcome, so there must be something going on."

And a month later, he called to tell me that X2 and the judge had gotten married and that this was a clear case of breach of judicial conduct, so he was going to call the state bar association and lots of other things. When he finally came up for air, I told him to just drop it. That judge was about to be punished more cruelly than any state bar association could ever manage.

The math on how to allocate my retirement pay was just a bit more than the finance clerk could figure out, so after a conference of several echelons of supervisors, we finally figured out that I would be getting 37 percent of my active duty pay, and I would authorize monthly allotments to X1 and X2 for their shares. And that's when the divorce hearing decisions became very real to me.

The finance clerk finished up her processing by confirming yet again my bank account information, had me sign another bunch of forms, handed me copies of everything, and provided a printout of what I could expect to receive for my first monthly retirement pay. I think I still have that printout, but because of the tear stains, it's pretty hard to read.

That was all that was on my schedule for the day, so I drove back to my room, changed clothes, and headed out to the local municipal golf course, figuring that there were wanted posters featuring my likeness plastered all around the MacDill course. The starter linked me up with an older couple who kept me entertained with stories of grandkids, gallbladders, and scandalous behavior at their retirement facility. We exchanged names but promptly forgot, so they were Sir and Ma'am, and I was Lefty, and a pleasant afternoon was had by all.

The next day I showed up at the base hospital for my retirement physical. The physical is one of the most important events for separating soldiers in that a military doctor will determine the extent, if any, of any physical disability that may be attributable to military service. For most soldiers being discharged, the disability pay the VA pays out, based on the doctor's disability percentage determination (and subsequent medical board review), is a tax-free monthly payment. The disability percentage requirement for this payment is pretty low—a determination of 10 percent disability is all it takes to get the check, and at this end of the determination spectrum, the docs are pretty lenient.

But for military retirees, things get more complicated. I'm not sure why I would have ever expected anything different. Even though the Army pays the retirement pay and the VA is responsible for disability benefits, most retirees only get the retirement pay (actually they get both, but the retirement pay is reduced by the disability pay amount). It might be the only example of collaboration between different government agencies. The rules can be explained in about ten pages (actually they can be explained in two pages, but if they *can* be explained in ten, they will be), but in a nutshell, here they are:

A. Retirees get both retirement and disability pay if the disability determination is 50 percent or greater.
B. If the disability is a result of combat wounds, the above number is 40 percent.
C. For the rest, "Thank you for your service. You should have been less careful."

And now the doctors aren't so lenient. The retiree finds himself in a sort of catch-22 situation; logically, over twenty years of physically and mentally strenuous, remote, and sometimes dangerous life will take their toll on joints, eyesight, hearing, nerves, and God knows what else. Maybe gallbladders. On the other hand, if that retiree has been passing annual physical exams and fitness tests and still serving on active duty, what half of him is disabled? And if he doesn't pass, he is discharged, likely before becoming retirement eligible. So barring some catastrophic accident or sudden illness that strikes twenty minutes before the retirement physical, it's awful tough to make the cut.

It's kind of like paying income taxes. For all but one day a year, you want to be one of the richest people in the world and play the market like Warren Buffett. On April 15, you want to be a minimum wage employee with twelve dependents and the guy on Wall Street that Warren Buffett keeps beating the crap out. And today was the "I want to be a physical and mental wreck" day.

I took a seat in the hospital lobby next to two sergeants first class waiting for their retirement physicals. It is a mark of Army professionalism that three days from rank becoming irrelevant, I was still "Sir," and they were still "Sergeant." But that didn't mean we couldn't become chummy, especially since the waiting time was running to about two hours. So after swapping some Army stories about been there, done that, we turned to gaming the retirement physical.

"Knees are the thing. Everybody over forty has bad knees. And hips, remember the hips."

"Eyes and ears are good too. Don't forget blood pressure. I drank four cups of coffee before coming here. How about you, sir? You got any good ideas?"

I offered up gallbladders while wishing the old golfing couple from yesterday could have had a few more serious afflictions. About ten years before, I had sprained my right ankle playing touch football, but other than that, my medical record was about as thin as a comic book. Even my vision was still twenty-twenty, and I could follow any conversation I cared to pay attention to.

"I think I'll try ankles. Maybe it's different enough the doc will give me some originality points."

That got some knowing nods. Officers are supposed to have all the good ideas, and I was happy that I didn't disappoint.

"Well, as long as you get ole Doc Swanson, you should do all right. Most of the other docs are too new to have a book on. If you get Patterson, forget it. You could come in with your head chopped off, and he'd still give you 10 percent because if you're infantry, you don't need a head. Ha, ha."

"And you get nothing if your dick got blown off because you don't need that either. Ha, ha."

I don't know what conversations civilians have, but I doubt they spend much time talking about getting their dicks blown off. Or if they do, they aren't laughing about it. I'm going to miss the camaraderie.

Oh, and fart jokes. A bunch of good guys sitting around with about 5 six-packs telling fart jokes with accompanying auditory and olfactory embellishments. Yeah, I'll miss that too.

After a while, each of the sergeants was called to the exam rooms and thirty or so minutes later came out, giving me a thumbs-up as they went out clutching thick folders of medical records and, presumably, favorable disability determinations. So maybe this would be my day after all.

When I had checked in, I was given a worksheet that guided me through all the things that I should discuss with the doctor if

I felt I might have an issue. It looked kind of like a Chinese menu, so I selected one from each column: skeletal and muscular—ankles, sensory—hearing and vision, mental—trouble sleeping at night, and threw in shortness of breath just because I was more tired after my five-mile runs than when I was twenty-one. I didn't find anything to check about gallbladders. I had to ponder the ankle business a little, trying to figure out whether I should mark right or left. I finally decided that they were both in this with me together and checked both.

After about two hours, it was my turn, and an orderly was standing by to escort me to the exam room. I hadn't thought the ankle business through carefully because while I can convincingly limp on one leg, I realized I didn't know how to fake limps in both legs at the same time. The best I could do was a kind of drunk old guy shuffle, mainly because I had some practice at that. The orderly shuffled along as well, keeping pace, and must have thought my problem was that I had to take a dump because he asked if I needed to use the restroom first. I said yes and crow-hopped into the men's room, where I banged each ankle against the stall several times and came out with a much more convincing shuffle.

We passed by Lt. Col. (Dr.) Swanson's office and several others and entered the exam room adjacent to Maj. (Dr.) Patterson's office. I tried to remember whether Patterson was the good or bad doc, and I concluded that because he was still only a major that he was either a hard-ass bucking for promotion or an *I don't give a shit guy* who had been passed over for promotion. When I got a crisp "Come in and sit down" from him when I entered the room, I knew I was screwed.

I'm not Catholic, and I have never been to Confession. But I kind of imagine that the priest isn't too interested in alibis and excuses. "Father, I have sinned, but it really wasn't my fault. You see, there I was . . ."

The mere act of entering the confessional booth and sitting down is a presumption of guilt. Just say your piece, receive your sentence, get the hell out (oops, get the heck out), and say your Hail Marys.

That's about how my session with Dr. Patterson went.

"Yeah, doc, my ankles have been bothering me for years."

"Uh-huh."

"You see, we were mortared every day, and I had night sweats, and some days I couldn't sleep at all."

"Hmm."

"Lately my headaches have been getting worse, my vision gets blurry, and sometimes I just don't know if I can go on."

"Oh."

"How do you come down on gallbladders? Good or bad?"

No comment, so I didn't tell him about the pain in the ass I was developing.

He finished making some marks in my record, closed it up, poked and prodded me a couple of times, and called for the orderly to take me to audiology for my hearing test. I didn't bother limping this time.

The audiologist sat me in the booth and told me that she would play a bunch of sounds that sounded either like beeps or hums or squeals and that if I heard something in my left ear, I should raise my left hand. Right ear sounds should bring about right-hand raisings, and if I heard sounds in both ears, I was to raise both hands. And if I heard music, I should do the hokeypokey. She didn't actually say that last part, but it seemed to follow.

She started the test, and I ignored the first couple of low hums and then the first couple of high-pitched squeals. She gave me a kind of quizzical look, so I mouthed: "Have you started yet?" At which point she gave the dial a wicked twist to the right, and I went from my seat to my knees while trying to rip the headphones off, nearly strangling myself in the attempt. At some point, she sneaked into the booth without me seeing her and smashed a meat cleaver into my brain.

Somehow, I made it back into the chair and kept both arms raised because the ringing in both ears was drowning out whatever beeps, hums, and squeals she was causing and the whimpering and sobbing that was all me. Apparently that was satisfactory behavior because the test was soon over, and the orderly came to lead me to the optometrist. I wasn't going to take any chances, so I read the damn eye chart to the 20/15 line and thanked everybody in the room several times. I think there was only the optometrist in the room, but there were several thousand voices, so they all got a thank you.

Back to meet again with Dr. Patterson. He reviewed the vision and hearing test results, registering nothing at the former, and I detected just a bit of a smile at the latter. He clipped them into my folder, closed it with a snap, and then swiveled his chair around to me and delivered the verdict.

"I'll give you ten percent for the ankles and ten for the hearing loss. (Mentally, I figured that was 1 percent for the hearing loss I had when I came in and 9 percent for the loss they inflicted.) A couple years down the road, you'll have to have something done to the right ankle, but most of the hearing loss will come back in a day or two."

And now the smile was clearly there. I suppose that if my new sergeant buddies were still in the lobby, I would give them a thumbs-up. It wasn't 50 percent, and in fact, from a net pay standpoint, it was the equivalent of zero, but I felt that I had beaten the system.

He proceeded to tell me that his determination was only preliminary and would have to be confirmed by a medical board. Their determination would be final, but if I thought it unfair, I could seek redress blah, blah, blah.

I still had a couple of hours left, so I headed back to my room to rest because although the pounding in my ears was subsiding, it had been replaced by a headache that was getting worse. And speaking of headaches, it reminded me that I needed to call my divorce lawyer and fill him in on the retirement pay calculations.

It took a couple of tries, but his secretary finally said that he was in and put me through. I wasn't sure he remembered me, but I brought him up to speed and asked if he or I needed to notify the courts about how much retirement pay I would be getting and what arrangements I had made for allotments. He started taking notes and asked how everything else was going.

"Oh, peachy. I'm retiring, haven't got a job, all my worldly possessions are hazardous waste, only got twenty percent disability, and I'm three days away from being homeless."

"Uh-huh. Okay, send me the retirement pay forms, and I'll make the notifications. Wait, what did you say about disability?"

That was odd. In my recitation of woes, that seemed to be the one that was almost good news, but that was what he'd latched on to.

"My medical evaluation resulted in a twenty percent disability determination. That's far short of what I need to get extra bucks."

"Wait. Hold on. I'll be right back."

He was back in two minutes.

"You idiot! Do you know what this means?"

Well, to me it meant that he remembered me after all, but that didn't feel like the ah-ha moment it seemed like he wanted me to have. Clearly he wanted more.

"Disability compensation is not retirement pay. Get it?" he said.

I did. I got that he didn't understand that although I got disability pay, that amount was offset by an equal amount of retirement pay being reduced. I explained that to him, but the explanation just got him more agitated.

"I got it, but you don't. Your divorce judgment says you have to give your ex-wife a portion of your retirement pay. It doesn't say anything about giving her disability compensation. So although you get less retirement pay, the percentage that you have to give to her doesn't change. And the disability compensation is all yours. And it isn't taxed. My friend, you just got a big pay raise—for life."

The headache and pounding went away. I think I heard bells. He had to go over that another time or two with me, but the story didn't change, and on the third time, everything sank in. He seemed only slightly less happy than I was; I guess X2 has that effect on people.

"So I guess you will do the notification paperwork pro bono?"

He wasn't *that* happy and cited his fee. It was high but well worth it. Maybe the first time in history a client ever was only too happy to pay a legal fee. We agreed that we had to wait until the medical board convened and confirmed the preliminary disability determination, but he advised me that if the final determination was the same as the preliminary one to not seek redress, blah, blah, blah because a review could actually reduce the percentage determination. Amen, brother.

I had scanned the judgment from my divorce from X1 into my computer and opened up the file. Same wording. I felt like I had just won a doubleheader. My headache had returned, but slighter now, so in addition to bells, the cannons were still firing, kind of like an orchestra between my ears was playing the "1812 Overture." I popped a couple of Tylenol and hoped they would fix the cannons. I kind of liked the bells.

The next day was VA Day. Death by PowerPoint, starting with the mission of the Veteran's Administration, the organization of the VA, where in your state the VA is located, benefits provided by the VA, and so on. And that was just the first two hours. Luckily, VA Days were really only VA Mornings because, really, who would want to follow that act? The more appropriate question was, "Who would really rather miss that act?" as several dozen of us lined up in front of the instructor to offer excuses about why we would have to miss his class. By the time I reached the front of the line, the instructor really wasn't interested anymore.

"You sick too?"

"Nope, I'm feeling fine." And I was. The orchestra that had been playing the crescendo part over and over in the concert hall between my ears had packed it up and gone home. "The general wants to see me."

That works even better in MacDill than in Kandahar because there are several dozen generals assigned to MacDill. If he got too curious and asked me which one, I would just tell him it's the one that he doesn't know, which isn't being rude. It's code for people assigned to Special Operations Command, which is also located in MacDill. The instructor just handed me the briefing packet and nodded.

I walked out into the parking lot, chucked the briefing packet into the dumpster, drove downtown, and bought a car.

If you think you are about to get a couple of funny stories about car buying, it won't be from me. There is absolutely nothing funny about it. It's just painful. The whole premise of the way Americans buy cars is that if the dealership accepts your bottom-line offer, you know you got screwed. And at the instant he agrees to the price, the salesman tells you to go sit somewhere else and wait for the business manager and then promptly forgets your name and the fact that you and he are best buddies, even though you just met. I always thought that if I were a car salesman, and somebody came up to me in the grocery store or golf course or wherever and asked, "Hey Griff, remember me?" I would look him in the eye and say, "Oh yeah. You were the guy that almost got me fired. My manager couldn't believe I let you have that car for such a sweet deal." And that's how to sell the next car. Maybe I have a knack for selling. But not cars; never cars.

Anyway, I bought a SUV. I really don't know why because on Friday, once I had thrown out all my old Army stuff, everything I owned could pretty much fit into the glove box. So buyer's remorse set in. I had never owned a new car. I always bought old clunkers, just like my old man, and most of those were pickups. The new car smell was beginning to bother me. A car should smell like stale food, dirty old clothes, and something that might be an exhaust leak but pretty much goes away if I roll down the windows and drive fast. And cars are not supposed to be quiet. A quiet car doesn't speak to the driver. A clunker is a pretty good conversationalist. I don't follow maintenance schedules since most of the time you end up paying a whole bunch to replace something that is working perfectly well just because some amount of time has passed. The knowledgeable driver and conversational car communicate; maintenance is only needed if there is a new squeal, the grinding noise gets louder, or there is smoke coming out from under the hood. Smoke is always a good indicator.

But now I had a silent, pleasant-smelling vehicle whether I liked it or not. And I was down to two days left in my Army career.

The final two days of out-processing is the Transition Assistance Program, or TAP, which sounds like "Taps," which is played when they bury you, and the similarity was only funny to the TAP moderator who kicked off the session on Thursday morning with that joke.

I hadn't sat in a classroom since college, and then I paid sufficient attention to pass my classes and keep my scholarships. Since my basic plan at this point was to get enough out of TAP to figure out how to make myself employable, I resolved to pay attention and even took a seat in the front of the room. That was an unaccustomed position for me, and I was close enough to see the presenter sweating slightly, which was less a reflection on his nerves than a result of the room air conditioning being just a bit off today. As in, completely off. So if the speaker needed to use the trick of imagining his audience in their underwear, in about twenty minutes his imagination would be able to take the rest of the day off.

We took a break while maintenance guys brought in a bunch of fans that were soon whirring away, making whatever the speaker was saying completely inaudible to everyone but the front row. So I was well positioned to keep my resolution about paying attention, even if I had to keep jabbing myself in the leg with my pencil to stay awake.

Unfortunately, the first speaker didn't make it easy for me. He was from the base psychiatry office and told us how perfectly normal it was to have feelings of being a bit lost, and uncertain, and anxious, and fearful, and a whole bunch of other things that I hadn't been feeling before but was now. He said that the base psychiatry office was open until the end of the day if we needed to see someone urgently, but they closed at four thirty and weren't open on Fridays. Luckily for us, there was a national suicide prevention hotline telephone number he had put in the paper copies of his slides, which he had thought the TAP administrators would provide but who insisted that it was the responsibility of the presenter, so we could just copy from the slide on the screen. And for emphasis, he read out the number, but what he read was different than what was on the screen, and by then the back two-thirds of the room was a concert of "What did he say?" until his time was mercifully over.

We were scheduled for a fifteen-minute break, so we all headed to our cars, cranked up the air conditioners, and stayed there for thirty minutes.

Our next speaker came at us from the other direction. His presentation was about how special we are, how valuable we would be to the nation's workforce, and how employers were just waiting to hire people with a demonstrated sense of responsibility, leadership, self-discipline, and initiative. His point was that these were more valuable than actual skills, and to prove that point, he began clicking through slides of quotes from various CEOs about how much they valued responsibility, etc., including one from a CEO that valued integrity, except the CEO had been ousted by stockholders the month before and promptly arrested by the FBI for fraud.

Fortunately, about halfway through his presentation, the building AC kicked on again, with a roar instead of a hum as if trying to make up for having slept in that morning by just going faster. Since Mr. AC had quite a bit of ground to make up, we adjourned again for our fifteen-minute break and spent the next forty-five minutes in our cars.

By the time the next session convened, the room was nearly habitable. First, a quick administrative announcement that because we had fallen behind, lunch hour would be curtailed to twenty minutes and that the PX snack bar was only about ten minutes away. And then a second quick administrative announcement that there was to be no eating in the classroom. The class agreed amongst ourselves that we would head to lunch and be back in an hour.

The third session promised to be valuable. "Elements of a Standout Resume." I had continued to polish my own résumé, but the results weren't getting any better. If an employer needed someone to lead an armed assault on a rival business or establish a company defensive position against that same rival, I was their man, but I hadn't yet stumbled upon any job postings listing those specific position criteria. I had seen several listings for former military interested in working in Afghanistan, but I remained firm in my resolve to never go back, although a little less firmly firm each day. So during lunch, I started thinking about how to slip initiative, leadership, etc. into the narrative, and maybe even integrity, although it seemed to be lower on the hiring priority list.

The session after lunch lived up to its billing. We learned the two cardinal rules about résumés, which to me seemed so profound I copied them verbatim:

I. Companies want to see results, so say what you have accomplished rather than a list of your duties.
II. Provide proof. Don't just say you improved the company's bottom line; provide the details of what you did to make things happen quicker, at less cost, and with better quality. The corollary to this is to use numbers because numbers mean the results are real, and you aren't just bullshitting. (This last part wasn't exactly verbatim, but he changed the slide before I finished copying, so this is the Finneganized version.)

The presenter even gave examples, but most of them weren't helpful since they were about improving manufacturing processes or cutting the cost of raw materials by finding new sources. Un-Army things. In fact, the more I considered the examples, the less positive I became about this approach. The Army isn't about efficiency, and Lord knows that cost saving isn't what the Army does well. We don't manufacture anything except chaos, and from what I could tell, most companies are perfectly capable of doing that on their own. At the end of the examples he clearly had copied from some internet page, he did provide a few ideas that were more relevant: improving maintenance procedure on F-16 fighters to reduce mean time between failures by 20 percent (which sounded pretty good unless it meant that only four out of five planes were now going to fall out of the sky) and reengineering the wash and rinse cycles of the clothes washers on board Navy ships so that they could use 40 percent less water than before (again great stuff but I didn't think nonpotable water shortages on Navy ships were big problems.) But it showed he was trying, and I was inspired enough to come up with one of my own that demonstrated initiative. I had put together, roughly, a cookbook in which the recipes used the ingredients of MREs to make meals that were almost edible (or quantifying the results, 35 percent more edible) and largely featured Tabasco sauce, small bottles of which are conveniently included in MRE packets. But I didn't share this with the class because I didn't want anyone to steal my good idea.

The rest of the day was spent preparing our own résumés, which we had to turn in before leaving. All but two of us promptly stood up and delivered their neatly typed, two-page résumés, probably just full of positively measured results and lists of merit badges earned for initiative, discipline, integrity, and starting campfires. The other holdover besides me hadn't even started his résumé, but he was going to work at his father's car dealership, so he just typed out a half page containing his name and address in extra-large font and turned it in. I almost asked him if he thought his dad might need any more help, but I figured I was at least two days away from being that desperate and besides, he would be in class tomorrow.

I stayed behind for another hour, hoping for another inspiration or two that never showed up, but I did work on my MRE initiative entry by adding it under special skills, then editing it, and finally deleting it because about the only people that would be interested would be Betty Crocker. And since my four-star recipes were pretty much limited to adding Tabasco sauce to everything, I didn't see much of a future there. I turned in what I had, apologizing for keeping the instructor so late, but he said he was an hourly employee, so we were cool. I wasn't looking forward to tomorrow.

I got back to my room and figured I would have one of my last two remaining steaks, one of my two remaining potatoes, and as many beers as I felt like having since I had replenished my supply and bought two more six-packs to leave for the next guy. I found a note on the door saying that the fire inspector had come by and found the disabled smoke detector and that I was a naughty boy and should never do that again. So I did, although I made a mental note to reconnect the smoke alarm. And then I got up and forgot about it because I never pay attention to my mental notes.

On Friday morning we were introduced to two important weapons in the arsenal of the job seeker. The phrasing was supposed to demonstrate how relevant the topics were to soon-to-be former members of the military, but it went right over our heads. Maybe the next group will get it.

The topics were networking and the fifteen- and thirty-second elevator speeches. The networking presentation was mercifully short, and our only participation requirement was to look at our contacts and identify the one most likely to help us land a job, and then the second most likely, and so on. "Remember, your network is your best resource!" I only had two contacts in my new phone, my parents and Jim Strack, so I ranked them fourth and fifth, respectively.

We weren't able to be passive participants for the next part. We were given ten minutes to prepare a short, to-the-point monologue that highlighted our qualifications and virtues and how good we would be at *fill in the blank*, to be delivered presumably to some poor stranger in the elevator. And then each of us, in turn, would stand up in front of the class and recite our speeches. We did not cover why a complete stranger, who just wanted to enjoy a few quiet moments between the hell of the office he just left and the hell of the traffic he was about to face, would want to receive the in-person version of a spam phone call.

I used my ten minutes to develop three versions, which began with "Good Morning," "Good Afternoon," or "Good Evening," and all three ended with "Hey man, don't call the cops," but the ten or twenty-five seconds in between were a bit squishy. I didn't even know whether to go with "Hi, I'm Griff," or whether the occasion warranted the more formal, "Allow me to introduce myself—I'm Griffin." I decided I would wait for others to do their presentation and plagiarize anything that sounded good. Unfortunately, this seemed to be the universal strategy, so lacking volunteers, the instructor started with the first row, and I was fourth in line.

The first three elevator speeches were pretty sad but got enthusiastic applause from the audience. The instructor just recommended: "Keep working on it. It will get better," but without any great conviction. During speech number two, I got an inspiration. I figured that if leadership, initiative, self-discipline, and integrity were key to a résumé, they had to be similarly important in an elevator speech, so I put together a sentence that jammed all these buzz words in, added another sentence with the same buzz words in a different order, dropped the original last line and added, "Thank you for your time."

The group gave me a standing ovation. I got the same "Keep working on it" treatment from the instructor but felt that he actually meant it when he said it would get better and sat down feeling pretty good about myself. That feeling only got better because everyone that followed plagiarized me. I could see *Summa Cum Laude* after my name on the TAP completion certificate.

After a fifteen-minute break, we reconvened and were introduced to a half dozen or so special guests who turned out to be retired business executives or personnel administrators. The last exercise was to conduct simulated one-on-one job interviews with these people, who would also provide feedback on our résumés. We were designated as Group A, Group B, etc. Then everyone but the first person in each group went out into the hall to await our turns to be interviewed.

I had chosen to be in Group C because our interviewer intrigued me. He was about sixty-five, tall, completely bald, and cadaverous-looking. He also had two of the biggest, bushiest eyebrows I had ever seen. More importantly, while the other interviewers were dressed in, to put it nicely, summertime Tampa casual, the Group C interviewer wore a starched long-sleeve dress shirt, dress slacks, and wing-tip shoes. His name was Walt, and he looked just like a Walt should look, so you have a pretty complete picture now. He looked like he meant business. Recall that the best plan I could come up with was to hope something fell into my lap this week, and we had about two hours to go, so although I didn't like the idea of him sitting in my lap, he was my best and final shot.

Walt started me out with questions he said were designed to relax me, like where I was from, where I served, what my political persuasion was, and then said that question was a red herring, and I shouldn't answer red herrings. I wasn't sure what a red herring was in this context, so he explained that they were questions that had nothing to do with my qualifications or the job I was applying for and shouldn't even be asked by a prospective employer. Good advice. Then he asked me how many times I had been married, and when I answered, he snapped that I needed to start paying attention since that was another red herring, and he didn't give a "flying fig" how many times I had been married. I was humbled.

Then we got into what he called my leadership traits since that would be my strongest set of credentials.

"How do you motivate underperforming employees?"

"I yell at them." I'm a big believer in the drill sergeant's unofficial motto: *Fear is a great motivator. Absolute terror works even better.* I've seen it in many a former drill sergeant's office. Walt's eyebrows arched upward magnificently.

"And if that doesn't work?"

"I yell louder." Walt's eyebrows were now in the middle of his forehead.

"And if yelling doesn't work?"

"I knife him." Okay, I blew that, but frankly, in the Army, motivation really isn't a problem because of the looming threat of extra work details and ultimately, a court-martial. And, there are plenty of former drill sergeants around to turn the matter over to.

Walt's eyebrows were standing straight up on the top of his bald head.

"Finnegan, I think we're done here. If you can't be serious, you'll never succeed. And cut the crap. I know you are scared stiff about what you are going to do next, and your résumé is crap, so you *should* be scared."

I apologized profusely and told him he was right and that humor was just my way of working through the fear and it wouldn't happen again and would he please give me another chance? Actually, I was somewhat sincere since, after all, he was right.

"Let's shift gears a bit. What are your goals?"

I had war-gamed what I thought were likely questions, and these touchy-feely questions were problematic. I felt comfortable with questions about where I had been, what I had done, and what my strengths were. Asking me questions about things I hadn't thought through was making me uneasy. So I almost blurted out that my goal was to end up with a good woman, a good bottle, and a good cigar, and then the same the next day, although not necessarily the same bottle, cigar, or even woman, for that matter. But I figured that answer would put his eyebrows somewhere on the ceiling, so I mumbled something about a meaningful job that would make me comfortable and a couple of other innocuous things I hoped would convince him that I was really sincere.

"That was horrible. Work on it. Okay, what do you want to do?"

Man, he was relentless. I am a degreed engineer and like math because all our problems have exact solutions, and we, well maybe not me, but other engineers and mathematicians, could work toward the solution, underline it twice, and be done.

So I pushed back. "Why is that important? Is that another red herring?"

The eyebrows returned to near eye-socket orbit, and he smiled, but just a little bit.

"Finnegan, I'm going to give you some good advice. Pay attention if you've a mind to, but I'm only going to say this once, and I won't accept any questions. First, lose the attitude. You aren't a general, which is its own calling card, so nobody cares if you were a lieutenant or a lieutenant colonel because rank won't do anything for them.

"Next, figure out what you want to do. Don't focus on what you think you can do best because even if you could do something valuable, which I doubt, it won't make you happy. When you find something you want to do, you'll see that, and you'll interview in a way that reflects how important it is to you, and the employer will see that.

"Write this down. USAJOBS.gov. It is the government employment website. I don't know if you'll find what you want to do there, but what's there will be more familiar.

"Finally, you've left out what might be your most important qualification. Do you still have a security clearance, or did the Army come to its senses and determine that you must be an enemy agent to screw things up as much as you have?"

And then I figured it out. He was a former Marine. Or not *former* Marine since a Marine will tell you there are no former Marines. But he was definitely a Marine.

"It was just renewed last year. Top Secret." The Army had upped me to a higher security clearance because of my job in Kandahar. Which meant that the Top Secret clearance was still good for another five years.

"That's gold. It's taking two, three, or more years to get clearances now. Check out USAJOBs and see how many of the positions require at least Secret.

A quick personal note. The Department of Defense does a thorough job checking backgrounds. That check includes interviewing neighbors, coworkers, and others the applicant includes on a list of references. It is *always* a good idea to let the neighbors et al., know you've done that, so if a couple of federal agents show up at their door and start asking questions about you, there aren't any bad surprises.

Anyway, I could have just hugged Walt, but since he was a Marine, we settled for a firm handshake.

"And Finnegan, one other thing. You're looking for a job. And in a few years, you'll get bored and be looking for another. Don't expect a second career. Guys like us have had a career, and all the rest are just jobs. You'll find that out. Good luck."

I went out into the hall and summoned the next interviewee, stopped by the instructor's desk to pick up my TAP Completion Certificate (no Summa Cum Laude) and filled out an evaluation form with no comment for all the questions, and headed to the parking lot.

And that was it. My Army career was over, and I had a certificate that essentially said the Army had determined that I was suitable for employment somewhere, just not with them.

PART II
Limbo

CHAPTER 6

Interlude

I GOT BACK TO MY ROOM and found another note, this time telling me that I had to check out of the VIP Transient Quarters by noon on Saturday so that the room could be prepared for the next incoming out-processor.

I had expected that, so it wasn't a problem. The problem was where to go next. After I got my new phone, I had called my parents to report my safe arrival and to see if I could come home for a couple of weeks after out processing. They were ecstatic, but that might have been because they weren't going to be home for those couple of weeks.

Mom had finally hit the lottery. She was one of thirty-seven winners in the statewide lottery, picking the week after the Mega Millions jackpot payout to win. So she got an eight thousand dollar share, which to her seemed like a million bucks and more importantly, a divine reward after all the years of questioning why God wasn't backing her play. A vacation was in order, and Dad suggested Las Vegas, but Mom had decided to attend the annual Southern Baptist Convention in Memphis. Dad was okay with this because he figured there would be more sinning going on in Memphis than in Vegas—for those two weeks, anyway.

"Please do come home. The key will be in the Snake Pit, and I'll leave a big bowl of Magic Stew for you in the freezer."

It was just like I had never left. We had Magic Stew every Friday.

Mom said its name came from her list of secret ingredients, which included a dash of this and a pinch of that and a large dab of magic. Dad said it was called Magic Stew because when it was put in the bowl in front of him, his appetite magically disappeared.

I was sort of in the middle. When I was younger, the name alone made it mysteriously good, and while the charm wore off when I was a teenager, it was at least filling enough that I didn't have to go out partying on Friday nights on an empty stomach. And now it was pure nostalgia. I reminded myself to bring a bottle of Tabasco.

The Snake Pit is the northern Missouri ADT Home Security System. Dad had dug a large hole in our backyard, about four feet wide and two feet deep, and put up a hand-lettered sign that said 'Snake Pit' right next to it. When they went out, he and Mom would put their most prized possessions into the pit. She stashed her notions, potions, lotions, waffle iron, and her lottery ledger, which was a forty-five-year record of the weekly lottery winning numbers. Every week she would make an entry and comb over the years of results, looking for a pattern that she just knew was there. Dad called it a waste of time because everybody knew the lottery was random, but Mom called it science because everybody knew there was no such thing as random. Dad put his Colt Peacemaker pistol with the pearl handles (they were plastic) in a gun box, his torque wrench, and engine timing light into the pit. Then he would throw a couple of shovelfuls of dirt on top, half bury a length of black garden hose, and place some rabbit bones nearby. I don't know if it ever fooled anybody, but for forty-five years, all of these family heirlooms went untouched, so who knows?

Every once in a while a real snake would get curious enough to drop in, so Dad would take a long pry bar and poke around the pit before reaching in, and if the ground started to squirm around, he would take the bar, lift out the gun box and begin blazing away at the snake. Dad was always a more enthusiastic than accurate shooter, so every couple of years, Dad would get a new timing light for Christmas.

"By the way son, you got an invitation to your thirtieth high school reunion. It's in two weeks in the gym."

Oh boy. If she had said that the National Lepers Association was having its annual Meet and Greet, I would have signed up in a heartbeat rather than go to my high school reunion. It's not that I didn't like some of my old schoolmates; it's just that time and distance had softened some of the memories, and I was all for maintaining the distance.

A bit of an explanation. First, for those who are paying close attention, you may be wondering how we could be celebrating our thirtieth graduation anniversary if I had joined the Army twenty-two years ago, straight out of a four-year college. Technically, you would have me there, but technically, it wasn't the thirtieth anniversary of our *graduation*. The class had tried typical reunions for the first couple of years, but not many were showing up, not surprising given that only about half the class graduated, so the class leaders decided to celebrate when we first entered high school because that would include a whole lot more people, including those that were more fun anyway. So we went from our fifth reunion directly to our ninth reunion the next year.

Our thirtieth was going to be special because we would "honor" the Most Likely To's. That would be relatively benign and no great threat to me since I wasn't one of them. But some of us had another competition pool going. A couple dozen of us had paid twenty bucks apiece into the pool, payable to the guy who had accumulated the most jail time by our thirtieth. It was a pretty serious competition since we had multiple front-runners, so we had put an effort into codifying the rules: the years had to be actually served since sentenced years could be overturned on appeal, and you had to be present to win, which meant that strategically, you had to plan on being a bad guy but not so bad as to end up with a life sentence. So lots of assaults but no murders.

One consequence of so many assaults, often upon each other, is that everyone was carrying at least one grudge, and the average was about three or four. I had been gone for over a quarter of a century, and I didn't remember there being any grudges against me before I left, but then again, what I thought really wasn't relevant. What did seem likely was that a couple of the old boys would consider my lack of jail time as proof that I had not demonstrated the proper spirit of the competition in our little contest. And because our rules hadn't envisioned the possibility of a tie, a couple of the boys just might figure I was available in the event they had to go to extra innings.

So, all things considered, I decided to pass, wished my parents well on their vacation, packed up my things, left a six-pack in the refrigerator for the next guy, and checked out on Saturday morning. And then checked in to my new room because I had decided to spend what was left of my terminal leave here.

The new room was in a different complex and was called transient quarters, dropping the VIP for real good reasons. The room was quite a bit smaller, which didn't really bother me, with furniture that had been new in the '70s (which also didn't bother me) and a half-size refrigerator (no big deal). But it had an electric hot plate instead of a stove, oven, and microwave (bothersome, but at least it worked, which means it was better than an Army facility). What really turned my ass red was that there was no coffee maker. I was so upset that I started calling local motels to check rates, just on principle, and I found out pretty soon that my principles had a price ceiling, so I drove to the PX to pick up a coffee maker. And then drove back because I forgot filters, and then drove back again, but this time I drove off base to the Publix grocery store for coffee because the thought of going back to the commissary on a Saturday was more than my faltering courage would allow.

What the room did have was good internet service, and I resolved to spend three hours per day on my job search; then on second thought, I decided to average three hours per day, which meant that on rainy days I could make up time spent golfing on nice days. The first thing I did was revise my résumé and add my security clearance information. I considered sticking that right after my name but decided it was a little too obvious. But I did put it in the first paragraph, where I listed my objectives. I started with, "I want to be able to use my experience, skills, and Top Secret clearance to enhance your capabilities," but something about that didn't quite seem right. So I decided to take a break and went on a run. Some people use runs to clarify their thinking; I just do a brain dump and don't think about anything at all.

I got back, showered, and took another look at my objectives. The run served its purpose, and I figured out that if I didn't want a string of job offers that paid in Chinese currency, that sentence would have to be revised. I finally moved the clearance information down to my qualifications paragraph and hoped that prospective employers would read at least that far to find it but not think I was offering to commit treason.

I then opened USAJOBS.com to see whether old Walt had given me a gold nugget or a plugged nickel, and frankly, thought that the plugged nickel made the site overpriced, but then remembered I was supposed to be looking at USAJOBS.gov. And also remembered that I really did need to start writing stuff down. I had to go through the create account, choose user name, enter password, your password doesn't satisfy criteria, enter different password, your password still doesn't . . . nonsense just to see what the site had to offer, but it was ultimately worth the hassle.

I say ultimately because my first impression wasn't positive. USAJOBS is the job announcement website for the entire federal government, and announcements are listed with the most recent first. So after reading the first several, only a couple of which were interesting, I figured out a couple of things:

A. I would have to refine my search to either the agency, the location, or the job position I was after or be prepared to read a couple of million announcements.

B. I had to go directly to the eligibility paragraph of the announcement and specifically look for the "any US citizen" jobs.

Although it looked like the federal government was hiring like crazy, it soon became apparent they weren't going to line up to hire me. Many agencies must feel that they have been so efficient for the last 220 years or so that they would only hire from within and not run the risk of ever getting any new ideas accidentally introduced into the workforce. Some agencies had seemingly good intentions and announced that all US citizens were eligible but then said the announcement would close three days after it opened, which meant that somebody high in the chain had those good intentions, but at least one stalwart beneath him said, "Oh hell no."

A lesser man might have been discouraged. I was impressed, at least sort of. After twenty-two years in the Army, a federal bureaucracy without peers, I admired that some lower-level administration weenies had gotten their instructions, nodded in understanding, and then had completely thwarted the intent of some senior bureaucrat that never even checked to see if what he had ordered had been implemented. Reminded me of myself. Besides, there is no point in being frustrated with the federal government. Everybody is, and it doesn't make a damn bit of difference to them. But the benefit was that I was able to cross off a whole bunch of agencies in which I had no chance of employment and ultimately saved myself a lot of time.

And it left me with a handful of agencies with which I thought I stood a chance. So I spent Sunday racking up a bunch of credit toward my three-hours-per-day resolution, bombarding those few agencies with applications and résumés. I even went so far as to tailor the résumé, putting *sense of responsibility* first on résumés sent to agencies I thought could use some, *integrity* first for those I thought in dire need, and *initiative* first for the rest because they all need that. So on Monday I played golf, but again avoided the MacDill course just in case.

By Tuesday, there were several more announcements and with my now-streamlined processes, I was able to whip out a couple of more applications in about an hour.

Feeling a bit cocky, I decided to retry some of the regular job boards to see if I could similarly unlock their mysteries. No such luck. Whereas government agencies are relatively transparent and tell you what they want, who they don't want, how to apply, what the pay or grade was, and when the opening would close, civilians are all over the place. There were lots of requirements for business developers and operations managers, but the companies must have felt that the title was descriptive enough for the applicants, and their websites didn't give enough information for me to figure out what their businesses and operations were. Some of the job boards were good enough to identify how long the announcement had been open, but I couldn't tell if a position open 140 days meant that the company was incredibly picky or had hired someone 139 days ago and had forgotten to close the announcement.

So just as I had for government announcements, I developed the Finnegan method for identifying real civilian opportunities. Patent pending. First, the announcement could not be more than seven days old, or fourteen if it was a big business, because it just took them longer. If I couldn't tell what the job was, it was trashed. Nobody was talking money, so that didn't cull the field any. And if they required a government security clearance, they went to the top of the list. But it was a long list, so the Finnegan method still needs some refinement. Next, I cut out all the ones that required that I submit a cover letter because I didn't know how to write one other than provide a summary of what was already in the résumé followed by *See résumé*. It felt like progress, so I decided to take another run, hoping to clear the clutter again and come back with a new perspective. It didn't work; the run just tired me out, so I went to bed early.

It rained all day the next day, so I decided to bank more hours and started applying for a whole bunch of the jobs on my civilian opportunities list. The engineer in me considered how best to utilize the five or so hours I was going to spend on this task; was it better to try and get to the 100 percent solution on each application and accompanying résumé and end up applying to five companies, each with a 5 percent chance of success, or go into mass production and send the same résumé to fifty companies, each with a 2 percent chance of success? I didn't really bother with the math because hitting their reply button and attaching the same résumé was the least amount of effort, so I applied fifty times and was satisfied with this scientific approach.

It may have been less work than the alternative, but it was still exhausting, so I decided that maybe I would chance a return engagement at the MacDill golf course. Unfortunately, the clubhouse manager recognized me, so when I tried to sign up for eighteen holes, he said they were out of carts, even though there were about a dozen parked in front. Damn, I don't know what the statute of limitations is on plowing through a golf bunker and green, but evidently it was more than a week, so I bought a dozen golf balls and a couple of range tokens and casually asked him if he was working this weekend. He was, so I went to the range and hacked up a dozen or so cubic yards of turf and called it a day.

But I didn't call it a night. When I had actually been stationed in Tampa in years past, I had found a little bar I liked not too far from MacDill. I won't tell you the name because one of the reasons I like it is that it isn't crowded. Also, it's quiet, not frequented by twenty-one-year-olds, and has bar snacks but doesn't serve food, probably because it wouldn't pass the state health inspection. Yeah, that kind of place. But the main reason I like it is because of the bartender, Guy. I don't even know if that's his real name, but whenever somebody he knows comes in he yells out, "Hey, Guy," so people just started yelling "Hey, Guy" back.

Guy was missing the last two fingers on his left hand and wasn't very talkative about it.

Where? "Nam."

How? "Grenade."

Ours or theirs? "Ours."

I changed the subject before we got into whether he was throwing the grenade at them or us. The next subject was baseball, and Guy is a hardcore Yankee fan. Lots of people in Tampa are because the Yankees play their spring training games there, and they are better attended than the real games of the hometown Tampa Bay Rays. So when I wandered in with my Red Sox cap on, we just naturally launched into debates that were pretty evenly contested. He had the advantage on overall record, number of championships, head-to-head contests, and Hall of Fame members, and I had the advantage of being a paying customer, so he always stopped just short of pissing me off completely. But he wouldn't let me wear my *Yankees Suck* T-shirt.

What made Guy tolerable, barely, was that he made the best vodka martini I have ever had anywhere. It's not really much of a competition because I don't drink martinis anywhere else, and I really don't remember how I started there, but at least once every couple of weeks my regular fare was three of the world's best martinis, a bowl of the world's stalest pretzels, and being left completely alone unless Guy decided he wanted to start in on me again.

So I decided to see if old Guy was still around and to let him know that even though I didn't think it was possible, he was even uglier than the last time I'd been in, and the Yankees still sucked. This wouldn't win the game, but it would put a couple of early runs on the board, and he'd have to play catch up. Then he beat me to it.

"Hey, guy. Long time. You're uglier than ever and the Red Sox suck."

"Hey, Guy. Foul ball. You're the home team and I get to bat first. Even a dumbass like you knows that."

"Well then, get out and come in again. We'll start over."

So I did.

"Hey, guy. Long time. You're uglier than ever and the Red Sox suck. And who's the dumbass now?"

"Shut up and give me the usual. Dry and dirty, just like your place."

It was just like I had never been away. I sat down and was about to take some practice swings by remarking that the place hadn't been cleaned since I was last in, which would be more of a factual observation than a jab, and his customers all looked like they needed rabies shots, which when I actually looked around, turned out to not be completely true.

There were three good-looking women sitting at one of the tables. Two blondes and a brunette that looked like about twenty years earlier they could have been vying for Miss Tampa. They still looked pretty hot, and although one of the blondes was trending toward Miss Tampa and Most of St. Petersburg, the other two had maintained their figures.

"How did they get in here? Did you kidnap them and chain them to the table?"

Guy approached with the martini. "No, but now that you are here, they'll clear out in a hurry."

And that seemed to be the case, but only one of them got up and, instead of leaving, actually approached me.

"Shaken not stirred?"

I presumed that she was addressing the martini and not me, so instead of answering, I just dipped my finger in the glass and swirled.

"Aren't you afraid of bruising the vodka?" So she was flirting, and the game was James Bond meets Bond girl.

"Well, I'm about to throw this down my throat, swallow hard, it will run through my system, and in about twenty minutes I'm going to go out to the parking lot and piss it on somebody's car. A little bruising now will just toughen it up for the ride."

Game over. Smooth and sophisticated James had turned into rude and crude me. Her face went from flirtatious to puzzlement to shock to disgust in two seconds, and she about-faced and headed for the door, with the blondes following a few seconds later.

Guy had no mercy.

"Well that was smooth, Romeo. Mr. Bullshit just missed a layup. You suck as bad as the Red Sox."

"Wrong again, my man. She'll be back in four minutes. She's just gone to move her car."

I missed by thirty seconds, and she came back in, sans the blondes. She and I reconvened at a table and in twenty minutes we were on our way out, headed to her place. I flipped Guy the bird on the way out just to let him know there were no hard feelings. Or the alternate translation: Yankees suck.

I don't talk about sex. I resolved long ago to only talk about things I know at least a little something about, like baseball, golf, cigars, booze, soldiering, and war. This is ironic because the way I wage it, sex is just like war, but without the Geneva Convention that prohibits atrocities. Still, it's my rule. I could have told you that, as a gentleman, I would refrain from any discussion of intimate details, but you've read too much about me to believe that.

The house was large, too large for a single person, and half-filled. They don't call me Sherlock Finnegan for nothing (most often in a "No shit, Sherlock" context), and all the clues pointed in a direction I didn't care for. The too-white band on her ring finger was the smoking gun; too white as in not six months or six weeks old but somewhere between six hours and six days. Continuing my spot-on ratiocination (that's what Sherlock Holmes would call it), I figured that since women generally ditch the ring soon after starting divorce proceedings, my new friend was only unofficially divorced, or as they say in court, married.

I couldn't think of a single favorable outcome, so I said a quick goodbye in the morning and deleted the contact information she had entered into my phone. My only regret was that I would have to stay clear of Guy's place for a while.

No, that's not quite right. I also regret not practicing my thirty-second elevator speech with her. But then again, you know how women are; she probably would have said it was only fifteen seconds.

PART III
Army

CHAPTER 7

Opening Battle

MY EMAIL INBOX WAS ON FIRE. Fourteen spam messages; three from my car dealer: a thank you, a coupon for the next service (expires in thirty days), and an offer to trade in for a deal on another model; one from the MacDill transient quarters saying my weekly rent was due; a couple from buddies in Kandahar saying they missed me and wished I was there; and one from the US Army Corps of Engineers, New England District. I waited ten minutes before opening it while googling whether federal agencies sent out rejection emails. Apparently not.

I remembered applying for Resident Engineer, Westover Air Reserve Base. The opening had come up because *Army* and *engineer* were in my search string, but I almost didn't apply because there wasn't a requirement for security clearance. But I took a flyer, and what do you know, the blind squirrel found the nut. The email was an invitation to interview at the Corps HQ in Concord, Mass. I could just feel the love.

I, of course, had run into lots of Army engineers—the kind that blow things up, put in minefields and barbed wire fences, install bridges, and, if we were real nice to them, dug our foxholes with their bucket loaders. Somehow, I didn't think these were the same guys as the ones that wanted to interview me. I tried to recall my classmates at Ft. Leavenworth and whether any were Corps of Engineers-types, but I was drawing a blank. I hit the websites.

The US Army Corps of Engineers is a very different organization. Definitely a part of the big "A" Army, which means it is mostly civilians with a couple of uniformed senior engineer Army officers sprinkled around as the nominal commanders of what looked to be about forty or more different organizations. This is the organization that builds dams and levees and canals and locks and hurricane barriers, whatever they are, but mostly it's the organization that everybody wants to yell at. It seems that the US is full of people very unhappy with the Corps because their dams are retaining too much water and not enough water (at the same time), they move too slow or too fast (at the same time), they are environmentally reckless or their requirements for protecting natural resources are too demanding and too costly (on the same projects), and guilty of a whole host of other sins. I couldn't find a single reference to anything they've done right, but that just means they are part of the federal government, so no surprise there. I guess they aren't too different.

In addition to frustrating the general public, the Corps manages all the Army's construction. So why is there a position for a resident engineer at an Air Force base? To my surprise, I found that the Army Corps manages about 90 percent of the Air Force construction too, and (play a couple of bugle notes here to indicate that a mind-blowing fact is about to follow) the Air Force has to ask the Corps' permission to do any of its own construction. I could see myself in charge of that: "Well, General, at the moment I am not inclined to let you build that officer's club, but perhaps we can adjourn somewhere, have a few drinks and a cigar, and talk about it."

Except that's not exactly what a resident engineer does. I am clear on that. I am less clear on what the resident engineer does do. Other than reside at or near where something is being built and supervise the construction, which includes several duties, not the least of which is authorizing payment to the contractor. I could also see myself doing that: "Well, Mr. Contractor, at the moment I am not inclined to authorize payment for that new officer's club, but perhaps..."

Since it looked like whatever the job entailed, a good resident engineer gets to be a real dick a lot of the time. I'd have to remember at the interview to work in something about my superior skills at that.

Westover ARB looked like a pretty good place, surrounded by several towns, each calling themselves the Gateway to the Berkshires, which also looked like a real good place. I really liked that Westover was about ninety miles from the Concord HQ, which is about as close as I want to get to a HQ, and probably vice versa.

I called the POC on the email. A lady answered (at least I think so; I had two choices and that seemed the closest), and we carried on a conversation for about fifteen minutes. Which should have been five minutes, but we each had to repeat ourselves several times because neither of us could understand the other's accent. Finally I got the gist of my reason for calling through to her and she kindly thanked me for the call, but they were about to make a selection, and could I possibly be there in two days or less? But they would understand if I couldn't make it.

I assured her I was a *can-do* guy, and she assured me that they would reimburse my travel expenses because immediately after saying I was a *can-do* guy, I began to wonder if I wasn't, but if they were footing the bill, I was going to give it a hell of a try.

Before I move on, let me give you one piece of advice. Never, ever ask someone for driving directions in and around Boston. There is no sane way to get from one point to another, and if you somehow manage to get to where you want to go, you can't go back the same way. From the directions, delivered 100 miles per hour with an accent that only allowed me to catch every other word, I gathered that there were two routes from the airport to the Corps HQ, each with a tunnel named after somebody, including what sounded like Ted Williams but could have been Ted Callahan, and at some point, I would take Route 2, but maybe it was 2A, but in either case I should turn at the Alewife station, which I later found out was a subway station named for a fish, not a retail outlet for perfect spouses—unless I was on the other route, which was a straight shot on the Mass Pike to 128, which I couldn't find anywhere on a map but turned out to be I-95, and then a series of directions that came at me like a machine-gun burst. When she finally came up for air, I thanked her and said I would send on my travel arrangements.

If you have ever driven in Boston you know I am not exaggerating, and it's not like GPS is any help because you get enough nonstop "recalculating" to make you want to drive into Boston Harbor and drown the bitch.

It took some doing, but I finally was able to book a seat on the next day's last flight out of Tampa, nonstop to Boston, arriving around midnight. I dashed off to Walmart and picked up a cheap suitcase. I packed my suit, tie, shoes, socks, underwear, and toiletries, double-checking that I had everything. I found out that there is an Air Force base right next to the Corps headquarters, which certainly took me by surprise and probably takes most people who live outside a two-mile radius of the place. Hanscom Air Force Base is probably only about a mile wide and, get this, has no airplanes despite being adjacent to an airport called Hanscom Field. I know you are confused, but I can't explain it. Anyway, at Hanscom, the Air Force develops several advanced communications systems that have almost all of the features of Facetime on your phone but aren't as easy to use. I was able to reserve a room at their guest house for two nights, just in case.

I spent the next day studying and practicing. I had a good feeling about this, and I was becoming enthusiastic about settling in New England—and with a lot of effort, I figured I could learn the language in a couple of years. In the meantime, I would just swallow a bunch of syllables while pronouncing place names and carry around a card that said I had a service-related hearing disability.

I made it without a problem, discovering that between one and two o'clock in the morning is the best time to drive in Boston, not only because there is less traffic but also because not many people get upset at you driving a rental car the wrong way down one-way streets. Thrifty is going to get a nice set of traffic photos that I'm sure they'll just have a good laugh over and then toss out.

I arrived at Hanscom at about three-thirty and found out that having a retired military ID card was a good thing after all because once I woke the guard at the gate up, he sort of cheerfully waved me through. Check-in at the guest house was not a problem since there was an envelope on the front desk with my name on the outside and a key card on the inside. I had about six hours to sleep before getting ready for my eleven o'clock appointment and used every minute.

I got ready, not feeling a bit nervous, until I discovered that I had forgotten my dress belt and my tie had Tabasco bottles all over it. I had never used checklists before, but after twenty-two years of never having to decide what I was going to wear to work, dressing myself was proving problematic. Nothing I could do about it at this point, so I hoped that the Corps interviewers would have a sense of humor. Given everything I had read, it wasn't a rational hope, but it was all I could cling to.

The Corps HQ building (actually two buildings) wasn't all that impressive, considering there were supposed to be close to six hundred people assigned to the New England organization, and it looked like about four hundred and fifty were playing hooky. Or maybe since there weren't any dams, canals, or construction projects in sight, the others were actually out somewhere doing something. There might have been a hurricane barrier nearby, but since I didn't know what one looked like, I couldn't tell for sure. But I guessed it would have to be real tall and wide and waterproof, and nothing nearby fit the description.

The receptionist signed me in, gave me a badge, and showed me to a hallway outside a conference room.

"They're waiting for you."

Without thinking, I kind of automatically said: "Well, wish me luck."

She walked away.

I knocked on the door and waited for someone to tell me to come in, and when that didn't happen, I opened the door and walked in. Four big, beefy guys in short-sleeve shirts, blue jeans, and work boots were seated around a table, and an open seat was at the head of the table. No notepads, no pens, no Finnegan résumé in front of them.

"Good morning, Mr. Finnegan. Please take a seat. May we call you Griffin?"

"Nope. But you can call me Griff," I said with a big smile that got a couple of weak smiles in return. One was polite enough to say, "Nice tie."

Well, here goes nothing. "Yeah, I decided to go formal today. The hula girl tie was a bit too casual."

That seemed to do the trick and drew a few chuckles, and the four sides of beef noticeably relaxed. As did I, and on the spot, I decided to shoot the works.

The oldest and beefiest one spoke. "Griff, we're glad to meet you. Hope you had a pleasant trip. Tampa, huh?"

"The trip was fine, and thanks for the opportunity. So great to be in the heart of Red Sox Nation."

That was me shooting the works. Preparing for one of my earlier debates with Guy, topic: best fans, I learned that Red Sox fans are the most rabid anywhere (contrary to Guy's stupid opinion) and that the most listened-to daytime radio program was sports talk radio and even during the offseason, even when the Patriots were winning Super Bowls every year, callers only wanted to talk about the Red Sox.

Ha! Like ducks on a pond. We talked for fifteen minutes about the pitchers (mixed bag: the starters were okay, but the relievers were killing us), the hitters (right players, wrong lineup), the manager (split vote: two for "pushing the right buttons" and two for "shit for brains"), the organization, the fans, and ticket prices. When the conversation started to wane, I told them about my debates with Guy and whether, as engineers, they knew of a way to measure "suckiness" or whether we had to invent our own ten-point scale and put the

Yankees at eleven. That took another ten minutes because they took that task seriously and got onto the topic of suction pressure and measuring it in newtons, but before we actually developed a scale, Old Beefy interrupted and indicated that they had just a few questions of me, if that was all right.

Since my only question was going to be, "When do I start?" I told him to go ahead, expecting something like who I thought the Red Sox should sign as free agents next year.

"How has your experience in the Corps prepared you for the responsibilities of resident engineer?"

The suction pressure on me must have been about a million newtons because I deflated immediately.

"Give me a second." It would take longer than that to pull something out of my butt that sounded reasonable, and I had nothing, so I politely reminded him that I had never been in the Corps but that I was a quick learner and had a great sense of responsibility, not to mention integrity, initiative, and that other thing that I couldn't remember at the moment.

"Oh, right. Sorry about that. No Corps experience. Of course. We'll move on.

"How would you rate your abilities to use CEFMS and RMS?"

I found out later that these were proprietary Corps of Engineers software systems, which meant that nobody other than Corps of Engineers employees had any abilities whatsoever.

"Well, again, I am at a slight disadvantage since I never have been in the Corps, but you know, with my sense of responsibility, integrity, initiative, and that other thing that's on the tip of my tongue, I'll be a bona fide ace in no time."

"Well, Griff, that's all the time we have. Thank you for applying. Please turn in your badge to the receptionist on the way out.

"Oh, and Griff, frankly we are a little disappointed that you weren't better prepared for the interview."

Driving back onto Hanscom Air Base and the guest house, I kept telling myself that I shouldn't be disappointed, that maybe I had set my expectations too high to think I would hit one out on my first trip to the plate, and I would be a winner the next time. If you think about it, you really can't give yourself a pep talk because if you need one, there isn't a part of you that is peppy enough to give it. So I just told myself to shut up.

I changed my clothes, packed up, and headed to the front desk to check out. The clerk said that I had missed check-out time so that I would have to pay for an extra day, which was the wrong thing to say at the wrong time. So he was a bit shocked at the intensity of my reaction, and I got my additional sixty-five bucks worth and headed back to my room.

But not for long. As they say in Italy, when in Boston, do as the Bostonians do. I decided to join thirty-five thousand Bostonians at Fenway Park that evening and take in a game; ironically, the Tampa Bay Rays were in town and they and the Red Sox were battling for the lead in the American League East Division. Expecting the worst as far as traffic was concerned, I left early and for once that day, my expectations were realized. Twenty miles and three hours later, I was circling around looking for a parking space. There are more parking spaces at your kid's Little League field than at Fenway Park itself. If there are *no* parking spaces at your kid's field, then it's a tie. Parking is on the street or apartment complexes or people's driveways or near some distant subway stop. I managed to find a spot in somebody's driveway, paid them forty dollars, and walked a mile or so to the park.

Fenway Park is always sold out. That doesn't mean that tickets aren't available. Scalping tickets is illegal, but so was booze during Prohibition and cirrhosis of the liver wasn't eradicated, was it? I found a guy who said he had tickets for tonight's game and he would sell them at face value, but when he looked around and didn't see anyone who looked like they might arrest him, he told me he had the kind of face he valued at two hundred and fifty bucks per, and it was a good seat down the third base line. Given the nature of the transaction, he looked like he wasn't going to stand around and haggle, so I forked over the two fifty, went inside and found my seat. I watched a little batting practice, grabbed a couple of Fenway Franks, a beer, and a program and settled in for the game.

Fenway Park is the best place in the major leagues to watch a game. Fenway is the oldest park in baseball, and although the seats are about three inches smaller than the average butt, the park's old-time character, the intimacy of the crowd, and their unforgettably colorful language make for a bucket-list type of experience.

Fenway Park is the worst place in the major leagues to be during a rain delay. At the start of the second inning, the skies opened up and about half of the fans were able to cram into some sort of sheltered space, but I wasn't one of them. After five minutes, it didn't matter, so I just hunkered down and decided to wait it out. After thirty minutes, the rain went from buckets to fire hose intensity and the umpires still hadn't called the game. Finally, after ninety-eight minutes, they called it without even consulting me, a consideration I thought I was entitled to since I was about the only fan still there. But my ticket would be good for the rescheduled game on a date TBD. The afternoon wasn't a total waste, as I was able to memorize every Red Sox major and minor league player's bio, batting average, hometown, and thoughts about being a member of the organization up through the P's, when the program got so soggy it just fell apart in my hands.

By that time it was dark, and I sloshed around for about an hour trying to remember where I parked. By that time, any ideas I might have had about spending a night in some of Boston's famous Irish bars had literally, or at least extremely figuratively, been swept out to sea or Boston Harbor, so when I finally found my car, I headed back to Hanscom.

The trip from Hanscom to Logan Airport the next day was uneventful, as was the return flight. The whole experience was a bust, but I learned a valuable lesson: it's too damned expensive to look for a job.

CHAPTER 8

Sweet Home

DO YOU KNOW THAT IF YOU RETIRE on a lieutenant colonel's pension, even one as devalued as mine, you don't qualify for unemployment benefits? Those were the kinds of searches I did for the next couple of days because worrying about money was better than worrying about money *and* knocking my head against the wall looking for a job. I wasn't too bad off, yet, as I was still drawing active duty pay for another month or so, and my checking account was healthy, given that I had just spent a year in Afghanistan and my poker losses were the sum total of my expenses. But, if there is such a thing as a psychiatric economist, the diagnosis would be that I was in a recession heading toward a deep depression. Even golf didn't appeal to me. I had enough good sense to lay off the booze, and I began to wonder who that old man in the mirror was. It certainly wasn't me.

I decided to ditch USAJOBS.gov and only scanned the job boards, more out of a sense of obligation than interest. I got a few notices from some of the sites about jobs I might be interested in, but I wasn't. Fortunately, it was the weekend, or I would have called Old Jim Buddy to see if Duke and Sticks were still looking for a mortar target to send to Afghanistan. But on Monday, I would.

On Monday morning I took a run to clear my head and settle my nerves. I had decided to tell Jim that my sense of duty to the nation was so strong that despite several lucrative offers, I was willing to sacrifice, etc. He wouldn't believe it, but at least I wouldn't have to come straight out and admit I was desperate. Which he would figure out anyway.

I usually never take my phone on a run. This was *me* time and I have never, ever received a phone call that I couldn't just as easily receive an hour later. So I really wasn't paying attention when my Lone Ranger theme song ringtone went off and my running shorts started to vibrate. I was in the zone, so I ignored it. Two minutes later, another ring and another ignored call. There aren't many hills around Tampa, but I was on a pretty good upward incline when it rang again, and I at least looked at who was calling and didn't recognize the 256 area code caller. But it was the same number for all three calls, so I decided to answer; spam callers aren't this persistent.

"What?" I panted into the phone.

"Mr. Finnegan, this is Della from the Tiger Corporation. Am I calling at a good time?"

"No. I'm running."

"Oh my goodness. Who are you running from?"

Well that put me off my stride, literally, so I pulled up.

"What can I do for you?"

"Ma'am would like to know if you are still interested in working for Tiger Corporation and would want to come here for an interview."

"And where is here?"

"Why, Huntsville."

Not ringing a bell. The accent was deeply Southern, sort of Scarlett O'Hara as a three-pack-a-day gal, so I had two choices.

"It's a pretty long way to Texas."

Pause. Really long pause.

"I believe so. Are you running to Texas?"

"You know, I just might, after I stop by to visit you in Alabama."

"Oh. How nice. I'll tell Ma'am you will be coming here for an interview. I'll call you back."

I was left standing there holding a dead silent phone. I continued running and got another mile in before the phone rang again.

"Mr. Finnegan? Ma'am wants to know if next Thursday or Friday is good for you."

"Tell Ma'am that either is good, but if she wants me to choose, I'll take Friday."

"Thank you, Mr. Finnegan. I'll let her know and call you back."

This conversation wasn't trending toward ending any time soon, as we still had the details of the trip to discuss, and I wasn't up to the two-marathon distance it was likely to take to get there, so I took the shortcut heading back to the transient quarters. I had just made it back when Della rang again.

"Hello, Della."

"Hello, Mr. Finnegan. Did you get away?"

Huh? "Get away from what?"

"Why, whoever was chasing you."

"Yes, yes, I did. Left him in the dust."

"Oh, I'm so glad. I was praying for you."

"That must have done the trick, Della. Thank you very much. What did Ma'am say?"

"Ma'am says she will meet with you at eleven o'clock next Friday morning. I will make a reservation for you at the Embassy Suites on Thursday night. Some of the vice presidents will come by and take you to dinner then, and someone will come to pick you up at nine thirty the next morning."

"Ok, thanks, Della. Say, could you send me an email with those details?" Something didn't sound right; either Huntsville, Alabama, was so small that the nearest motel was ninety minutes away or they had some hellacious traffic problems.

"Of course, Mr. Finnegan and I look forward to meeting you. Have a blessed day."

How, uh, quaint? Or maybe the automobile hadn't yet come to Alabama, and it would take Ole Bessie and the horse cart an hour and a half to plod around the cotton fields and up Main Street to the office.

I had applied to Tiger Corporation. My job board account showed the status as pending, right among the sixty or so total applications also listed as pending, but fifty-nine of those companies hadn't contacted me. Yet?

Tiger had been incorporated the previous year. Its website identified it as a science and technology firm that supported the federal government, including the military and NASA. Corporate officers were Mamzelle Reynard (Aha! Ma'am.), president and CEO, and several Jacksons that were assorted and various vice presidents, including Della Jackson, who was vice president of administration. No vice president or director of business development was listed. And that was it. No links to bios or current contracts or accomplishments. The one site photo was of a three-story building that was identified as corporate headquarters, but Tiger's address was Suite 311, so somebody was fibbing a little.

There was a lot more to be found out about Huntsville, and it was all good. As in really good. As in one of the best places in the country to live, as rated by about a dozen organizations that make those types of ratings. So, on average, once a month, they were on an annual best place to live list. Keeps the Chamber of Commerce busy.

And there is a military installation, Redstone Arsenal, run by the Army and home to a bunch of organizations I had never heard of; organizations that develop rockets, missiles, helicopters, and probably lots of secret spook kinds of gadgets that wouldn't be listed on the official Arsenal website but most certainly have been leaked and are lurking somewhere on the internet. One number jumped out at me: about $10 billion federal bucks pass through Redstone each year.

To think that Huntsville's claim to fame was once "The Watercress Capital of the World." Because some place has to be, and I guess all of the other much cooler leafy green vegetables were already taken. Frankly, watercress looks like a weed to me. So back when, if you were one of the Huntsville muckety-mucks you had to figure that watercress was not something to build a future on. Round about

World War II, the Army decided to make its chemical munitions at Redstone Arsenal, but the mucks were slower than the Germans in claiming the title of "Poisonous Gas Capital of the World." So for a while, Huntsville was without a nickname because the locals who had been part of the Arsenal of Democracy just couldn't get into weeds anymore.

After the war, the Army pulled off one of the great con games in history. The Army rounded up all of the German rocket scientists and waved a wand over their records, making any Nazi past disappear, smuggled them into the US, and put them to work building rockets for our team. Impressive, but a minor con at best. The real con, an all-time winner, was to set up the scientists by taking them first to White Sands Missile Range (aka the great Southwest desert) and after a few years, convincing them that northern Alabama was just like their homeland in Germany with forests and rolling hills and fräuleins carrying steins of beer while yodeling. And compared to White Sands, it is, if you aren't too particular about the yodeling.

So the Nazi, er, German, scientists came to Huntsville to build rockets for the Army and, later, NASA, which by the way, has a large center at Redstone Arsenal, and somebody got the great idea to call Huntsville the "Rocket City," which is a cool enough nickname to catch on. Because if that had failed, they probably would have gone through a few more fainthearted iterations and ended up as the Nickname Capital of the World.

One of the best things about Huntsville isn't found on a website. It's found on a map. Huntsville is less than fifty miles from Mecca. Not the real Mecca, but a place of similarly fervent religious significance. Lynchburg, Tennessee, is the home of the Jack Daniels Distillery. Mark your calendars for our semiannual pilgrimages.

Over the next couple of days, I got even more familiar with Huntsville, played some more golf—the statute of limitations at MacDill's course must have expired, and although I was on my best behavior, my golf game wasn't, and I quit after nine holes. My parents had come back from Memphis, and while Mom said she was disappointed, Dad said he wasn't. Mom's report on the class reunion was about what I expected: nine arrests, and it ended early because someone had set a restroom trash can on fire. The class president was in it at the time. So pretty much an average weekend in northern Missouri. No word on who'd won the jail time lottery.

I did get a couple of invitations to interview for jobs, but I wasn't wild about either of them. One was from the border patrol, who must have thought that my experiences in the Southwest Asia deserts keeping illegals from sneaking into US installations and blowing us up was a good matching experience for sitting in the American Southwest desert keeping illegals from sneaking into US cities and mowing our lawns.

The other was from a company that was bidding to build border walls in the American Southwest desert to keep . . . well, you get the idea. But it wasn't a real offer; the job was contingent on them getting a contract from the US Government to build the wall. And they were optimistic that it wouldn't take more than two years.

I hadn't yet gotten to a short list of what I wanted to do or where I wanted to be, but my list of places I didn't want to be and things I didn't want to do was growing. And these were two more to add to that list. If the great American desert wasn't good enough for refugee German scientists, and their only other options were to be prosecuted for war crimes or turned over to the Russians, then Mrs. Finnegan's little boy wasn't going there either.

I did get an email from Della. My room reservation was now at the Holiday Inn and not the Embassy Suites, there wouldn't be any dinner with the VPs, and I could make my own way to the office. Be there at nine thirty. She was so sorry for the change of plans.

I arrived in Huntsville on Thursday afternoon, got a rental, and tried to check into the Holiday Inn. Wrong hotel. The desk clerk had to call around to a couple of other Holiday Inns to see if they had a reservation for Finnegan, but none did. And none of them had any vacancies. I was about to call Della and give her a stern talking to, but paused and asked the clerk if he had a reservation for a Della Jackson. Right hotel, wrong name. It took twenty minutes, a three-way conversation with Della, and my credit card for the clerk to allow me to be Della, but just for that one night. "Have a nice stay, Mr. Jackson."

I was having second thoughts about turning down the desert interviews, so I ate dinner at a Mexican restaurant because I can't stand Mexican food and that would squash the second thoughts. My mind at work. Unfortunately, and fortunately, the food was real good, and so were both extra-large margaritas, so I forgot all about the desert jobs. Mission accomplished.

Tiger Corporation is located in Research Park. There's the three-thousand-acre Research Park, home to all of the biggest aerospace and defense companies in the country. (Step right up—we got your Boeings, Lockheeds, Northrups, Raytheons, SAICs, and 300 assorted companies in nine million square feet of office space. Come see your second-largest research park in the whole U-S-of-A! Admission is free, unless you count the trillions of your tax dollars spent here.) And it's a park. Beautifully landscaped with flowering trees, ponds, and manicured lawns. Hoo boy. Sure beats sitting in a Humvee in the desert with a night-vision scope looking for border crossers.

Except Tiger wasn't located in that Research Park. It was in what the locals called "the old research park," which was a couple of nondescript office buildings to the northeast of the new park. I pulled in at 9:15, took the elevator to the third floor, and looked around for Suite 311.

I took a peek into the office door and saw a little old Black lady at the front desk. And she saw me, so I was committed.

"Mr. Finnegan? Welcome to Huntsville." The voice was magnolia-scented gravel.

"Hello, Della. Happy to be here and to meet you. I'm a little bit early, if that's okay."

"Why, no problem at all. Let me just see if your first appointment is ready. Would you like a cup of coffee?"

First appointment? "How many appointments are scheduled?"

"Well, let's see. One, two, three, four, five. Five."

"Then I'll pass on the coffee." Some people say that coffee runs right through them. I'm not one of them, but even at a slow amble, the coffee would have reached its destination before five interviews were over, so I decided not to take a chance.

My first appointment was with Regina Jackson, the vice president of personnel. Della ushered me to her office, first one on the left, and introduced us. Regina was in her early thirties, well-dressed, an attractive African American lady.

"What did Mam say?"

"I haven't met with her yet. In fact, I haven't even spoken to her."

"Oh. Did you have a pleasant trip?"

We went on for ten minutes like that. My trip, my family, my wife—Regina clearly frowned when I mentioned that I was twice divorced. Not a word on the job, my qualifications, my experience, my goals, or anything else that I had rehearsed for about four hours. It was starting to feel like the Corps of Engineers interview all over again—a waste of time. I considered starting a conversation about baseball, but that didn't work last time, and besides, she didn't look the type. Or maybe it was some newly developing maturity, finally, that allowed me to maintain my cool. Nah, probably just that I hadn't had any coffee this morning to stoke the fires.

My next appointment, in the adjacent office, was with Reginald. Reginald, the vice president of operations, was Regina's twin and, not surprisingly, as much a spellbinding conversationalist as Regina. In fact, the twins must have been given the same script.

"What did Mam say?" Etcetera. I even got the same frown when talk turned to my marriages.

Next door on the left was Reginald Jackson, vice president of finance. That would be Reginald, Senior, an older version of Regina and Reginald. Of the group, Senior was the most engaging conversationalist. Not that the script had changed, but Senior had the engaging, turning to annoying, habit of chuckling after each of my answers. I got the feeling that when he asked me about my trip, if I had answered that the plane had crashed and that I was the only survivor, he would still have chuckled. He even chuckled when frowning at my marital history.

"Mr. Jackson, do you mind me asking, is this a family-owned business?"

Chuckle. "No, Mam owns the business one hundred percent."

"Well, there seems to be more than a few Jacksons in important positions here. Kind of suggests a family arrangement of some sort."

That brought two chuckles. I couldn't wait to see what happened when I broke out my really good material.

"You might say that. I'm Mam's uncle, Reggie and Regina are cousins, and Della is an aunt but from another part of the family. Mam's real good about takin' care of family."

"Isn't that nice. So, as VP of finance, how's business?"

No chuckle. "Fine, really good. Lookin' to expand. Yes, sir. Really good."

I felt that I was really going to like it here. The Jacksons are such lousy liars that someone like me would be able to walk all over them. So for future reference: "Real good" means real bad, and "expansion" means that there are a couple of other cousins in line for jobs. Hmmm.

"Say, Mr. Jackson, we have a couple of Jacksons in our family. Any of your kin ever make it to Missouri?"

The chuckle was back; is there such a thing as a thoughtful chuckle? "No, not that I can think of. Kind of a common name, you know."

"Yes, I suppose so. But you never know. Just thought I'd ask." So I wasn't a cousin, even several times removed. I was about to ask him if there were any Finnegans in the Jackson family line, but Della interrupted us to tell me that Mam was ready to see me. Right-hand side of the hall.

I haven't said much about the building or offices. I know some writers will try and give their readers a sense of being there by detailing carpet, ceiling tiles, water coolers, and the like, but frankly, I don't really pay attention to these things. It was just a building; the offices were just offices. The veeps all sat in identical offices with an L-shaped desk configuration, a computer, a desk chair for them, an armchair for me, and nothing on the walls. Pretty much as if cubicle modular furniture had escaped and sought sanctuary in a regular office. I suppose there were ceiling tiles. I walked on something that may have been carpet, tile, or something else, and I don't remember seeing a water fountain.

So why mention it now? Well, for one thing, Mamzelle Reynard's office was huge, the same length as the reception area, three vice presidents' offices, two restrooms, a janitor's closet, and the mechanical/electrical room combined. And its size is just the third thing one notices.

Start with: "That's a hell of a lot of purple."
Move on to: "Are the baseboards and ceiling gold?"
Arrive at: "This is a huge room with purple walls and gold trim."
Finish with a flourish: "What in the hell kind of place is this?"
"Would you like to come in, Mr. Finnegan?"

To tell you the truth, I really wasn't sure. Stepping into the office would require that I set foot on a purple carpet with a large gold LSU in the middle. That's pretty intimidating.

But not nearly as intimidating as what awaited me at the other end of the carpet. Mamzelle Reynard sat at the end of a huge desk festooned with Mardi Gras beads, a purple lamp with a gold lampshade, and a computer monitor with a LSU sticker on the back. She was surrounded by three walls of pictures of LSU notables, including Nick Saban, who had guided LSU to a national championship in 2003. On her bookshelf was what looked to be a replica of that 2003 trophy. At least I think it was a replica. Looked pretty real.

The room was overwhelming, but I suspect that if I came in often enough, it would become less and less so. But Mamzelle Reynard was imposing, and I don't suppose that would ever diminish. From behind her desk, she looked like a block of granite, with short, curly blond hair (that probably was supposed to be gold to go with her purple blouse), a square face accented by a square jaw, broad shoulders and her hand placed flat on her desk. Damnedest optical illusion ever, because when she stood up to shake my hand, she must have been all of five feet, four inches tall.

"Mr. Finnegan, I am considering you as our business development manager. What is your experience in business development?"

Direct, to the point. She wasn't interested in my flight, my family, or anything else.

"None. But I know the military, and if you are interested in doing business with the military, especially the Army, I can help you." A direct answer. Probably stretching a bit; well, maybe more than a bit, but I kind of felt she would appreciate my confidence.

"Your résumé doesn't speak to any experience in military procurement. Do you know any of the decision-makers at Redstone Arsenal?"

And there went my confidence.

"Not that I am aware of." No point in BSing. This was going to be a short interview.

"Hmm. Do you think that your military credentials will open doors for us? We have great potential and some ideas about how to support the military. What we don't have is the access that will allow us to sell ourselves."

That sounded like a lifeline. "I understand your problem. The military is a fraternity; if you're in, you're in, but the fraternity doesn't admit others too readily."

That sounded really good. Mature, intuitive, and probably true, but I wasn't really sure that the fraternity here at Redstone granted reciprocity to members of my part of the fraternity. Kind of like keg bubbas crashing a wine-tasting party.

We stayed on the subject for more than half an hour. I was ready to let go, but she wasn't, so she ran through the whole list of all the Army activities at Redstone and then moved on to NASA and others. My contributions to the conversation consisted of what I hoped were astute-looking head nods. I thought I was pulling it off well until I must have overdone it and my neck cracked.

Change of subject. "Are you aware that we are a Small Disadvantaged Business?"

"I'm sorry to hear that." It seemed appropriate. I was going to add that I didn't hold that against her but something in her eyes told me to shut up. So I did.

"Do you know what that is?"

The inference was that I really should know what that was. But I didn't. I seemed to recall something about that on their website, but at that time, it didn't seem important. At that time.

A knock on the door interrupted us and probably saved my ass. Definitely saved my ass.

"Mam, Henry's here." Della to the rescue.

And with that, everyone filed in and headed to the conference table on the far side of the room. They were followed by an older, gray-haired Black man wheeling a cart of aluminum foil-wrapped trays, paper plates, plastic utensils, napkins, and six Styrofoam cups.

"Mr. Finnegan, will you join us for lunch? I don't know if you are partial to barbecue."

"Ms. Reynard, it would be my pleasure. May I use the restroom first to wash my hands?"

I didn't give a damn about my hands, but I ducked into a stall and googled "Small Disadvantaged Business." Seems like the federal government and what looked to be most, if not all, states allowed minority-owned small businesses to claim that designation and thus receive a preference for government contracts. So they became Small Disadvantaged Businesses and gained an advantage.

I returned to the office, which had now become a dining room. There were six places, one of which was filled by Henry, and I took a seat in the empty chair; in front of me was a plate full of pulled pork, coleslaw, and potato salad. I instinctively grabbed for my fork and felt ten eyes blazing away at me.

"Della, will you kindly say the blessing?"

"Yes, Mam. Lord..." Della proceeded to bless the food, everyone at the table, individually, saving me for last, but with what I thought was extra relish, and then a couple of other Jacksons, some of which were ailing and some of which were having babies, and then Tiger Corporation, the governments (federal and Alabama), several other institutions including "our military boys and girls," and closed with a flourish. "War Eagle."

Regina added an emphatic "Amen."

There was a chorus of "Roll Tide" from the Reggies.

"Go Tigers," Mamzelle offered as a closing comment. "And we will have a civil conversation at lunch. That means no football."

"That's cause you ain't got nothin' to talk about!" the Jacksons chorused.

And so we had a decidedly uncivil conversation about football. After all, the college season was to kick off the next day.

There are dozens of books about how to speak Southern and dozens more Southern dictionaries, but there are no books about how to have a conversation with Southerners. That's because it would be a very, very short book. There are only three topics of conversation: religion, politics, and football. And if you are too lazy to become conversant in the first two, just learn Southeastern Conference Football because you can always turn conversations about religion and politics into a conversation about football. If you don't, someone else will. Even preachers and politicians.

Regina broke down the strengths (lots) and weaknesses (none) of the Auburn offensive line, Reggie covered the various defensive schemes Nick Saban would employ at Alabama, and Della and Senior debated whether Alabama or Auburn had the stronger running game. Henry, who, as far as I could tell, hadn't declared a side, offered no opinion but listened politely. Mamzelle listened, but not politely, judging by the various grunts and snorts she frequently offered. I guess if you haven't won a national championship or two in the last five years, you aren't credible, so the best you can do is make annoyed noises every once in a while.

At halftime, they remembered that I was there and asked who my team was.

"I'll have to side with Ms. Reynard on this one. Go Tigers. Missouri Tigers."

That set the whole table into roars of laughter, with comments like: "We meant college, not high school," and from Della: "Oh bless your heart."

I took it all good-naturedly, then told them that we were applying to the NCAA for Small Disadvantaged Football Team status, which means that the other teams would have to spot us a touchdown each game. That got confused looks from everyone but Mamzelle, who snorted, and Senior, who chuckled, but I couldn't tell if he got it or not. Della asked Reggie if we could really do that.

We polished off lunch and the remaining football analyses, which consisted of special teams and the good and bad qualities of the two sets of fans, including how well they can put on a game-day tailgate party, and somewhere along the line I became Griff to everyone but Mamzelle, so she remained Ms. Reynard to me.

"Mr. Finnegan, shall we continue our conversation?" she said, pushing away from the table. Everyone else filed out. "It occurs to me that you might have some questions for me." All business again.

"Ms. Reynard. Thank you. Do you have any current business with the government, or anyone else for that matter?"

"No."

"So you have no income?"

"That is correct."

"Well then, forgive me for asking, but how are you going to pay for all of this until you can get something going? Just curious, you know."

"Mr. Finnegan, have you done your research on me?"

I felt like she was dodging the question. Google may give me some particulars on her life story, but it's not like I'd be able to see her bank statement. There might be an item listing the top two or three richest persons in a state, but . . .

Oh.

Time for another bathroom break.

"Thank you, Ms. Reynard. That's all the questions I have."

"Can you come back in half an hour?"

"Of course." And with that, it was down the hall to the second stall.

Mamzelle Reynard. Barbecue Queen of the Southeast. The picture was a little dated, but it was her all right. The other information was current enough. Second-wealthiest person in Alabama.

I headed downstairs to the back of the building, where there was a bench where I could serve my half-hour time-out. Henry was already sitting there, so I asked if I could join him.

"Sure, Mr. Griff. I's been waiting for you to joins me."

"Henry, that was the best barbecue I've ever had. And I've had barbecue all over the States; all over the world, for that matter."

"Thank you for that, Mr. Griff. I do take great pleasure when folks enjoy my 'cue. You ate 'cue all over, sure 'nough?"

And then he gave me his tutorial on Texas, Kansas City, Memphis, Carolina, and various other regional barbecue, and how Alabama (and he grudgingly included Mississippi and Georgia) barbecue was best because it was pork-based (mo' flavuhful) and prepared with better wood and smoked longer at the right temperature. I thought I was just passing the time, but he made it so interesting, I actually lost track of the time. By the way, for you readers that live in the above-named places that want to invite me to your barbecue, I'll graciously accept and tell you yours is the second best in the whole world. I hope that's good enough. Except for you Carolinians—you know why. Vinegar? Really?

"You know how to tell if you is gettin' good 'cue, Mr. Griff?"

I admitted I didn't—I just knew what I liked.

"No, no. You gots to get up real early, say four in the morning, and watch for the smoke. If they isn't smokin' by then, they won't be ready for lunch. Too many places jus' boil the meats and puts them in the smokehouse for jus' a couple of hours."

He said it like it should be a capital offense.

"Well Henry, that's good advice. A bit early for me, though. Any other way to tell?"

He considered the question for a while and then slowly shook his head.

"No, I'm afraid that's the only way. You can come by and look at the wood an' if it ain't hickory, you'll get some mighty sorry smoke. Some people swears by mesquite, and then you gots your exotics like apple and cherry, but hickory is the best."

"Say Henry. I read that Mam is the Barbecue Queen of the Southeast. Does she own your place?"

A big smile. "No suh. That's my last place. Has been for nigh on ten years. She owns all the others, though."

Wait. What? "Henry, did you own all the other barbecue places that Mam now owns?"

He considered that for a while. "I suppose so. Least ways, me and Mam did."

"Henry, how did Mam get all those other places and leave you with only one?" I was getting a whole new picture of Mamzelle Reynard, and it wasn't very flattering.

He looked at me like I was the prize idiot at the fair. Complete with a blue ribbon glued to my ear.

"Well, Mr. Griff. That's what she wanted." As if that explained everything.

"Henry, I think you're leaving a few things out. Did she just walk into one of your restaurants one day, order a rib platter, and then say: 'I'll take the restaurant to go?'"

Henry got a bit of a kick from that. "Pretty much that was the way it was. She done walked into my place in Mobile one day, a skinny little girl of sixteen, and told me she was goin' to be my waitress, and it didn't matter if I was hiring or not. And then in a couple of months, she told me she was going to be my bookkeeper, and then my business manager, and the next thing I knew, we was partners and gettin' married."

I got the feeling that this was the most words that Henry had ever put together at one time in his life, which was convenient as far as keeping the conversation going, because I was too stunned to talk.

"You and Mam were married?"

"Still are as far as I know. Never did see any papers. Anyways, Mam just started buying up other barbecue places, and then started franchising, and pretty soon we was a corporation, with a board and a whole bunch of folks that knew business but nothin' 'bout 'cue. But Mam made all them other restaurants cook like I does, so they all was successful, and Mam wanted me to go out and inspec' 'em all so as to make sure they did what she told 'em. Well, no sir, that ain't me, so I jus' asked for my own little place, and she could have the rest. And that was fine with her, so I moved up here. Wasn't going to be happy without the cooking and serving good folks anyway. Got me my place up toward Hazel Green, and you is welcome any ole time."

I always thought that X1 and X2 were at the top of the class, but from what Henry said, Mam made them look like Girl Scouts. Well, maybe Girl Scouts with merit badges in the dark arts, but definitely not in Mam's league.

"When did Mam go to LSU?"

"Oh she ain't never been to school there. Didn't even graduate from high school. She just like the colors—has to be purple for the Queen, you know." And now he looked almost embarrassed, like he was telling stories out of school. "Don't tell her I told you that, or we'll both be sorry."

Della had come down and interrupted. "Mr. Griff, you ought not to keep Mam waiting."

Having delivered her message, she gave a look at Henry, turned on her heel, and marched back to the office. I said a quick goodbye to Henry and hustled after her.

"Della, I'm so sorry, I just lost track of time. Is Mam angry at me?"

"Not half as angry as she is at me and Henry. Says it's our fault since we were supposed to be minding you."

Not very flattering, but then again, maybe it did appear that I needed minding.

"Della, you said I was supposed to have five interviews. Are you the fifth?"

"Oh my Lord, Mr. Griff. Heavens no."

"Well, who was number five? I've met three Jacksons and Mam."

"Why, Henry, of course."

Of course. "Why Henry?"

"Henry knows people. Mam trusts Henry's judgment of people."

I knocked on Mam's door and came in when I heard the growl.

"What did you and Henry talk about for so long?"

"Barbecue. Did you know the man's a genius? A Rembrandt with a basting brush. A Hemingway of the hickory. A—"

"Shut up. The only thing that old fool knows is barbecue. I don't know why anybody wastes their time with him. I have my hands full with that one old idiot and I don't need another."

I just gave her my idiot grin, which is pretty much like my normal grin, except I cross my eyes a little.

"I'm probably going to regret this, but if we can agree on a few things, I'm prepared to offer you the position. You'll start at 90K."

"How about we start with six figures since I have to relocate here and find a place to live and—"

"Ninety."

"How about if I waive health coverage and sick days and other benefits? Does that get me to a hundred?"

"I am not offering any benefits. Ninety."

Apparently, agreeing on a salary is not the same thing as

negotiating a salary. I could see the danger ahead. You may or may not have picked up on this already (and if you haven't, did you just skip right to here in the book?), but I have this whole Irish thing about being too stubborn to just roll over good-naturedly. She needed to know who she was dealing with.

"Okay, I accept, but I couldn't possibly begin work before nine. I'll be out and around starting at four to see what barbecue places have started smoking."

"Two damn fools. That's what I got, two old damn fools. Get out of here."

So I did but lingered just long enough in the hallway to hear her yell: "You start two weeks from next Monday."

I thought Henry and I would look pretty good in our matching *Old Damn Fool* T-shirts.

Della had the offer letter ready for my signature. The date reminded me that today was the last day of my active duty service. Tomorrow, I was retired from the Army, but today, I had a job in hand.

CHAPTER 9

Getting Down to Business

YES, THE XES AND I HAD OUR DIFFERENCES, with the principal difference being our opinions of me, ranging from about average or maybe just a bit slower than average (my opinion) to utterly worthless (their opinion). Actually, there was no range—those were the two choices. But, despite those differences, I used to admit that when it came to planning and conducting our several household moves, they were the best. Turns out that all their planning and coordination were necessary only because 90 percent of the things we moved were theirs. What I had to move fit into my SUV, with two seats to spare, not even counting mine.

Finding a place to live and setting it up was going to be a different story. Since I had joined the Army, I never had any choice about where to stay. The Army either assigned me living quarters or a tent. Setting up a tent was easy (see: cot, folding, army green). Frankly, the unmarried quarters I lived in didn't feature much more than that, and any furniture I had in married quarters went to one of the Xes. So far my list consisted of a bed, a TV and something to put the TV on, and a chair. I was thinking of a table to put next to the chair, but if the chair had cup holders, the table would be redundant. I finally just made a list of everything I remembered being in the MacDill visiting officers' quarters, threw in some towels and sheets, and considered it a good effort.

Which brings me back to a place to live. Obviously, rent not buy; I wasn't ready for that type of commitment. There were several apartment complexes that offered one- or two-bedroom apartments, but none that were furnished, which was okay with me. About time I started accumulating the trappings of a settled middle-aged man. Even if I wasn't sure I was all that settled yet.

One bedroom seemed too confining, but two seemed like an extravagance, especially since I hadn't considered buying anything to put into a second bedroom, certainly not another bed. I decided to make appointments with several of the apartment managers and just see how I felt at the time.

In the meantime, I would hang around Tampa and try to figure some things out. The first mission was to try and figure out what a business developer did. It's not like we do that type of thing in the Army. Considering what our business is. On the other hand, somebody has to start a war, and that's pretty much like business development if your business is fighting wars.

I did find something that I thought was important. There is a government marketplace where everything that the government is shopping for is posted. The website is FEDBIZOPS.gov, and like everything else in the government, it's overwhelming. Every federal agency posts every single solicitation, announcement of pending solicitations, changes to existing solicitations, and contract awards on this website, which is updated daily. I bought a couple of spiral notebooks and started entering into them all the words, phrases, and terms that I didn't understand and filled four notebooks in the week I spent digging into the site. The last couple of hours of each day I spent looking up everything that sounded like a great idea, but almost every definition used words, phrases, and terms that I didn't understand to explain the original word, phrase, or term I didn't understand. The whole process reminded me of a computer program do-loop; if you don't know what that is, look it up, then look up all the terms in the definition you don't understand (and there will be plenty) and keep going until your head hurts and you feel like throwing this book at something. And then do it for a couple hours a day for a week. I was doing it because I felt like I had to; I have no idea why you would want to because do-loops aren't all that fascinating, and it turns out that neither is page after page of government solicitations.

It didn't help that the solicitations are written in the type of legalese that readers may recognize as vaguely English, but an English that would have persuaded Shakespeare to write in Portuguese. It was as if a linguist had given a lawyer a list of the most obscure words in the English language, and the lawyer then put them all on a dart board and threw darts to determine the order. As with a game of darts in a pub, there must have been a lot of drinking involved.

I could sense my piece of cake turning stale.

A couple of the items on FedBizOps were different than the rest. There was one that looked like an invitation, extended by a half dozen or so federal organizations at Redstone, to an Open House, where these organizations would "present their programs for the upcoming fiscal year." The event was scheduled for mid-October, after the beginning of the fiscal year and well past the point that Congress is supposed to pass the spending bills that fund the government. Except that lately, that doesn't happen, and because Congress gets F's on its kindergarten *Plays Well With Others* report card, it instead passes continuing resolutions that allow federal agencies to keep the lights on but not buy new light bulbs. A couple of years ago, a continuing resolution lasted 217 days, so most of the government was literally, as well as figuratively, in the dark for a long time.

But the agencies play the game anyway, and there was a link in the announcement to sign up for the event. The link took me to a web page for the headquarters of the Army Materiel Command and a two-page attendance form to be filled out, which I dutifully did. I also checked the box asking if I wanted to schedule a meeting with a government representative. Once I submitted it, I received an email confirmation and a notice that the attendance limit had been reached, but I would be put on a standby list, just in case there were cancellations. The announcement had been posted the day before. I checked to see if the Rolling Stones had been booked as the opening act, but it appeared the attraction was the government representatives themselves, so they must be a hell of a band.

In the evenings, I broke up the monotony by stopping by Guy's bar. Before entering I took a sneak peek inside just to make sure that the coast was clear of any recent friends, but it was the regular crowd, only fewer. Guy wasn't in a talkative mood; his Yankees were trailing my Red Sox going into the home stretch of the pennant race, but even when I volunteered to take baseball off the conversation table, Guy didn't perk up. He was only faintly interested when I said I was leaving for Alabama, and all I got was something about rednecks and dumbasses and my impeccable qualifications for both, but his heart wasn't really in it.

"Look, I've been saving some good ones about how ugly you are and how your Yankees suck and how even the rats won't set foot in your bar anymore, but if all you are going to do is act like they caught you watering down the booze again, I won't waste my time."

A vague smile turned downward. "Finnegan, they're kicking me out. I can't make the rent anymore; the place ain't drawing like it used to, and this bunch of losers just nurse one beer all night. They extended me all they said they were going to. Come the first of October, I'm closing down."

"Ouch. How much are you down?"

He gave me a figure that even if I was so inclined, I couldn't make much of a dent in.

"What will you do? Do you have enough to open a new place?"

"Nah. I've got nothing here. Thinking of heading down to the islands, maybe tend bar in some coconut shack on the beach. Maybe just do nothing."

"Mankind's loss. You're a pretty sorry excuse for a human, but not many can make a vodka martini like you can, and speaking for those discerning few who appreciate that kind of skill, I don't know how we can overcome the loss if you cut and run."

"Thanks, Finnegan. I know you probably don't mean it, but I appreciate the thought. It's the nicest thing that somebody I don't like has ever said to me."

I thought that might earn me one on the house, for old times' sake, but Guy asked me what part of not liking me I didn't understand. So I paid full price and gave him a nickel tip, and we shook hands and said we'd stay in touch; one last lie.

The next day I packed up and headed toward Huntsville. I avoided the pleasure of driving through Atlanta; instead, I picked my way northwest on secondary roads, overnighting at the Ft. Benning visitor's quarters in Columbus, detouring through the Talladega National Forest, and taking a tour at the Superspeedway. I arrived at Huntsville in plenty of time to make the apartment tours. I took a second-floor, two-bedroom apartment in a complex behind a shopping center close to Research Park; the manager gave me a discount and charged me only forty-five dollars a month more for the second bedroom, calling it a military discount, which I figure was about one-tenth for me being former military and nine-tenths because the elevator didn't work. On the other hand, it had free Wi-Fi as long as I stood in the doorway.

There was a Target in the shopping center, so I picked up a cot, some sheets and a pillow, a folding chair, kitchen stuff, and some towels to get me through the next couple of nights. Or more because the furniture I bought the next day wouldn't be delivered for three weeks.

I had a couple of days to see the sights, which for the most part consisted of the Space and Rocket Center. I am not usually a museum kind of guy, but this place was fascinating, and I spent the whole day looking at the exhibits, which ranged from the early days of Army missile development to the entire history of America's space exploration. The guides were super friendly up to a point; they said I was too old to sign up for Space Camp, where kids from all over the world "train" to become astronauts. I kept telling them I was just big for my age, so they said I could go on the rides and simulators if I had my parents' permission, or without permission if I'd just quit bugging them about it. The most interesting story the guides didn't tell, but a fellow tourist did, was about the former CEO who had left the Center twenty-six million dollars of debt and then split for Texas. I was going to ask if I could go on that ride, but there were kids present, so all I said was how horrible that must have been. And besides, I didn't want to risk getting kicked off the real rides.

The next day I drove onto Redstone Arsenal and used my retired ID card for the first time to get through the gate. I asked the guard where they made the chemical munitions. He said he didn't know, so he asked the other guard, who also didn't know but said I could pull over and wait for the MPs to come by and they would be glad to help me. I didn't like the way he said it, so I told them it was just something I read and I really only wanted to go to the PX. The guards conferenced a little bit, but the people in line behind me were getting impatient, so the older one said I could go on, gave me some directions, and strongly recommended that I drive straight there. I waved at them, waved at the people behind me, and drove on at a steady clip a full five miles per hour slower than the posted limit.

I didn't really want to go to the PX, but I figured the Class VI store would be nearby, and it was, so I packed the SUV cargo area full, headed back to the apartment, and settled in, waiting for Monday morning.

I showed up at Tiger at eight on the dot. And for half an hour I admired the door, walls, ceiling, floor, and the small hallway window that was too high to look out.

Della showed up around eight thirty and let me in. We began about an hour and a half of paperwork. She issued me a key, set up automatic deposit, and finished converting me from soldier to civilian. Somewhere along the line, the rest of the Reggies (male and female) wandered in, said hello, entered their offices, and closed their doors. I asked Della what time Mamzelle would show up.

"Why, Mr. Griff, LSU played a home game on Saturday. Days when LSU plays at home, Mam don't show up until Tuesday. Before she left, she did say that I was supposed to collect up your security clearance."

She looked at me expectantly, like I was supposed to pull a piece of paper or a badge or something official out of my back pocket and hand it over. I explained that a clearance wasn't something I carried around; there is a big database called JPAS that she would have to access to check or transfer my clearance. We fooled around with that for a while and finally concluded that the government probably wasn't going to let just anybody jump online and see who in the federal government had a clearance; the instructions indicated that a company had to have a federal contract that required someone to have a security clearance in order to get authorization to access JPAS.

Della wasn't all too happy about that.

"Mam was thinking that if we was to hire you, with your security clearance and all, that you could get some of those contracts for us. Now you are saying that we need to have one of those contracts to even find out if you have a security clearance. Mam isn't going to like this one bit."

I could see her point. Telling her that it wasn't me saying it wouldn't help.

By this time, it was getting close to noon, so the Reggies filed out of their offices. Each got the full explanation, and each contributed a "Better call Mam" to the solution and headed out to lunch. Reggie Senior also pitched in with a couple of chuckles, a habit that was moving rapidly from mildly amusing to aggravating and destined for a "knock that shit off" real quickly.

So Della called Mam, put us on speaker, and explained the problem.

"And you're sure he doesn't have a piece of paper or a badge or something official?"

"Why, no Mam. That's what he says."

"And we can't get into that whatever website because we don't have any contract that requires us to have classified documents?"

"That's what it says, Mam."

"But if Griffin were to have to talk to someone who has a classified document for him to see, then they would have access to that website and could check on him?"

Della and I exchanged looks. Mine was sort of a "Hey, that makes sense" look. Hers was more of a "Hey, aren't you supposed to know that?" look.

"Pardon me, ladies, while I go out into the hall and kick myself."

"Della, you go with him and make sure he doesn't miss. See you tomorrow."

After Mam hung up, I looked at Della.

"She realizes that kicking myself is just a figure of speech, right? I mean, she doesn't really expect me to do that, does she?"

"Why, Mr. Griff, bless your heart. Of course not."

She pondered that for a little while. "On the other hand, maybe you should limp a little when she comes in tomorrow."

I could have told her that my fake limps weren't worth a damn, but that was too long a story.

We finished up the administration paperwork and Della led me back to the end of the hallway, past the Jackson family offices, the Reynard suite, the bathrooms, and the mechanical rooms, to an unmarked door. She knocked twice, heard nothing, unlocked the door, and walked in.

The room was huge, about fifty feet long and almost as wide, and completely unfinished, with sheetrock walls, a concrete floor, and no ceiling, so you could see all the roof structure, mechanical ducts, and electrical conduit. But no windows. To say it was sparsely furnished is a hell of an exaggeration. At the far end of the room there was a desk, and behind the three computer monitors was a headphoned head that paid absolutely no attention to us.

"That's Derek. We don't bother him when he's in the zone."

"How often is that?"

"Oh, about all the time."

"Why do you lock him in? Is he dangerous?"

"Why, Mr. Griff. We don't lock him in; he locks himself in. We have to unlock it to come in because he don't pay attention to anything else when he is in the zone. This is your desk."

She didn't answer the question about Derek being dangerous.

For years, government offices were furnished with gray steel desks, straight-backed chairs padded with something that might have resembled fake gray leather when it was new, and, if you were important, a swivel chair on four rollers. If you ever wondered what happened to all that furniture, I have a partial answer for you. And the real thing: the desk was missing one of its six drawers, two were stuck and wouldn't open, and there was a wad of paper under one of the legs to keep it from wobbling, somewhat. Which made the desk the better of the two pieces. The chair padding was torn and there were two missing wheels, so the chair rested lopsided on two casters and two wheels. Apparently the craftsman who had engineered the wobbly desk fix only specialized in desks.

Della gave me a smile and a shrug. "I suppose we ought to replace this. I'll speak to Mam about it."

There was a computer monitor on the desktop and a large tower on the floor. Della pulled a keyboard and mouse out of one of the drawers and gave me a piece of paper with logon and password credentials for the computer. She did the same for the company email system, gave me another shrug, and told me to give her a shout if I needed any more help.

It took me two hours, but I finally got things working. Except working was another one of those exaggerations. There may be another computer in the world still running Windows Vista and Microsoft Office XP, but if so, it's in a country we not-so-politely call *third world* and send millions in foreign aid to. My first inclination for an email password was WhatTheHELLDidIGetMYselfInto??!!

but besides being too long, I figured it would be too easily hacked since all things considered, it's the obvious choice. So I settled on my birthday. I found an old spiral notebook in one of the desk drawers, ripped out half the pages, and stuck one of the halves under each chair caster, which kept me somewhat upright as long as I put most of my weight on my left butt cheek.

Derek hadn't budged, so I settled into my chair to do some heavy-duty executive thinking. Somehow, executives are supposed to be able to do that. Grand strategies about new products and business deals and stock prices, dividends, and customer relations. Et cetera. Me, I had nothing. Except my left butt cheek was starting to get sore.

I decided that my problem was that the far end of the room was too far away for me to focus. I decided to swivel my chair around to the nearby wall, which was two feet away, to bring the focus closer. Except it wasn't a swivel; I picked up the chair, turned it, set it back down, and reinserted the notebook paper props.

Well hello. I had completely missed it because I had never faced this wall. The whole time, looking down at me, was a full-sized angel. That was at first glance. At second, and many, many subsequent glances, it was an almost life-sized poster of a long-haired blond in a white bikini, with a perfect tan, a perfect white-toothed smile, and all the other things that make a perfect girl perfect, standing on a ski slope. After a while I got around to the caption: *Think Snow!* Nice try, but there isn't a red-blooded male over fourteen who would be thinking about snow.

I decided to name her Heidi because she deserved a name, a unique name—which ruled out Jennifer and Meagan and Kaitlin/Caitlin because they were just too common. And Heidi, the girl, wasn't common at all. The poster was kind of yellowish around the edges and clearly had been around a while, maybe from the time when the furniture here was new. Now, that was a sobering thought because that would make Heidi about seventy now. There was also a torn corner, with the local area code written down and the rest of the telephone number missing, and I remember thinking that it was sacrilegious, the equivalent of defacing the Mona Lisa, only worse because Mona isn't wearing a bikini.

So Heidi and I began conversing about snow, and standing in the snow with a bikini on, and whether she was a good skier, and whether it was hard to ski with just a bikini on, and generally getting along real well when I snapped out of it and realized that it was dark, Derek had gone, and both my butt cheeks hurt like hell.

Now, I know that this was just an imaginary conversation, so don't go calling the guys in the white uniforms. The reason I know is that there was nobody in the room with me; Heidi is just a poster. Also, every extended conversation I've ever had with a blonde got me into trouble and I didn't feel like I was in trouble. I'd had a very nonproductive first day, but I didn't get into trouble.

Good night, Heidi.

CHAPTER 10

The Business I'm Getting Down To Is Funky

I GOT IN EARLY THE NEXT DAY, but Derek beat me. He was already hard at doing whatever it was he was doing, with his headphones on and smoke literally coming from his computer monitors. He barely looked up when I came in, but it was long enough for him to see me pointing at the smoke. So he pointed back at me, gave me a 'thumbs-up,' nodded his head, and kept on keeping on.

I rushed over, but as I got closer I could both see and smell that the smoke was from incense burning on a stand behind his desk, so I slowed down and tried to appear casual. In a moment, he looked up, resignedly took the earphones off, stood up, and extended his hand.

Derek is a big guy. It wasn't obvious when all I could see was the top of his head peeking over the computer monitors, but Derek runs about six feet, five inches, and 230 or so pounds, of which, maybe, one or so is fat. He had on a T-shirt and jeans and a pair of beat-up work boots. That's all he ever wore, even in winter, although he periodically switched out the T-shirt. I can't say the same for the jeans. A shaved head completed the picture. Except for the black-framed eyeglasses. I am way out of date; they look like the type the Army used to issue, and which had the nickname "birth control devices" because of how ugly they are, and now they are apparently in style. Could it be that the shaved-head Army recruits with the

BCDs were really cool all along? Nope.

Don't get me wrong, it's not the shaved head and BCDs that made Derek cool. Obviously. It was the three chipped front teeth, or more accurately, it's how he got two chipped front teeth. Big hint: Derek is from Canada. Believe it or not, collegiate hockey is played in Huntsville, Alabama. The University of Alabama-Huntsville competed in Division I NCAA hockey and even got as far as the annual NCAA tournament semifinal game in 2010. All in all, pretty good for a bunch of Southerners. Well, they were mostly southern Canadians, including Derek, who played defense and who some hockey fans would call a goon. But not me, definitely not me, even though he led the team in penalty minutes for two straight years. By a wide margin. But he earned two varsity letters—and three chipped teeth.

Unfortunately, the conference they were in dropped them the following year; although hockey is played in Huntsville, it isn't played anywhere else close to Huntsville, so the UAH Chargers had a hard time finding games to play and almost terminated the program.

Derek decided to switch to basketball instead and was welcomed warmly by the coach, who cooled noticeably when he found out that Derek had no ball-handling skills and although his two-hand set shot was, uh, entertaining, it wasn't very accurate. But Derek had found his niche as a fierce rebounder and aggressive defender and broke school records for most fouls, even though he usually had fouled out within the game's first five minutes. His best, and final, moment came when he absolutely leveled an opponent, a hit so devastating it broke that guy's collarbone and two ribs. The refs had to huddle for a while and finally called cross-checking, which, although a hockey penalty and not a basketball foul, was closer to what happened than anything else they could think of. The league ultimately reviewed the play and concurred with the call, although those officials also considered calling it aggravated assault, making Derek the first and so far only player subject to the NCAA Basketball rulebook, the NCAA Hockey rulebook, and the Alabama state penal code, all for the same infraction.

Part III: Army

The conference and the team suspended Derek, which was moot because when the other team articulately explained to the Charger players the nature of "payback," the Chargers just as articulately explained to Derek that this wasn't the NBA, and the UAH Victims wasn't a healthy team name, so Derek left the team to do other things. Needless to say, he didn't earn a letter, but he did chip another tooth.

Three diplomas on the wall behind him were evidence of what those other things were. Derek earned doctorate degrees in Mechanical Engineering, Aerospace Engineering, and Computer Engineering. And yeah, that's pretty cool too. So if a shaved head and BCDs are part of the whole package, then by the associative property of coolness, they must be cool too. On some people.

I didn't find out about all this about Derek until later. The immediate discussion, after introductions, was about what he was currently working on.

He opened a file and started moving his cursor around. Nothing happened. He continued moving the cursor and still, nothing happened.

"Uh, Derek, I might be missing something, but you are falling just a bit short of keeping me entertained."

"Don't you see it? It's a plane."

It looked just like a Microsoft Word document. I don't even think the word "plane" was in the document.

"Is it a stealth plane?"

"No, an F-16. A C-model. The Flying Falcon."

I felt like I was on *Jeopardy* and had been given more clues than any other contestant ever, and everyone in the audience knew the answer but me. Soon there would be millions of shares of memes of me staring at a computer monitor and screaming, "I don't see a plane."

"It's the cursor!"

It was. The cursor was a little plane, and it was a remarkably detailed F-16.

"Now watch this!"

And Derek hit the ALT, FUNCTION, and CTRL keys, and the cursor became a ship.

"A Destroyer. Arleigh Burke class. What do you think of that?"

"I love it." I lied. I mean, it looked sort of realistic, considering I had no clue what an Arleigh Burke-class destroyer was supposed to look like, but it was a ship with some guns sticking out, and it could be moved around like a cursor. Why I should care was the issue.

"So, can you play Battleship with it? Sink the other guy's ships on his computer?"

Derek ignored that. "I need your help with the Army part. What kind of icons should I use?"

I had no answer. Partly because I didn't understand the question, but mainly because I still couldn't figure out why we were having the conversation.

"Icons for what?"

I guess I am sort of a bellwether for these kinds of things; whenever I am made part of a stupid conversation, I just act confused so that pretty soon everyone else understands that the conversation is stupid. It's a gift. Most of the time it works. Sometimes it just convinces others that the conversation is fine—it's just me that is stupid.

This time, it worked. Now it was Derek's turn to be confused.

"Icons for the Army set of cursors. The Air Force and Navy have all kinds of planes and ships. As far as I know, the Army just has one kind of tank, and I don't know what else."

I got it. Derek wanted me to give him ideas of Army stuff to put on his computer and move around when he wiggled his mouse. And he wanted me to do it before my second cup of coffee and my morning conversation with Heidi. Not happening.

"Hey Derek, I've got some things going on I have to get to. Can we circle back on that?"

"Sure, sure. No problem. See you in a bit."

It was to be a short bit since at that moment, Della stuck her head in and said that Mam was back and wanted to see both of us.

We trooped on down to her office; the door was open, so we walked in. LSU had just thumped Mississippi State, so I figured Mam would be in a good mood. And she was because the scowl was almost gone, and she even nodded when we both said hello.

"You boys getting along? What do you think? Are you going to be able to sell it?"

She was looking at me, but her mistake was in not specifically naming me as the person she wanted the answer from.

"Great. What do you think, Derek?"

Derek was willing, able, and eager, and for the next five minutes he gave us a blow by blow of how he had completed the Air Force and Navy cursor libraries and how he and I would get together to do the Army systems and a bunch of other technical things. In the meantime, it was dawning on me that I had been hired to sell computer doodads to the Army, Navy, and Air Force. He hadn't mentioned the Marines; please not the Marines. The other three would just laugh at me and show me to the door, but mostly politely. The Marines would likely think I was making fun of them, and since *Semper Fi* is really just short for *Semper Fighting*—at least based on how I've seen them behave in bars—I really hoped he wouldn't mention the Marines.

"And then we'll work on the Marines, but I think I can use a lot of the stuff from the Army, so it should go quickly."

"Are you okay, Griffin? It looks like you were just punched in the stomach."

"I was just thinking about packaging and marketing brochures and how we would demo it. That's how I look when I think. My contemplating look is almost the same, but less so. Ruminating makes me break out in hives, and I suspect that if I ever get to cogitation, I'll have complete organ failure."

That earned a snort.

Now I was just babbling. It's my second go-to technique for stupid conversations that I can't just walk away from, and since both Mam and Derek seemed convinced that we were having a serious, rational conversation, my confusion act wasn't going to work.

"What are we going to call it?"

Mam answered: "My Click. Maybe without the *K*. Maybe with a hyphen, maybe not."

"Yes, yes. I like it. Good hard sounds. K is always memorable. Like Kalashnikov. No one remembers any of the Soviet tank designations, but everyone remembers AK-47. It's the K sound."

The thing about babbling is that there is a fine line between regular, standard babbling and drooling, insane babbling, and I felt that I was getting close. So I shut up.

Derek was just beaming. He would tell me later that he admired just how quickly I had picked up on so many key things and was already forming a plan to sell My Click. Or My Clic. Or My-Clic. And each time he said it, he emphasized the K. And I always thought that they made you wear helmets in college hockey.

Mam wasn't exactly beaming, but she wasn't scowling either, which was about as much a sign of approval as anyone remembers her ever showing, so it was time to get out before I screwed it up.

"Come on, Derek. We've got a lot of work to do, man."

He took me literally. When we got back to our office, he stopped by my desk, hoisted himself onto a corner, and waited for my pearls of wisdom.

"Army stuff. Hmmm. Well, we have helicopters and Bradley Fighting Vehicles and artillery. How does that sound?"

"Good. Okay. It's just that, well, you know, it's not jet fighters. Or aircraft carriers."

"I get it. No ZIP. No POW. How about a grenade?"

It looked like I was going to get a Marine Corps-type reaction from Derek, and I hoped it would only be a ten-minute major penalty and not a game misconduct and ejection infraction. Those are hockey terms, with the significant difference being that I might survive the former.

"Whoa, take it easy big guy," I reassured him. "I was thinking a grenade cursor, but when you double-clicked, like to open a file, it explodes."

And just like that, anger changed to awe, bypassing admiration altogether. I know because his only verbal response was "Awesome!" with a K sound, and he sprinted, literally sprinted, back to his desk.

I began to wonder if Heidi and I were the only sane ones around here, and she was standing in the snow with just a bikini on.

I checked my email, looking especially for whether or not I would have a space at the Federal Open House that was scheduled for next Monday. Nothing in the inbox or spam folder, so I called the POC at Materiel Command. She was very sorry, but they were still at full capacity, and there wouldn't be any room for me unless there were some last-minute cancellations. Specifically, if there were 124 cancellations since that's how many people were in front of me on the waiting list.

I spent a couple of hours going through FBO.gov, including some of the opportunities that I had passed on before, but given that my immediate future consisted of selling cursors to the military, some of those passes might look a whole lot better. For the most part they didn't; on Saturday night, no matter how desperate you are, there are still some girls you just won't dance with. A couple were maybes.

NASA's Marshall Space Flight Center, on Redstone, had an announcement for Administrative Services. I had to read it a couple of times, but each time it seemed like MSFC was looking for someone to hire secretaries for them. I don't get it; why not hire your own damn secretaries? The announcement didn't provide any hints, but even after one more reading, it was still asking for someone to hire their secretaries. And they only wanted small businesses to respond; it's what the government calls a "Set-Aside." And the next day at the Space and Rocket Center, there was to be a preproposal conference by MSFC on the solicitation. I had no idea what preproposal meant, but there was a number to call to register for attendance, and I figured that the worst that could happen would be that I got completely bored and then I would wander around the museum. So I called, figuring that I wouldn't get in anyway, but a nice lady said there was plenty of room and that she looked forward to meeting me tomorrow.

I don't know, but I guess that I should have asked Mam for permission to miss most of the next day. Part of me sort of resented having to ask for permission all the time (we'll call that my petulant side), part of me said this would be a good opportunity to show her some of the things I had uncovered on my own and get some feedback on what she considered legitimate business opportunities (we'll call that my professional side), and a small part of me thought it would be a good idea to say I was going to the conference and play golf instead (and we'll call that my Finnegan side). It took a great deal of effort to convince myself that I ought to at least give my professional side a chance and maybe get some of the considerable rust off. So I grabbed my laptop and walked down the hall.

"Derek seems to think you are some type of a marketing genius based on figuring out that we can use an exploding grenade. Is that so?"

"Well, yes, grenades explode, but a lot of people figured that out well before I did. Most intentionally, some not."

I only got a half-hearted snort for that, probably because she figured that she had set me up for that and so was only getting what she deserved.

I started by showing her FBO.gov and how one could search for opportunities locally, nationally, or by type of work, whether it was set aside for small businesses, etc.

"Do you mean that the government just advertises for all the things it wants on this website, and I can just open it up and tell them that I am willing to sell to them? Why do I need you?"

"Fair question. Let's open one up and see."

I showed her the MSFC Administrative Services item and let her read through it. And then read through it again. And one more time.

"What the hell are they asking for? This is the craziest thing I've ever seen. I cannot understand a single thing they are trying to say."

"They want us to hire secretaries to work for them. About fifty, as far as I can tell."

"Why don't they hire their own secretaries?"

"That will be my first question. There is a conference tomorrow that I plan on attending to see if this is something we might be interested in."

"Well I'm not. Where would I even put fifty secretaries?"

"They wouldn't work here; they would work at Marshall Space Flight Center in the NASA offices. Why should you? Because the government pays you back for what you pay the secretaries, pays you for the work you have to do to hire and pay them, and then pays you a little extra that we'll call profit, but they'll think of as something you get to pay corporate taxes on. And that is why you need me."

That earned a fully hearted, and then some, snort.

"Okay, let me know how the conference goes. And Griffin, you don't need my permission every time to go do your job."

And since I never intended to ask her permission every time I didn't intend to do my job, I was 100 percent covered. I printed out the NASA solicitation for Administrative Services, all 154 pages, and went home intending to read through it. I'd like to say I made it all the way through, so I will. Give or take about 150 pages.

Awaking well-refreshed, I decided to dress in "business casual" because "preproposal conference" just sounded way more informal than the sure-to-follow proposal conference, but I stuck a tie into my jacket pocket, just in case. Turns out I didn't need to worry about the tie or reserving a place at the conference. It's probably depressing to reserve a large place and then have such a small turnout, so the government brought along about twenty representatives, far outnumbering the seven business representatives. So the auditorium was only about 250 people short of being half full.

I checked in at the reception desk and the very bored government representative had a hard time finding my name tag, which, considering it was on top of the four remaining, was no small feat.

She smiled at me. "I guess I have a hard time reading them upside down."

They were right side up for her. I smiled back. "It happens sometimes. Where can I get some coffee?"

I suppose it was a trick question. There was a table with three coffee urns right behind her. She held up her arms in the "I don't have a clue" position.

"Sorry, I'm new here."

I don't know why I expected more of NASA employees. After all, they are still federal civil servants. Still, it's NASA, rocket scientists and all. Wouldn't you think they had a better candidate pool to choose from? For the next four hours, NASA would answer my question. Painstakingly.

The attendees mingled in the lobby of the auditorium while waiting for the doors to open. Most were Black, a few looked Hispanic, and there were a couple of women. I introduced myself to a few who seemed to be intimidated by the whole thing.

"Do you think they'll be giving us the contracts here?"

Are you asking me? Really? My guess is that there are at least six other people in this lobby who are better qualified than me to answer that. But looking around, I think I guessed wrong.

"No, I'm pretty sure that today they are just going to tell you what they want and then tell you the things you have to do to win the contract."

I guess that sounded pretty authoritative because they all started congregating around me.

"Will we all get a contract?"

"Nope. Just one of you. Us."

"Will they tell us how much our price needs to be?"

"I'm pretty sure that you tell them your price and they use that to figure out who gets the contract."

Each of my sage answers got head nods. I have to say that it felt pretty good to know things that others didn't. I hadn't felt that way in a long time.

One guy looked out of place. He was about my age but about 180 pounds heavier. He kept looking at me and appeared about to come over when the auditorium doors swung open, and we all filed in. Of course, the seven of us all went to different areas in the auditorium so that there were no fewer than forty seats and a dozen rows between any of us while the government personnel all sat shoulder to shoulder in the first row. All of which I could see clearly from my seat in the far right of the back row.

As soon as we got settled, one of the government reps, who later introduced herself as the contracting officer, grabbed a microphone and asked everyone to move down to the first three rows since the sound system wasn't working right, a point she proceeded to emphasize by banging the microphone on a table several times. At which point, the microphone, which had been working perfectly well before, stopped working altogether.

So we all trooped down to the first three rows, and I picked a seat behind the big guy who had been staring at me in the lobby. I figured that if I picked a good covered and concealed position, I could play with my phone or nap if it got too dull. Hearing me sit down, the guy in front twisted around, looked at me, looked at my name tag, repeated the maneuver twice, and broke into a grin.

"Finnegan!"

That was either recognition of some sort, or he was way too proud to have read my name tag. In either case, I didn't recognize him, and he hadn't twisted around enough for me to see his name tag.

"Finnegan!"

Still nothing.

"It's me, Sanders. We were in Korea together!"

That was twenty years ago. If I were a computer, my screen would say *Processing*, but since I've been told, in so many words, that I'm a few bits shy of a byte, the little wheel was just spinning.

Mr. Sanders must have taken my silence to mean: "Yeah, sure, come back here and sit beside me," because that's just what he did. These were comfortable seats, but there is not an auditorium seat in the world that is built for a 350-pounder, so about a hundred pounds worth was lopped over into my seat. We were the only ones sitting in the entire row.

In the meantime, all twenty of the MSFC team members were introducing themselves and identifying their roles in either contract preparation, evaluation, or management, which all boiled down to twenty people supervising one contractor. Sanders kept trying to lean over to continue our conversation, but I shushed him and pretended that the government introductions were the most fascinating thing I had ever heard, and I was going to give them my utmost attention.

"You're not going after this contract, are you?"

Some people are just oblivious to shushing.

"Thinking about it."

"How many small businesses do you think there are in this area?"

"I don't know. A couple hundred, maybe a thousand?"

"At least. And there are six here. Do they look like the industry's leading lights to you?"

The government was still introducing themselves. We only give the enemy our name, rank, and serial number, but these folks felt that, as a friendly audience, we were entitled to their name, job, number of years at MSFC, college attended, an appropriate Roll Tide or War Eagle, major, and maybe favorite color, and a bunch of other things, but I could never concentrate enough to last that long into the introduction. I wanted to raise my hand and ask if I could switch allegiance to the enemy side.

"Can't say one way or the other. I'm new here."

"Well, they're not. Anyone with any understanding of this contract wouldn't come near this. The last three incumbent contractors won't compete again. Two are leaving town. The other folded his company and opened up a tattoo and piercing parlor because he said he wanted to only associate with normal people."

Mercifully, the MSFC reps had finished introducing themselves and were about to start the presentation, so I pulled out my copy of the solicitation, where I had marked a few sections I had questions about.

The first slide was the cover page of the solicitation and the presenter read the whole thing and then popped up the second page, the third, and the fourth, each of which was read in its entirety.

"Sanders, are they going to read the whole thing?"

"Yep, word for word. All hundred and fifty-four pages."

That explained why there were twenty MSFC reps; it was a tag team event.

"Sanders, I give up. I don't remember you at all, from Korea or anywhere else."

He grinned. "Tell you later. You seem too interested in this for me to interrupt."

I was about to tell him that he would be my friend forever if he would please interrupt, but then I got it.

"Sad Sack! Sad Sack Sanders!"

Sad Sack Sanders was a lieutenant in the same company I was in; we both were assigned to the DMZ in Korea. Sad Sack presumably had a legitimate first name, but if so, no one ever used it. Sad Sack, then, was about 120 pounds with a full rucksack, helmet, and heavy machine gun. He had big ears then too; today, the ears looked, relatively speaking, pretty normal.

Sad Sack earned his nickname, and I was glad to have him around. The real Sad Sack fit the cartoon Sad Sack to a T; he was the Army's version of a really short and skinny Elmer Fudd, only less competent and without the speech issue. Compared to Sad Sack Sanders, I was the second coming of George S. Patton, who coincidentally believed in reincarnation, so I could very well be him. And if he was none too happy about sitting in a nearly empty auditorium having a 154-page solicitation about hiring secretaries read to him, join the club, George. That's life. Or, in this case, that's afterlife. But hey, you could have come back as Sad Sack Sanders.

"Sad Sack, how did you end up here? What happened to you?"

"Wait, we're coming to a good part."

I looked up at the screen and saw that we were only on page five. I completely agreed that up to this point there had been no good parts, but frankly, pages six through one hundred and fifty-four didn't look any more promising.

The presenter got to the bottom of the page where the words *This is not a Personal Services Contract* were printed in bold type. The presenter dutifully emphasized, loudly, each word.

Sad Sack's hand shot up.

"I have a question."

"Sir, I'm sorry, but we will only take questions at the end."

"Well then, I request a clarification."

The MSFC team huddled. After a few minutes they must have concluded that a question and a clarification weren't the same thing, so they solemnly announced that they would permit occasional requests for clarification but insisted that all questions must be asked at the end.

"Sir, what can we clarify?"

"What's a Personal Services contract?" he questioned.

"Sir, a Personal Services contract is when the contractor provides personal services to the government."

I shot Sad Sack a dirty look. He was making an already painfully long and worthless day even longer and more worthless.

"Ok, well, thanks for that. But, for clarity's sake, how can someone tell what are and what aren't personal services? For example, will the secretaries work in the contractor's offices or in the government offices? If they work in your offices, do I provide the computer, paper, desk, chair, etc.?"

"Sir, your employees will work in government spaces, and we will provide all of those things."

"Good, good. So if I'm the contractor, do I give my employees their instructions?"

Before the presenter could answer, she was yanked back into a conference. After three minutes, a different person stepped forward to respond.

"Sir, the government will instruct the contractor to instruct his employees that they are to follow the government's instructions."

"Oh, yes, well, that just makes sense. And do I, as the contractor, assign my employees to their government office?"

"Sir, you will assign your employees based on the assignment instructions the government provides you."

"Excellent, thank you so much. I am completely clarified now."

"Sad Sack, what was the point of all that?" I whispered.

"Personal Services contracts are illegal."

"But this isn't one. It says so right in the solicitation."

"Precisely. If it isn't a Personal Services contract, there wouldn't be any need to say so. Since they included a statement that says it isn't, then it is."

At this point, the presenter announced that since we had been there for an hour, it was time for a break. One hour, five of 154 pages; the math was terrifying. But things had gotten quite a bit more interesting.

I quickly headed back into the lobby looking for another cup of coffee, but the urns were gone. The Geneva Convention that prohibits inhumane treatment of prisoners of war needs an update.

Sad Sack caught up with me.

"You wanted to know what happened to me? After Korea and my next assignment, I transferred to the Acquisition Corps and became an Army contracting officer. I got out after five years, got hired by a big aerospace contractor to help manage their large contracts, and moved here. What about you?"

While I was giving him the rundown of my last twenty years, I was recalling the day back when I was at the Officer Advanced Course training to be a captain, and we were all ushered into an auditorium and a lieutenant colonel with some strange branch insignia briefed us on the Acquisition Corps and how important it was going to be and how they were looking for just the right people to transfer over. His incentive, so that any transferees wouldn't be disadvantaged by switching branches, was that the promotion rates for Acquisition Corps officers would have the same average as the rest of the Army.

Okay class, here's a quick quiz. Which of the following are most likely to throw away what they had achieved and trained for over the last several years for a desk job shuffling papers and the chance to be average?

A. The Above Average
B. The Already Average
C. Neither of the Above

If you listen to the John Boy and Billy Big Show on the radio in the morning, you know that the answer to the Current Events Quiz is always "C." If you don't listen, you are missing out, but the answer is still the same. Sad Sack Sanders must have been the poster boy for the Acquisition Corps.

He suggested we get out of there, have a cup of coffee, and catch up. "Trust me, you'll thank me later."

We found a coffee shop nearby, one Sad Sack evidently was familiar with because he made a beeline straight to the very oversized stuffed chair in the corner. So I asked what he wanted; I was embarrassed to ask for it but told the barista emphatically that the large black coffee was for me and the decidedly unmanly drink was for Sad Sack. The barista wasn't at all interested; he just asked what names to put on the cups.

"Hey, Sad Sack. What is your first name?"

"Just have him write Sanders."

I ask you, what kind of first name can be so bad that he would rather I call him Sad Sack than tell me what it is?

So I asked, but he wouldn't budge and went so far as to clamp his mouth shut tightly and didn't say anything for several minutes. I let it go.

"Tell me why I don't want to go after the MSFC secretary contract?"

"You mean other than it's illegal? Well, picture fifty hormonal—or worse—menopausal women that are bitching to the government manager they work for about how hard they are working, and they never get a raise or time off, and it's too hot in the office, but it was too cold yesterday and so on. And finally the government manager can't stand anymore and calls you and starts bitching to you, and then you are getting fifty bitching calls a day. And when you explain you can't do anything about it, they all go bitching to the MSFC contracting officer who becomes your fifty-first call each day."

"Can't I just pay them more and then ask the government to reimburse me?"

"Yes and no. In that order. The government doesn't care what you pay your employees. But they won't give you a penny more than what is in the contract."

Gulp. I considered whether I should race back to the conference and warn the other five contractors about the hell that was awaiting them, but I didn't. They can find their own Sad Sack and buy him coffee.

"Here's the question I was going to ask. Why doesn't the government hire its own secretaries? Especially if having someone else hire them is illegal?"

"Aaaah. That goes back to the beginning. So I'll need another." And he held up his cup.

Sad Sack boiled it down for me. The beginning was the start of the Army Acquisition Corps. Previously, each Army organization had its own acquisition staff, and it generally worked just fine. Sure, there were a few cases of contracting officers taking bribes, but they were invariably caught, and the amounts embezzled were relatively very small.

Then, in the late 1980s, the Army said to itself, "Army, we need a professional, independent acquisition organization made up of people with unimpeachable integrity, and because we will be independent and professional, we'll be much more efficient and save the Army lots of money."

That's generally how things work in the Army. Someone comes up with a good idea, writes a briefing paper, prepares dozens of PowerPoint slides, and promises results orders of magnitude better than the current method. The idea is implemented, and the idea guy gets a medal.

The trouble is that no one knew how to measure efficiency, and in fact, it really wasn't measured, and neither was the efficiency of the new system, so no one really knew if anybody was saving money. And besides, no one ever explained how changing the shoulder patch of the contracting officer and putting him in a new organization would make him any more honest if he was already inclined to take bribes. So we don't really measure that either. Which makes it real easy to claim any results you want.

Regardless, the Army Acquisition Corps was stood up in 1989 or so, and even after taking the cream of the crop of the Army's commissioned and noncommissioned officers (Sad Sack gave me a wink), found itself thousands of people short of a full staff so they went on a hiring binge and classified most of the positions as "administrative."

Now, the Army, and the rest of the federal government, has a pretty set way of hiring; it prefers to hire within its own organization and transfer laterally between like jobs when possible. And most of the people in Army administrative positions were secretaries who saw an opportunity to upgrade from administrative assistant to acquisition professional at a higher pay grade. So, the acquisition organizations got full, and the secretarial positions took a hit. And this was taking place in a lot of, if not most, federal agencies.

At the same time, throughout government, everybody was doing the hokey-pokey, which was another name for the A-76 studies that were designed to determine things like whether it was more cost-effective to hire some positions directly or contract for those functions. And the math said that it was cheaper to hire contract secretaries than pay them and the hiring, paying, and managing staff needed as well, and then pay all their pensions when they retired.

"And that, Finnegan, is how we got here. And if Subpart Thirty-Seven of the FAR says what the government was contracting for was personal services and those aren't legal, as long as everybody is doing it and nobody complains, then no harm, no foul."

The FAR is the Federal Acquisition Regulation, the two-thousand-plus page set of instructions on how to procure within the federal government. I had a pretty basic understanding of the FAR already, and if I were to read about 1,950-plus more pages, and remembered what I read, I would understand a whole lot more. And since Sad Sack didn't look like he was able to get up out of the chair without a crane, here was my chance.

He held up his cup again. But I made up my mind that this had to be the last; I wasn't going to be around when all that coffee kicked in and he had to get out of his chair and make it to the bathroom.

"Here's some advice. If a government contracting officer tells you what to do and says you have to do it because it is in the FAR, ask what subpart or paragraph it's in. Ninety-nine times out of a hundred they just made it up. Hardly anyone has really read the entire FAR."

Except him, and he had read it six times. And he gave me the *Reader's Digest* version, which still pretty much went over my head but at a much lesser altitude than previously, so I felt that I could become a midgrade contracting officer, at least the way Sad Sack described them.

Sad Sack was wiggling around like he was positioning himself to get up, but it wasn't even noon, and I had no intention of going back to the office yet. So, recognizing that he was pretty much at my mercy until I helped yank him up, he held up his cup again. I just shook my head and went and got him a muffin instead. A bran muffin. So this last discussion would have to be quick before things went nuclear.

"Sad Sack, aren't there any good contracting officers?"

"Sure there are. They just don't stay around. Businesses figure out quickly who the good ones are and then hire them away. That's what happened to me."

And he proceeded to answer my earlier question about what had happened to him, about how he had served for about five years in the Army Acquisition Corps and then his current company came calling with big promises and bigger checks. And he did a good job and got more responsibility, and the checks got bigger, until he became the go-to guy to deal with problematic contracts or problematic contracting officers.

"One time, we had a problem with a contract and kept asking the contracting officer for an answer. It went on for months. Each time we met, she kept telling me how much work she had and how her desk was so full of work, and they kept giving her more work until I'd had enough and told her, 'It's only work if you do it.' She didn't get it right away, but when she did, she told her boss, who told her boss, who told my boss, who asked me why I had gone out of my way to insult the contracting officer. Of course, I told him that I didn't go out of my way; she was sitting right there. Apparently, one can be a smart ass with the government but not with company executives, so he sent me packing to the business development guy, who told me to go out to government conferences and if I found anything we might want to go after, to write up a report. So I go to these contract conferences that we aren't even eligible to compete for, and I don't have to write reports."

The last several sentences came out fast as he struggled to get out of the chair. His eyes were getting wild, and he started sweating—a lot.

"Gotta get going, Finnegan." And he made for the door.

"Sad Sack, there's a restroom right here."

"Can't use them. Can't get into the stall—and if I do, I can't get out."

As we went out the door, a cop stopped us and, pointing at a blue

Mini Cooper, asked if it was mine.

Sad Sack jumped in. "No officer, it's mine. Why?"

"Sir, your driver's side-view mirror is broken, and I can't let you drive away as it is. If you do, I'll have to ticket you."

He can't fit into a public restroom but drives a Mini Cooper. And his side-view mirror was dangling from its bracket.

By this time, Sad Sack was beyond desperate.

"Finnegan, it's really bad. I need to borrow your car right now."

No was the obvious answer. No was the right answer. No was on the tip of my tongue and moving to my lips. While my hand was moving to my pocket for my keys. I did aid and abet in the situation, but it wasn't the guilt. I had weighed the alternatives and calculated that the considerable collateral damage my car was likely to suffer was less problematic than what was going to happen to Sad Sack, me, and the cop in about thirty seconds. If in Alabama a dangling side mirror gets you a ticket, Sad Sack would be facing life in prison.

My hand came out of my pocket without the keys but with my tie. A quick couple of wraps and a square knot got the mirror into something close to the right position. Sad Sack asked the cop if that was okay, but because the cop took longer than three-tenths of a second to answer, Sad Sack didn't wait and, faster than I thought possible, got into the Mini Cooper and was pulling away.

And as he drove off, he shouted: "Finnegan, I owe you one." I didn't know how to take that.

I looked at the cop and shrugged. "Family emergency."

I don't know if he made it or not. If he lived more than thirty yards away, probably not. If there was a blue Mini Cooper for sale the next day, it was buyer beware.

I got back to the office just in time for Henry's weekly visit. And the Jackson clan's weekly appearance outside their offices. College football season was in full swing, Henry had delivered the works, as usual, and even Mam, while not in what anybody would say was a good mood, was at least not in a bad mood. There was the usual give and take; Alabama had just beaten the snot out of Texas A&M, and Missouri was on the schedule in three weeks with just Louisiana (not LSU) and Arkansas in between, which is to say, essentially two bye weeks. So I was to be a target for three weeks.

I don't know why they thought I wouldn't be prepared; after all, this wasn't a surprise attack. I reminded them that Missouri was undefeated to this point, having scored forty or more points in each of its three games. More importantly, as I also reminded them, our next opponent was Alabama's SEC rival, Georgia, which brought out a couple of "Go Tigers" and relative peace for the rest of lunch.

Henry, as usual, remained pretty quiet throughout lunch, but during the lull when everybody else had gone back to the cart for seconds, he asked if I might want to attend the monthly Veterans of Foreign Wars meeting on Saturday with him. My answer, which I tried to mumble through a mouthful of pulled pork, wasn't exactly no, but it sure wasn't yes, which Henry seemed to accept for what it was. But Mam called it an excellent idea and assured Henry that of course I would be there. To which I mumbled, through another mouthful, something that could have been interpreted either as "Love to" or "Like hell," but in either case ended the conversation with the return of the reloaded Jacksons.

After lunch I gave Mam the rundown of the Administrative Services preproposal conference and some of what Sad Sack had told me about the contract and the FAR. My strong recommendation was that we not go after that contract.

Thankfully, Mam agreed. "That's not consistent with our corporate vision."

We had a corporate vision? I mean, the Army, Microsoft, GM, and GE have corporate visions. Your lawn guy probably has a vision. But Tiger? I wasn't sure I wanted to know, but I asked anyway.

"I didn't know we had a corporate vision. What is it?"

"Tiger Corporation is an advanced technology company that . . . There's some more I'm thinking about but haven't quite decided on yet."

Well, I've heard worse. At least it didn't start: "Tiger Corporation is an Administrative Services company that will hire and manage secretaries for you regardless of how painful that might be."

What Mam really wanted to talk about was the FAR and how the government solicits, accepts, and evaluates proposals for work it needs done and advertises on FBO.gov. There were a couple of things that really seemed to bother her. First, she now realized that I wasn't going to be able to walk right up to some honcho in the Navy and sell him battleship mouse cursors. And second, the whole complicated process was in the hands of government acquisition managers that, at least according to Sad Sack, were likely to screw it up.

"We need to find out what happens if—when—the government makes a mistake in their solicitation and how we would be compensated for the government's mistake."

I already had the answer. She wasn't going to like it, but since she'd just volunteered away my Saturday, there was that whole thing about payback again.

"Short answer is: you get to eat it. Long answer is that somewhere along the line, Congress became so infatuated with the FAR that they incorporated it into law, in the Federal Code. But they still call it a regulation instead of a law because the government hates change more than it hates confusing people, which is something they actually like. Anyway, because it's a law, there's an automatic assumption that a government employee wouldn't intentionally break the law, so there is no culpability there, and ignorance of the law isn't a defense, so you are responsible for knowing the law and if you don't, it's on you." Whew.

Mam stared hard at me, and I suspected she was thinking about excusing me from the VFW meeting and dragging me down to LSU for tackling practice.

"You made that up."

"No, I did not. It's called the Christian Doctrine, likely because when people heard about it, they shouted: 'Jesus Christ!' or 'Holy shit!' but even more likely because someone named Christian was involved somehow, although he is to this day probably walking around and saying, 'Holy shit!' a whole lot himself. And you know what else? I think we need to hire someone like Sanders because there's no way either you or I will know enough about the FAR to stay out of serious trouble."

Mam considered that for a while. "I'm not sure we're ready yet. Do you think he is going anywhere?"

I thought back to the last time I had seen him. "Well, he is a man in a hurry. But no, I don't think he'll be taking off for somewhere else in the near future."

CHAPTER 11

You Say Toe-May-Toe, I Say— Wait, What Did You Say?

SATURDAY NIGHT AT THE VFW wasn't as bad as I thought it would be. Granted, I had low expectations, but, well ... it wasn't bad.

I showed up what I thought would be fashionably late, found a parking spot amongst all the pickups and Harleys, and saw that Henry had saved me a seat, so I slid right in. The current post president, readily identifiable by his blue garrison cap that said *Post President*, had just about finished introducing all the distinguished guests, which consisted completely of all the previous post presidents, readily identifiable by their blue hats that said *Past Post President*. So, more than half the room got introduced. Henry was also wearing a hat—I hadn't realized he was a vet—but his said *Mess Daddy* on it, and as I looked around at the long tables full of aluminum foil-covered trays, I guessed his status was honorary, no doubt by overwhelming acclamation.

The post president next introduced today's guest speaker, a colonel from the Army's Aviation Program Office stationed at Redstone Arsenal. The Army, when developing new systems, assigns the designs, production, testing, and fielding responsibilities to a Program Executive Office, headed by a program executive, usually a general officer, at least for the major programs. The colonel's presentation consisted of a series of slides that showed various concepts for the Army's new attack helicopters, a development timeline, and cost estimates. The audience was respectful and asked good questions about roll, pitch, and that other thing, and collectives and cyclics and firing rates, and the former mechanics asked about phase maintenance and all those other things important to aviators. The colonel answered each question, except for the ones he said were classified, and even took a few notes. I was duly impressed, but I also noticed that what I thought would be a beer-guzzling session lacked one important element: the beer. There were pitchers of sweet tea on the table, and most were sipping the tea, which will make most anyone pretty mellow, but the fact that the Army sends out its "ambassadors" to keep the veteran community engaged and feeling important was mostly responsible for the business-like atmosphere.

Afterward, Henry introduced me around. I met Grunt, DAT, Redleg, Whirlybird, Grease Monkey, a few Docs, and Lieutenant Dan, who hadn't been a lieutenant, wasn't named Dan, and didn't look like Gary Sinise. Most of the attendees were Vietnam vets, with a handful of Desert Storm vets and ones and twos that had served in some of our other adventures over the last fifty years or so. The Korean War and World War II Vets had faded away, and the newer Iraq and Afghanistan vets hadn't yet shown up, so I was one of the younger attendees, which attracted a lot of attention because everyone wanted to know what the current Army was up to and how was it that they could get so screwed up after the previous generations had worked so hard to get it straight, and my best answer, with my mouth full of barbecue, was a shrug.

Yaw! That was the other thing. Roll, pitch, and yaw. I have no idea what they are, but they somehow keep a helicopter in the air, right side up, and flying straight ahead, and if you ask a question about helicopters with those buzzwords, everyone will think you are smart. Or an aviator, which definitely isn't the same.

Monday morning I drove to the University of Alabama in Huntsville (UAH) campus and parked at the far end of the lot. The

Open House conference was to be held in the UAH auditorium, and by the time I got there, the parking lot was about half full. I waited until the lot was almost completely full, picked out my target, and as he was closing his car door and gathering his briefcase, I sauntered over. He was about my age, weight, and height, and we looked enough alike for my purposes.

"Hey, good morning. I'm really looking forward to this. How about you?"

He looked up. "Yeah, sure. Not sure how much good intel we'll get since they haven't approved a budget, and none of these agencies are going to commit to any program that doesn't have congressional authorization yet."

"True that, but you never know where you'll find a nugget, am I right? I'm Sa . . . m, Sam Sanders. Son. Sam Sanderson." Barely caught that; introducing myself as Sad Sack Sanders wouldn't do if I wanted to be as anonymous as possible. Which I did.

"Bill Elliot. Boeing. Who are you with Sam? I don't recall seeing you before."

"Hey Bill, gotta run. I'm meeting my boss here and I'm late already. Nice meeting you."

And I skedaddled, beating him to the auditorium and the check-in line by a good two and a half minutes. I found the shortest line and started talking to the distinguished-looking guy in front of me, and when Bill Elliot, Boeing, came in, I waved.

I got to the front of the line and good morning-ed the young lady checking in attendees. Her name tag said *Courtney*, so I tagged it to the end of my good morning, and she didn't flinch. A good thing.

"Bill Elliot, Boeing."

Courtney started going through her list, but her head came up suddenly.

"Hey, you're not Mr. Elliot."

She had me. The accusation just kind of hung there. A lesser man might have panicked. An even lesser man might have run. Luckily, the Finnegans are made of sterner stuff. The key is remembering to smile; no one but car salesmen and politicians can lie when they are smiling. And they can only do it because of all the practice they get.

"Absolutely right. Bill got called into a meeting at the last minute and asked me to come in his place. Say, you're *Courtney*. Bill said to say hello if I ran into you. So, hello."

"Oh, that is so nice. Mr. Elliot is always so nice, isn't he? Tell him 'Courtney says hi,' and enjoy the Open House, Mr. Uhh . . . Will you be attending the one-on-one sessions?"

Okay. Decision time. I decided to jump in with both feet.

"Finnegan. Griffin Finnegan. And yes, please sign me up for a one-on-one session. I think. What is it?"

"Oh, you get to meet with a small business deputy from one of our agencies and ask questions and tell him about your company. Of course, they probably have already heard of Boeing. Hah! So you probably don't need these sessions."

"Well, you never know. Of course, everybody has heard of Boeing, but have they heard about all the new things we are doing?"

She paused, but just a second.

"You are so right, Mr. Finnegan. So I'll sign you up for a two o'clock session?"

I gave her a thumbs-up and moved on because the real Bill Elliot was nearing the front of his line, and I didn't want to be around when someone told a senior Boeing executive that he had already checked in. So I headed for the coffee and donut tables, where there was a big crowd to mingle with. Pausing to slip the name card out of its plastic clip-on case, I wrote my name and *Tiger Corp* on the reverse and slipped it back in. I did notice that quite a few people had inked in rather than printed names, so either there was a lot of substituting, or I wasn't the only one in town playing this dodge.

The conference was okay, as far as it went, which wasn't very far, at least for Tiger Corp. I did get to learn a little about the considerable number of federal organizations that spend a very considerable amount of federal dollars here. I would be able to give you a more definitive number—it's in the bazillions and maybe even gazillions—but even though the moderator had said all attendees would be able to access the slides online, about halfway through, he interrupted, apologized, and announced that because the numbers were projections and not yet approved, there would be no slides provided. So, all I remember is that each slide had lots of zeroes on it.

The problem was that all of these organizations were doing things that were way over what Tiger Corp could help them with. Lots and lots of missile defense, helicopters, space, information management, and all the supplies and matériel that the Army procures. Even the FBI was introduced and had a few slides about the new training facility they were going to build on Redstone. No computer doodads, and believe me, I was looking. Everyone else was oohing and aahing, and there was even periodic applause whenever what must have been new programs were introduced. The biggest applause was when it was announced that the new US Space Command had narrowed down its list of headquarters locations to six sites, and Redstone Arsenal was one of them.

There were a couple of coffee and socializing breaks, and I hunted around for Sad Sack. I caught a glimpse of him in a crowd, and he waved me over, but Bill Elliott was part of the throng, so I decided not to take the chance he would remember me and put one and one together to come up with me as the guy who'd swiped his spot. But he got in anyway, so no harm, no foul, right? Not worth the chance, just in case Bill Elliott isn't as nice as Courtney thinks he is. I saw a couple of the contractors that had attended the MSFC Administrative Services conference and hung around them for a while, but mostly slurped the coffee and munched on the donuts.

As a result, when the presentations were over and everybody broke for lunch before the one-on-one sessions, I wasn't really hungry, had no place I needed to be or wanted to go, and had about two hours to kill. Mostly I sat in the empty auditorium going over my notes and trying to think of what to tell Mam about opportunities I uncovered while "developing business" here. I usually like to start out the good news-bad news presentations with the good news, and that's where I was stuck. The bad news was easy; it was basically the agenda that listed all the federal organizations in Huntsville. So I took that list and put a checkmark next to the ones that did things I basically understood, or at least almost understood. I put X's next to the ones that I had sat and listened to and still had no idea what they did. And at the end of that drill, I was still no closer to figuring out how we could get any business from these organizations, whether I did or didn't know what they did.

So I tried a different approach. Most of the organizations, as part of their pitches, gave a presentation on how much work they gave small businesses. Now, a small business isn't easy to define. First, small in one industry isn't necessarily small in another. Second, being small doesn't count very much. You have to be woman-owned, or service-disabled-veteran-owned, or a special kind of minority-owned business called 8(a)—after some provision of some law that set this all up—and then the feds will give you special consideration for contracts, like setting some aside exclusively for your category. And they assign themselves goals to give so much work each year to each of these categories.

I sorted the federal organizations based on how well they reported they were doing in meeting their goals, which most of them did, mostly. That is, most of the organizations met most of their goals, some met some of their goals, a few met all of their goals, and some didn't report at all. I felt like I was onto something.

But then, I flamed out. Because there were still too many things I didn't know. For example, is it better to go after organizations that had good small-business participation records because they seemed to think it was important, or does the fact that they were successful mean that they aren't very interested in bringing on new small-business contractors? Conversely, are organizations that weren't doing well trying to do better, or is it that they just didn't care? I mean, except for the guy who has to keep the statistics and put small-business participation slides together every once in a while. And I suspect he is just going through the motions.

And finally, if I can't figure out what Tiger can do for any of them, does my analysis really even matter? Well the good news about this question was that I could answer it. Which was also the bad news.

Courtney came by to tell me it was time for my one-on-one appointment and led me to a classroom where several pairs of desks had been set up. I sat down opposite a young man with a nametag that read *PEO, IEW&S*. It was probably his organization, which I had never heard of, but then again, it could be Hungarian or some Slavic name, and I was about to extend my hand and greet Mr. Peeyo with a good afternoon when Courtney came to my aid.

"Mr. McCarthy, this is Mr. Finnegan from Boeing. He works with Mr. Elliott."

We shook hands, and McCarthy said, "Good afternoon, Mr. Finnegan, from Boeing," while his eyes were on my nametag, particularly the Tiger Corp part.

I was about to dial up another Finnegan BSer, but he had already moved on.

"Well, Mr. Finnegan. From the *auld sod*, I presume? What can I do for you today?"

"Mr. McCarthy, I represent Tiger Corp and we are a small disadvantaged business . . ."

"Right. 8(a)?"

"Well, no, not yet."

Mam and I had discussed this. The federal 8(a) program is a business development program for socially and economically disadvantaged businesses that offers several benefits, the principal of which is the opportunity to compete for contracts set aside, or reserved, exclusively for 8(a) businesses. A business can be an 8(a) for up to nine years, which sounds like a long time, but since a company can only be an 8(a) business one time, it has to maximize its success during that time and emerge capable of competing and winning in full and open contract competition. Which means it needs to have had several successful contracts and made a lot of money. And that's what had given Mam something to consider, which she did for almost half an hour.

It might have been longer, but that's when I told her the other part, the part about the owner qualifications, which included limitations on net worth. That earned me a snort and a glare, but not any questions about what those specific limitations were since we both knew it wouldn't matter.

"We're not ready yet."

And that was that.

McCarthy kept moving. "What does Tiger Corp do?"

"Tiger is an advanced technology company—"

It's a good thing that McCarthy interrupted at that point because that was all I had.

He was rolling his eyes. "Oh God, not another one. You can't throw a rock in Huntsville without hitting an advanced technology company and then having it ricochet and hit another. We gave a contract to a janitorial company last week that said it was an advanced technology company because it used electric floor buffers."

He recovered. Slightly. "Sorry, it's been a long day. Okay, an advanced technology company. Good for you. What do you do?"

The session was supposed to last fifteen minutes. We had used about two, and if I left then and said, "Have a nice day," but real slowly, I could maybe get to twelve minutes left. So I would only have wasted three minutes and McCarthy shouldn't hold that against me. Should he?

I just couldn't help myself. "Well, a little of this, a little of that. Working on a little project we call My Click..."

McCarthy's eyes stopped rolling. Instead, they were bugging straight out and staring at me. Intently.

"What do you know about My Click?"

Only he didn't really say My Click. It came out more like "Mick-Click." At least, I think so, but he had dropped his voice considerably and was sort of hissing at me now.

"Oh, pretty much just the basics. We have a couple of modules just about ready . . . working the others. You know. It's looking good."

"Ssshh. Lower your voice. Are you working the detect or the neutralize piece?"

It's not like I had been shouting or anything. But, okay, if that's what you want.

"Uhhmm, the software piece. Wait. You got me. You know Derek, don't you? This is about my Battleship suggestion. Did he sink your computer battleship? That's it, right?"

That last part wasn't a whisper. I've been the butt of jokes before, and I usually play along, but I had gotten all dressed up in a suit and then waited around for two hours to talk to this guy, only to find out that he and Derek had set me up, and I damned sure wasn't going to take it in a whisper.

McCarthy, for all I know, may be a man of very few talents, but if so, at least he was amazing with his eyes. I had gotten the rolling, the bugging, the staring, and now I got the wide-eyed shock look. Followed by a narrowing and then a wink. "You're right. We can't talk about Mick-Lick in here. Wait and I'll be right back."

I didn't have much of a choice since he had hustled off to the exit and was standing in the doorway talking to another suit.

But he had said it again, and this time I had heard him distinctly. Mick-Click. Or maybe Mick-Lick. McCarthy didn't sound Southern, and if he was, it would have come out Maah-Click. And if he and Derek were pranking me, that train had gone off the rails and was headed for a wreck. I don't care what McCarthy said—I was out of there.

McCarthy and his nice suit buddy showed up just as I was getting out of my chair, so Suit must have thought I was being polite and stuck out his hand.

"Mr. Finnegan, I'm Chuck Bergen. I don't know everything Ed told you, but if he was out of line, I'm sure he didn't mean it. Isn't that right, Ed?"

"Mr. Finnegan, I didn't mean to upset you. I'm so sorry if you took anything I said the wrong way."

"Ed," Bergen said quietly, "let's have everybody sit back down and get to know each other a bit."

"Yes, Mr. Bergen. Please have a seat, Mr. Finnegan."

So, I did, but I kept my weight on my feet just in case I had to make a quick exit. McCarthy wasn't close to being my match, but Bergen was in a different weight class, and if he was going to beat the crap out of me with kindness jabs and politeness hooks, I was resolved to bleed all over his nice suit before throwing in the towel and heading for the exit.

"Ed, why don't you tell Mr. Finnegan a little about what mutual interests we might have?"

"Yes, Mr. Bergen. Mr. Finnegan, do you know what PEO, IEW&S does? Oh, pardon me. Of course you do. That's why you're here."

I thought Bergen was going to yank him out of his chair and throw him out the window.

"Tell you what, Mr. McCarthy, uh—Ed. Let's just start with a nice chat, so why don't you tell me about PE EIEIO?"

McCarthy looked like the condemned prisoner who had just gotten the 11:59 phone call from the governor, but Bergen still had his hand on the switch. He took a deep breath, kind of surprised that he was still able to.

"Mr. Finnegan, the Program Executive Office, Intelligence, Electronic Warfare and Sensors, is responsible for several programs, including our Terrestrial Sensors Program. Mr. Bergen is the deputy program manager for TS as well as the product manager for our counter-explosive hazards work. Now you realize that Mick-Lick is just a concept at this point, and we haven't yet committed to making this a program, as of yet. So our discussion is, shall I say, hypothetical, at least so far?"

I gave him a nod, wink, and smile, which seemed to relax him a little, and Bergen too. A little.

At this point, Courtney came bustling up and impatiently reminded McCarthy that he had a two-customer backlog, and if he would please send me on my way, they could all try and get back on schedule.

Bergen began to get out of his chair, and as he did, he asked me if we could meet again the next day at his offices on Redstone. McCarthy also popped up.

"Mr. Bergen, uuhh, you know we have that *thing* tomorrow."

Bergen didn't look like he knew. "What?" he said, sounding rather short.

"That, uuhh thing. That event. The activity."

Bergen turned to me. "Mr. Finnegan, do you play golf? The RSA Scramble is tomorrow, and our team just got an opening for a fourth."

I figured out who the dropped fourth was about three seconds before McCarthy did.

"Well, Mr. Bergen, I'd be delighted, that is, if Mr. McCarthy is sure that he isn't able to make it."

"He's sure." And that's when McCarthy figured it out.

"Well then, Mr. Bergen, I'll see you then. Have a good evening. And you too, Ed."

Although I figured he wouldn't.

I drove back to the office to get Mam caught up on my day, and while I was driving, I tried to make sense of it. I circled the block three times, but I felt that I was getting further and further from anything halfway sensible, so I parked and decided to tell Mam the truth: everyone in the federal government who wasn't already there had gone insane.

Everyone had gone home but Mam, and she was meeting with a couple of slick-haired, middle-aged White guys in suits, one of whom I was pretty sure I had seen before because his name and face were plastered all over billboards. It's Silly Season again this year—

midterm elections at the federal level and everything from mayor to county coroner at the local level.

Politics in Alabama isn't very sophisticated. To be sure, there are registered Democrats in Alabama, and some even run for elected office. It's just that nobody knows why. So the real competitions are the Republican primaries, and there are only two issues, regardless of the office.

Issue One: Trump is Good.

Issue Two: Obama is Bad.

About a month before the primaries, the issues become more focused.

Issue One: Trump is Great.

Issue Two: Obama is Evil.

One week before the primaries, the candidates lagging behind will go nuclear. And play the Hillary Card.

The winner will be the candidate that is most pro-Trump and most anti-Obama. Unless you believe the other candidates who labeled him or her as anti-Trump and pro-Obama. But you shouldn't believe them because the winner labeled them as very anti-Trump and radically pro-Obama. It's a remarkably versatile strategy; every four years, the names can be changed, but the strategy remains the same. And the Hillary Card is still devastating.

So that's why you see a Republican candidate for Limestone County coroner on TV, wearing camo hunting gear and toting a shotgun, looking you right in the eye and telling you that he is going to fight against Obama's interference with his sworn and sacred duties as county coroner, so help him, Trump. And your dollars.

Don't mock—because it works. I'm telling you now that Barack Obama did not win election as Limestone County, Alabama, county coroner.

But if these two were trying to pry checks out of Mam's checkbook, I didn't want to stick around because if the homicide detectives were to question me, I could honestly say I didn't see a thing.

CHAPTER 12

Playing Golf with the Devil

I SHOWED UP AT THE LINKS at Redstone golf course at seven thirty. The weather was great—a nippy 85 degrees, which felt like 106 because the humidity was 99 percent.

Alabama summers last from the beginning of April to mid-October. Every day, the TV weather forecasters will give you a forecast high, but it doesn't really matter when it feels like it's ninety degrees or more. So, for all intents and purposes, there's hot, Hell, and hotter than Hell. Today was shaping up to be a day the Devil would be proud of.

I registered in the clubhouse. I thought I would have to explain why I was playing for the IEW&S team instead of Ed McCarthy and hope that Bill Elliott wasn't standing near, which he was, but it didn't matter because my name was on the list. So I paid my greens fees and got a sheet of paper with the scramble rules.

This was a charity event, with the proceeds going to scholarships for local military families. A scramble is a best ball tournament, with all four players on a team hitting a shot and then playing the next shot from the position of the best ball. To keep it a team event and make sure that everyone had to contribute over the eighteen holes, the team had to use at least two drives of every player. There were prizes for best team score, longest drive, and straightest drive, and for a par-three hole, the tee shot closest to the hole. Each player could also buy a mulligan bag.

A mulligan bag isn't really a bag, but for ten bucks, a player got three mulligans (or do-overs if you're not a golfer), two of which could be used on drives and one of which could be used for a putt, and one power drive. A power drive allows a male golfer to tee off from the ladies' tee. Ladies just got an extra regular mulligan.

Purists don't like mulligans. They consider them to be a corruption of the ancient and honorable game, and nobody is as haughty as a purist golfer confronting a mulligan user. Which is why I don't play with purists. Because of all the things I enjoy about golf, one of them isn't stumbling through knee-high rough trying to find a beat-up old golf ball I absolutely shanked before a snake finds me. I'll just hit another, thank you. I asked for a dozen mulligan bags. They only let me have one.

I joined up with my team, and Chuck helped load my clubs into his cart. He introduced me to Hank and Larry, who were deputy program managers for other programs managed by PEO, IEW&S, notable only for their indecipherable acronyms. That is, the programs were acronyms. Larry was notable for the knickers and Ben Hogan-style cap he was wearing. A little pretentious as far as I was concerned, especially when he started calling his clubs "mashies and niblicks" and the like when they looked like top-of-the-line Callaways to me. People that dress and talk like Larry are just clowns, unless of course, they have the game to back it up. And Larry had game. So did Hank, but as far as I could tell, he didn't look notable or talk notably. Maybe he saved that for the office.

At the first hole, they graciously let me tee off first. So I cranked one 240 yards down the middle-ish of the fairway, setting up what would be an easy-ish shot to the green. If my ball hadn't rolled into a fairway sand trap. No matter, the rest of the team hit theirs easily 280 yards, right down the middle and so close together, I could have driven the golf cart over and covered up all three.

And that's the way it went for the rest of the round. Before each of their shots, they huddled up and gave each other advice like: "Put a little draw on this one, and if you hit the slope just right, you'll be on the right side, a hundred and forty from the pin." Their advice to me: "Just give it a good whack, Griff." Condescending bastards.

By the time we made the turn to start the back nine, I was feeling it. The temperature had climbed noticeably—it was ninety degrees by ten o'clock, and I started hitting my drives farther and farther into the rough because that was where what shade there was, was. At least, that's my story. I did sink a forty-eight-foot putt at the par 5 eleventh hole to give our team a birdie. We had all missed, and I was lining up my mulligan putt after having received all of their advice on speed, aim point, break, etc., and as I carefully drew back my putter, I clipped the grass a little, throwing my alignment off just a touch. As a result, the ball started rolling way off line and way too fast and way too much to the dissatisfaction of the others, except that it kept heading for the hole, banged into the flagstick and dropped. Highlight of my day.

The trouble with highlights is that they are a relative thing; that is, they are high relative to the other events of the day, which by comparison are usually much lower lights. And by the time we came to the eighteenth hole, I was just barely hanging on, as the temperature had hit ninety-six, although the humidity did go down all the way to 90 percent. I was all for letting the other guys bring us home to victory—or defeat—by this time I didn't care, but Hank pointed out that, by the rules, I had to contribute two drives, and so far, I was still stuck on one.

I proceeded to shank it, badly. We—that is, they—recovered well enough to earn us a par and a score of sixteen under. Normally, that's good enough to walk away with the win, but we ended up tied with the team from the Missile Defense Command. Our only two pars were the holes where my drives had to count, so I wasn't feeling good about that at all, but it could have been the incipient heatstroke.

The winner was decided by going in order down the list of the hardest holes, and the team that won the hardest hole would be the winner. We got all the way down to the fifth-hardest hole, the eleventh, and our birdie topped their par, so we collected the top prize, which consisted solely of bragging rights and a box of balls since all the proceeds went to charity. I was about to offer up my body to charity, or medical science, and if they were to wait about fifteen minutes, they could cart me away, but the clubhouse air conditioning and a couple of beers got me most of the way back to lucid. That was a good thing because the ambulance had already made two roundtrips with two other victims, and the paramedics were advancing on me. I was able to give them a thumbs-up and utter something that sounded like "I'm okay," but may have been closer to "Sunset Bay" or "Milky Way," but in any case, the paramedics peeled off to collect someone else who had given them a thumbs-up and then fainted and hit his head on the table.

Anyway, I'm telling you this not just because I thought you should know about our victory but also because the golf course is where business people discuss business, and I got a cartload. I'll give you the condensed version because you're probably not as interested in that stuff as you were the golf results.

As we drove together in the cart, Chuck Bergen apologized again for any misunderstanding that Ed McCarthy may have caused, but it all worked out okay because he and the team really enjoyed playing with me, even though Ed had been the captain of the Auburn golf club and had played with them in this tournament for the last three years.

He reiterated that MickLick was not a program and as such couldn't have contractor involvement, and any implications to the contrary were just a misunderstanding. And it wasn't MickLick, but MICLIC, which stood for *Multiplatform Identify and Clear Lanes In Combat*, which was all about finding and neutralizing hidden explosives or mines so that vehicles could pass through without blowing up. But they had high hopes that MICLIC would get to be a program in the next couple of years, and we could certainly compete at that time for a contract to support the program.

But anyway, his boss, Colonel Harvey, the program manager for Terrestrial Sensors, would be in town for the next couple of days and maybe we could come by and introduce ourselves, say tomorrow morning at nine? He added that I might not like Col. Harvey since she didn't understand things like he and I did, and she was too far out there trying new things, and that he constantly had to rein her in before she got too far out of the box. But I could judge for myself tomorrow. What about it?

I must have said something that sounded like "Yes" or "Glompf," which was close enough because it was accompanied by what Chuck thought was a head nod but was more of a momentary fainting spell.

Anyway, it was a heck of a putt, and now that I consider it, it might have been closer to fifty-five feet.

It took me two hours to recover, take a cold shower, and drink a gallon of water, and three trips to the bathroom before I was feeling well enough to come to work and fill in Mam on the last two days. As I came in, two more politicians were leaving, so I asked Della whether Mam was a Republican or a Democrat and whether she actually gave these sharks any money.

"Mr. Griff, Mam isn't partial to either party, but she is more than generous to both and not just in Alabama, but Mississippi, and Louisiana, and some even in Georgia and Tennessee too. Why, I think every incumbent in those states is beholden to her, and just about all those they beat out are too."

Good to know. But were they risking life, health, and heatstroke for her? Time to ask for a raise, and if I could only put a positive spin on what had happened the last two days, I believed I could pull it off. Except I really had no idea what had happened the last two days, and the only thing positive I could spin was the seventy-foot putt, and I didn't really expect that would get me even an extra buck.

I laid the last two days out to Mam. She sat there stoically, a periodic and almost imperceptible raising of an eyebrow the only sign she was paying attention. At the end of my recitation, she had only one comment and one question.

"Some of the big boys hit their golf balls over three hundred yards. I don't think hitting it seventy feet is much to brag about."

And, "Griffin, what have you gotten us into?"

I wished I could give her an answer.

CHAPTER 13

Surprise!

The Purpose of the Adaptive Acquisition Framework, DOD Instruction 5000.02

The AAF supports the Division of Administrative Services (DAS) with the objective of delivering effective, suitable, survivable, sustainable, and affordable solutions to the end user in a timely manner. To achieve those objectives, Milestone Decision Authorities (MDAs), other Decision Authorities (DAs), and Program Managers (PMs) have broad authority to plan and manage their programs consistent with sound business practices. The AAF acquisition pathways provide opportunities for MDAs/DAs and PMs to develop acquisition strategies and employ acquisition processes that match the characteristics of the capability being acquired.

I THOUGHT I'D TRY PUTTING IN one of those quotations that inspire or illuminate or present an original, deep thought or are just simply quotable, but as far as I can tell, nobody ever said or wrote anything inspirational, illuminating, original, deep, or quotable about how the military acquires or procures things. So here you go, straight from the source. Be inspired, illuminated, and thoughtful to your heart's content.

Anyway, as far as the quotation idea, all the real serious authors do it. Frankly, it doesn't do that much for me, so I don't know if I'll do this again. Probably not. Unless I can find a quote that explains what the hell this one says.

The Army doesn't buy things like you and I do. To make sure you understand that, they don't even use the term *buy*. Instead, the Army *acquires* things. Occasionally, they *procure* them. But if you expect to see the Army standing in line outside of Best Buy on Black Friday to get good deals on electronics, you'll be disappointed. Or relieved, because they probably would have *acquired out* everything in the store before you even got in.

If the FAR is the DOD Acquisition Bible, then the DOD 5000 series of instructions are the Catechism, Hymnal, and Book of Common Prayer. And that's as far as I'll take the analogy. In a nutshell, and it's a really large nutshell, these instructions tell the armed services how to manage the requirements, development, design, production, testing, procurement, deployment, and maintenance of everything from Humvees to missiles and lays out a step-by-step process for every action and decision that takes place along the way. By directing every step, the military can ensure several things, including consistency of process. It must work because what is acquired is consistently more expensive and less capable than what we ask for. And don't get me started on timeliness.

And that's how it used to be. More recently, the Department of Defense, startled by the blinding flash of the obvious, has been trying to reform its acquisition approaches. Some of the new approaches being considered include encouraging Program Managers to:

- Be more autonomous, flexible, and creative in their decision-making processes
- Network and collaborate with other acquisition activities and services
- Incorporate past experiences, new ideas, and creative problem-solving to translate concepts into novel applications
- Apply commercial innovation to government processes to

keep up with industry technology
- Engage nontraditional industry partners.

The sound you hear is paradigms breaking all over the place. And it's music to our ears.

But just because someone directs change doesn't mean that the change will be embraced. Or even tried. Change is hard in a bureaucracy, but you know that, so I won't beat a dead horse. Which is exactly what we would all be riding today if the bureaucrats had their way.

So, Mam and I set out to meet Col. Harvey. We wondered what her tune was.

We met Col. Harvey in a nondescript office in a nondescript building on Redstone Arsenal. She got up to greet us—broad-shouldered, tall, and impressive in her uniform, but her most distinctive feature was her overly large ears. Overall though, she looked like a soldier. That last part wasn't necessarily a compliment, and if you don't know what I mean, try snuggling up to your sweetie tonight and telling her she looks like a soldier. But Col. Harvey was impressive in my eyes, and it became pretty clear, pretty soon, that she was one of those new-era, progressive PMs the Army was trying to grow, which to me, put her at odds with Chuck Bergen, who was in the room as well. Both were nominally stationed in Fort Belvoir, Virginia, just outside of DC, but Chuck was in Huntsville because he thought she was in Fort Belvoir, and she was in Huntsville, at least for a few days, because it wasn't just outside DC.

Chuck introduced me and I introduced Mam and Chuck introduced Col. Harvey, who had already introduced herself. Col. Harvey then introduced us to the Terrestrial Sensors program and then turned to a discussion of MICLIC. She reiterated that MICLIC wasn't yet a program but that there was a great deal of interest in fielding a capability very soon and that she was looking for ways to streamline things. And in fact, they had made some significant progress already in that they already had an approved MNS.

A MNS is a mission needs statement, which identifies that there is a shortcoming the Army needs to address. It doesn't necessarily mean that the solution is a new system; in fact, the Army uses an analytical process to determine what a proper solution should be, with the idea that it is more efficient, cheaper, and timelier to find a solution that *doesn't* require a new developmental program. That process involves the analysis across a spectrum of paradigms that go by the acronym DTLOMS, which used to be DTLOM until someone said that the analysis necessarily had to include the Soldier, and Soldiers had to be first and foremost in how we think about things. So they put the S at the end.

The approved MNS, developed by a team in Afghanistan, is not classified, but it is *for official use only*. However, it went something like this:

> **MISSION NEED:**
>
> Combat operations in the Afghanistan Theater of Operations necessarily involve the transport of critical supplies over the few passable roads in the country. The predictability of the main supply routes has increased the likelihood of hostile interdiction, especially by means of conventional landmines (leftover by the Soviets) and improvised explosive devices (IEDs). Invariably, the first vehicle is targeted, and the resultant casualties have created an understandable hesitancy on the part of our truck drivers to be the first driver in the convoy. Specifically, this hesitation is based on a common theme, which overwhelmingly has been, to quote: "We are not idiots." There were several more colorful variations of this same theme. After canvassing the entire theater of operations, we uncovered, in fact, that there was a theater-wide shortage of idiots, the consequences of which, *sine qua non*, are a shortage of drivers to assign to the lead vehicle.

DOCTRINE:

We have researched our doctrine and determined that the responsibility for recruiting, training, and deploying idiots has not been assigned. Consequently, absent a designated idiot proponent, there is an absence of doctrine that addresses these responsibilities. Several Army branches come to mind as logical proponents, but to date, none have acknowledged any responsibility.

More broadly, we have inquired of the Air Force, Navy, and Marines about their approaches to idiot doctrine, which created some testy moments until we rephrased the inquiry to be about doctrine for the recruitment and training of idiots, at which point: the Air Force laughed and hung up, the Navy laughed and said they had the Marines, and the Marines said they were Marines but didn't laugh.

In summary, all the services have neglected this key doctrinal responsibility, and although we have enclosed certain recommendations in this regard, implementation will not provide the timely solution we seek.

TRAINING:

Consistent with the absence of an assigned proponent, no training Program Of Instruction (POI) has been developed. We took the initiative to develop our own POI here in Afghanistan, but we soon realized that we were faced with a conundrum. Once we identified trainee prequalifications, both physical and mental, outlined course material, and determined the nature of the qualification test, we realized:

If a trainee failed to meet the standards or pass the test, they would not be qualified to be idiots, and they would subsequently be washed out of the program.

If a trainee demonstrated that he or she could both meet the standards and pass the test, they would be certified as both qualified and trainable, which would, in fact, prove that they are not idiots, and they would subsequently be washed out of the program.

As a result, despite all our efforts, we could foresee that the net result would be zero (0) new idiots available for driving trucks.

LEADERSHIP:

This too proved to be a less than successful approach. Initially, accepting the Army's fundamental tenet that all problems could be solved by the implementation of good, sound leadership, we looked at this as a challenge. Our approach called for the application of both positive and negative motivation reinforcement measures:

Positive Measure: We offered three-day passes to those who accepted their assignments as first driver. These soldiers quickly pointed out that, in Afghanistan, a three-day pass has very limited positive substantive effect on motivation due to the fact that there is no place to go, and pass recipients just hang around their barracks all day.

Negative Measure: In addition to glaring with very stern faces, we threatened anyone who refused a first driver assignment with confinement to quarters, whereupon those very same soldiers cited above pointed out that, except for the stern glare, the result was exactly the same and that they were willing to live with the stern glares. Literally.

ORGANIZATION:

Initially, we felt that an innovative series of organizational changes offered the most probable means of satisfying our mission needs. We assembled all the drivers and explained that we accepted their premise that assignment as first driver involved certain distasteful consequences and that henceforth, drivers would only be designated as second, or following, drivers and assigned to the second, or following, spot in the convoy. With the caveat that in the event of the authorized or unauthorized absence of a first driver, the second driver would temporarily assume the first position, but, and we emphasized this point, only for the duration of the first driver's absence. After a very brief consultation amongst themselves, the newly designated second, or following, drivers informed us that they had concluded that we were, in fact, idiots, and that we ought to drive, and here I quote, "our own damn trucks." Despite what may seem to be the obvious merits of this particular solution, we dismissed this approach as impractical. And for other reasons.

MATÉRIEL:

The nature of this mission need did not suggest that we would find a solution in the Army's supply system, but we dutifully combed through all Army supply catalogs. We found what we thought just might be a matériel solution, but upon subsequent examination, determined that the lug nuts were not the type that we were looking for.

PS: However, please send us four gross lug nuts to replace the ones that have been blown off our wheels.

PPS: Also send one hundred fifty wheels to replace the ones that have been blown off our trucks.

PPPS: Also send forty trucks. Ditto.

SOLDIER:

We note the irony of investigating the Soldier paradigm as a means of satisfying our mission need in that our mission need resulted directly from our unsuccessful efforts to put soldiers first and foremost.

PPPPS: It occurred to us that given our lack of success

in finding doctrinal, training, leadership, organizational, or matériel solutions to satisfy our mission need, perhaps we were pursuing the wrong approach, so if you want to provide us with systems that detect and neutralize explosive hazards, that's A-okay with us.

Col. Harvey concluded her presentation of the MNS and then politely asked us to explain the nature of our achievements in developing a MICLIC-type capability.

Mam was on that. "Col. Harvey, I hope you appreciate our position in that, without a formal agreement between Tiger and the government, we can't fully divulge our approach, but suffice it to say that our entire technical staff, including PhDs in Computer Engineering, Mechanical Engineering, and Aerospace Engineering are working full-time on the project."

Translation: "If you ain't paying, I ain't talking. And you better be paying a lot."

I don't know if Col. Harvey appreciated her position, but at least she didn't seem too put out by it.

"I anticipated that response and have been thinking of an innovative way to streamline our next step, which is, as you know, to prepare the Operational Requirements Document or ORD."

At this point, Chuck started to cringe.

"Ma'am—I mean Col. Harvey, not you, Ms. Reynard—I must advise you of the implications of getting too far astray of accepted practices at this point. I recommend that we confine our thinking to the proverbial box and not jeopardize the program by adopting unconventional methods."

"Thank you, Chuck. And may I remind you, yet again, that I am the one who gets to say what the box is, proverbial or otherwise.

"Tiger has apparently done some groundwork to at least identify capabilities and requirements for a system and perhaps has gone as far as performing engineering work to design for these capabilities."

Mam gave a slight head nod as if to say, but be careful not to say, that Col. Harvey was exactly right and that perhaps Tiger had even gone beyond that point. My admiration for her was growing by leaps and bounds.

Col. Harvey continued: "Then it seems pointless, or at the very least, highly inefficient, to develop an ORD detailing operational capabilities, size, weight, mounting, and other technical requirements when Tiger has already gotten to that point. And at the worst, to create an ORD that is in conflict with what Tiger has already developed without considering whether their concepts might be better than ours."

Chuck rolled his eyes, but even he had to acknowledge the logic. But he didn't appreciate it, and he didn't appreciate what came next.

"Chuck, we're going to have to get Ms. Reynard a security clearance, Top Secret, before we go on. Let's get that started. Mr. Finnegan, you check out okay. Is there anybody else we need to read onto the program?"

I was about to say I didn't think so, but Mam interjected and asked if her chief of technical services could also be included and gave them Derek's name.

"Next, we are going to have to figure out how to get to you guys. Contractually, I mean. Chuck, any ideas?"

"Ma'am, I mean Col. Harvey, this is highly unorthodox. But . . . Ms. Reynard, Tiger is a Small Disadvantaged Business. Are you an 8(a)? If you are, we have a means of getting to you directly."

"Not at the moment, but I submitted my application to the SBA yesterday."

News to me. It didn't seem likely that Mam had just chucked all her wealth to get certified. I wonder if she had forgotten about that requirement.

"Well, Col. Harvey, there goes any hope of program acceleration. To the best of my knowledge, these applications can take years to be approved. By law, SBA has ninety days, but their favorite trick is to claim that there is some error in the application, send it back, and the clock starts all over again. Which means this could take years." If Chuck was trying to hide his smugness, he wasn't very good at it.

Mam was controlling herself quite well. But barely. I didn't know if she was more pissed off at the implication that she had made an error or the inference that she was just like all the other applicants. "Col. Harvey, if I may be permitted to make a phone call, I think we can find out quite quickly. And not have to speculate."

Col. Harvey nodded, and Chuck looked remarkably relaxed for a guy sitting in a room where two women were trying to keep themselves from tearing him to shreds.

"Loretta, this is Mam. Yes, it was good to catch up with you yesterday too. Uh-huh. Uh-huh. So, working it? Uh-huh. That long? Well, okay. Thanks, Loretta."

Mam addressed Col. Harvey but was looking at Chuck. "Loretta runs the Birmingham branch of the SBA. She apologizes that she won't be able to approve the application today. But she'll FedEx it to me tomorrow."

I need to anticipate moments like these and have my iPhone camera ready. Chuck's reaction was priceless. I thought you had to hold your breath to turn that purple, but since his jaw had just about hit the floor, I knew he was breathing. I suspected I would have other chances to get a picture.

Col. Harvey decided that we'd had enough for the day.

"I'll be here for two more days; I have a flight out Saturday morning. How about we get back together on Friday at 1300?"

Another jab back at Chuck since I suspected, in the great tradition of all civil servants, that he didn't work Friday afternoons. But he's a trooper.

On the way back to the office, I think Mam and I were both too stunned to talk. Much. I did point out that Derek was a Canadian citizen, and that might prove to be just a bit of a problem getting his clearance. And in this case, just a bit of a problem meant impossible.

Mam just smiled. "Griffin, can you get your friend Mr. Sanders to drop by sometime tomorrow?"

Of all the day's surprises, I think finding out that Mam could actually smile was the biggest of all.

I arranged for Sad Sack to come in at nine o'clock, and I arrived at seven thirty to check with Mam on what our game plan would be. She was on the phone, so I waited in the hall, and that's when I noticed that beneath the sign on Reginald's office that read *Vice President of Operations,* there was a new sign that said, *Owner.* I looked back at Mam's office and noticed the sign that said *President and CEO.*

I knocked and entered. Reginald was at his desk.

"Congratulations, Reginald. Let me be the first to say that the company couldn't be in better hands. And let me also take the opportunity to inquire whether the new ownership is inclined to give raises to its most valuable employees."

A couple of chuckles. "As owner, I will allow my president to continue to handle those matters."

"Well then, how about, in recognition of weeks of dedicated service, giving me another week of paid vacation?"

More chuckles. "As owner, I will allow my CEO to continue to handle those matters."

"Well then, in your capacity as owner, how about giving me my own office?"

A half chuckle, and then he stopped and appeared to study the question.

"Griff, I agree. That is a matter the owner should address directly. No."

While waiting for Sad Sack, I chatted up Derek for a little while. Apparently, he was making great progress on his cursor icons and had even developed a prototype minesweeper game that could be played between two users on the same server, with the added feature that both screens would morph into spreadsheets if anybody were to walk by.

I casually asked about some of his other interests and whether they might include, say, hypothetically, explosives detection and neutralization. Well, I couldn't slip it past him because he asked if that was what Mam and I had been working on together. But then again, he does have three PhDs. What was I thinking?

He pondered the question a bit and went off on a discussion of the chemical elements of explosives and how new "sniffer" technology was coming out, but that was as far as I understood because he went into chemical formulae and such. Turns out he had also gotten a master's degree in Chemical Engineering but didn't think it was appropriate to hang that diploma with the three PhDs.

Sad Sack showed up promptly at nine, and Della buzzed me to join him and Mam in her office. I made the introductions, and Sad Sack settled himself into the largest chair available.

Mam asked me to summarize our conversation with Col. Harvey and Chuck Bergen, but since I didn't know what was and what wasn't important, I pretty much related the whole afternoon verbatim, as best I recalled. Mam didn't interrupt, so I guess I got it mostly right.

Mam took over. "Mr. Sanders, thank you again for coming here. If you don't mind, I have some questions specifically about the contractual discussions you just heard about. Our 8(a) certification came today, so is it just a matter of Col. Harvey awarding us a contract directly?"

"Are you a Native American, Hawaiian, or Alaskan?"

"No." Mam didn't blink, but I thought it was a ridiculous question and didn't see how it related to our 8(a) status.

"Are you a community development corporation?"

"What's that?"

"A CDC is a nonprofit—"

"No!"

"Then, no. They can set aside the contract for 8(a) companies exclusively, but it would still be competed, not a direct award. And that would seem to defeat the purpose."

I chimed in. "Wouldn't Bergen know that?"

"Sure. Sounds like he set you up. Or Col. Harvey and he set you up. Or he set up you and Col. Harvey. And that's the one that I would bet on."

"What else?"

"Hmm. FAR Part 18 talks about contracting in emergencies, such as a war, but it wouldn't apply in this case since the capability you're after isn't readily available to be employed in the emergency. Expediency is the key."

Mam's face fell. This wasn't going the way she had hoped. And, I suppose my face fell too, for the same reason, but also because I had talked up how smart Sad Sack was, and I felt I was letting her down.

I took a shot. "Can we claim that what the government is getting from us is proprietary? Wouldn't that have to come directly from us if we are the only ones that have a MICLIC system?"

Sad Sack just smiled. But it was a sad smile.

"Yes, the FAR does have provisions for safeguarding proprietary information, like software, but the government isn't after information; it's after a physical capability. It hasn't specified any specific technology, and besides, you would have to present your case by describing the capability—which, from what I understand, you don't have."

Mam was clearly disappointed.

"Thank you, Mr. Sanders, for coming by. I'm sorry that we—"

"Wait, I wasn't through. It seems to me that you have only one last resort. A personal services contract."

Mam brightened up again, but I didn't.

"Aren't they illegal? They were on Monday, according to you," I reminded him. The thought of sharing a cell in Leavenworth prison popped into my head, and there was no way this kid was going to do anything that made that put me in that situation. Ten years of Sad Sack in the top bunk hovering over my head was beyond the call of duty. Way beyond.

"Very good, Griff. You were paying attention, after all. They *are* illegal, except under one condition. FAR Part 37 says that Congress can pass a law authorizing a PSC."

"But wouldn't it still have to be competed? The NASA secretaries contract still had to be competed."

Sad Sack just winked. But at Mam, not me.

"Depends on what the law says."

Mam had fully recovered and then some. Her second smile—in as many days. "Leave that to me. Mr. Sanders, you have been most helpful. Griffin, if you will excuse us, Mr. Sanders and I have some things to discuss."

Some people may have been put off by being kicked out of the big-people-only conversation. Not me. It occurred to me that I was becoming the moral conscience of this bunch—an unfamiliar and frightening thought—and my best strategy, when it became necessary to employ it, was the Sgt. Schultz defense: "Your Honor, I know nothing." German accent optional. (If you are too young to remember the TV show *Hogan's Heroes*, and you probably are, you won't get this reference. So, look it up.)

But I do know what happened in the meeting.

Sad Sack was hired as vice president of contracting and government relations. By the way, his first name is Harland. Yep, a third-generation descendant of Col. Sanders—or, as Sad Sack puts it, one generation out of the money. Turns out he didn't like to be the butt of the inevitable jokes and name-calling. He was okay with the obvious, like Chicken Man or even Chickenshit Man. He couldn't stand being called Colonel. He wants everybody to know that he works for a living. And he asked that I keep his first name a secret. But since he is pulling in forty thousand bucks a year more than me, he doesn't get any favors.

The next morning, I bumped into Reginald in the hallway outside his office. He was holding his *Owner* sign and looking like a bug someone had just stepped on.

"Sorry, big fella. I really enjoyed working for you all of yesterday."

He was so despondent he didn't recognize the sarcasm.

"Thanks, Griff. I really thought I could do it. And Mam also just stamped out the raises I was going to implement."

Now I was despondent and more than a little sorry for being a jerk.

"Reginald, I am truly sorry. So you put us all in for raises?"

Reginald nodded. "Yes. Well, not all of us. Not you. Or Derek. But all the rest of us."

And now I was more than a little sorry for not being a bigger jerk.

One month later, buried in the Water Resources Development Act of 2018, an innocuous little piece of legislation that authorizes projects and studies to develop, improve, and protect our nation's water resources, was a single-line amendment: "The Department of Defense is authorized to negotiate a contract with Tiger Corp, Huntsville, Alabama, for the purposes of obtaining personal services to develop vital programs for the United States military." Since Col. Harvey, and begrudgingly, Chuck Bergen, agreed that their program was already adequately funded to pay for program development, they didn't need any accompanying appropriation legislation, which suited certain members of Congress and a certain patron of theirs quite well. Especially considering, other than declaring war, which it hasn't done since World War II (not counting periodic wars on drugs, cancer, crime, and good taste in political advertising), Congress only has one job, and that is to pass annual appropriation bills. Not only do they not do that in anything close to a timely manner, they invented something called a continuing resolution just to avoid having to do their single job. Normally, most people would welcome the idea that Congress isn't spending our money, or more precisely, money that is in addition to the money the continuing resolution provides to just maintain the status quo. And no funding for new activities, which means that not only would we not be paid, we couldn't even get a contract because for some reason, the government draws the line at issuing contracts that spend money they don't have. As if that ever stopped them before. Ladies and Gentlemen, as Exhibit A, I present the National Debt.

On Friday afternoon, Mam and I headed to the Arsenal for our meeting with Col. Harvey and Chuck Bergen. En route, she brought me up to speed on the conversation she'd had with Sad Sack about what we could expect when (not if) we negotiated our contract.

The government has two basic types of contract payment schemes. If the government can well-define the scope of work and what is required of the contract (contract deliverables), it will ask for a firm, fixed price from the contractor. If the scope isn't well established, and the government can't identify specifically the contract deliverables, then the contractor has to take on a big risk. Contractors deal with risk in different ways; they charge lots more, or they charge a whole hell of a lot more, or they just ask for the keys to Fort Knox. So the government, rather than setting a firm, fixed price, agrees to reimburse the contractor for the effort expended—in other words, the government assumes the risk. The contractor and the government agree on rates for all costs: direct costs and overheads, or indirect costs, and profit. Sad Sack had told Mam that if the legislation came through, the negotiation would be to arrive at this cost-reimbursable contract.

Sad Sack also told her that she couldn't cheat, although I suspect that he didn't just start the conversation that way but rather responded to various of Mam's suggestions. All contractors are subject to official audits, and the Army Audit Agency, noting that Tiger was a brand new Army contractor, would be looking at fresh meat. Even before the contract award, Mam would have to establish a government-approved financial system, not only to satisfy the AAA but also because falsely certifying invoices to the government would cause Mam, on her way to the gold depository at Fort Knox, to have to make a substantial detour to the west to get to the federal penitentiary in Fort Leavenworth.

"And you, Griffin, will be the program manager."

I had anticipated that. I figured that I was the only one she knew who was halfway familiar with what needed to be done, had a security clearance, was available, and was relatively cheap. But that latter qualification didn't need to be a permanent condition. Besides, Mam would just pass that cost on to the government anyway. So I casually mentioned that perhaps her favorite program manager could use a raise.

Mam was silent for a moment.

"I've considered that. How much does a program manager make around here anyway?"

"From what I have heard, the average ones make about a hundred and forty, and the good ones get forty or more over that."

"Okay, we'll bump you to 120K. But only once the government starts reimbursing us."

A man can only take so much. And for thirty thousand dollars more a year, that was well within my limits, so I said okay. Of course, at that point, I didn't know what I didn't know—which turned out to be a whole bunch.

Our Friday afternoon meeting with Col. Harvey went well, not just because Chuck wasn't there, but that certainly didn't hurt. Col. Harvey had found out that he had set her up on the 8(a) direct award matter, so she'd excused him from the meeting. He did make up for his prank, at least partially, by processing an interim security clearance for Mam.

It was a good thing that Col. Harvey had kicked Chuck out of this session, especially if there wasn't a defibrillator nearby. Basically, she treated the fact that MICLIC wasn't yet a program as if it were, well, in fact, not a fact, and started laying out approaches for developing the operational requirements, designing and then prototyping a system, followed by all the other steps in the DOD 5000 instructions. She discussed how she would get funding, or in the vernacular, obtain different colors of money, which I knew to be just a phrase that means the money would come from different sources. Until she started talking about making this a joint effort with the Marines and began mentioning purple money as if it were really purple-colored money. Sensing that I was getting uneasy, she assured me that we would be paid in green money.

Turns out that purple money is just the phrase used to describe funds sourced from several of the military services, which makes sense because if you mix together the dark blue of the Navy, the lighter blue of the Air Force, and Army green, you get some yucky color that isn't purple, so actually, I don't know why it's called purple. As long as I don't have to spend it.

I had called Col. Harvey the day before and told her about Derek's Canadian citizenship, which I realized would be a security clearance problem. At first Col. Harvey was reluctant, but I insisted that he would be indispensable to the program, so finally I got a "Roger," which means that I had successfully passed my problem on to her, and she accepted it as her problem.

So Col. Harvey told Mam and me that in addition to making this a joint program, she would approach her counterpart in the Canadian Army about making this a combined program. *Combined* is the term the military uses for operations involving the United States and other countries. As allies, not enemies. Operations involving enemies we call war. Presumably, the Canadians would provide Canadian money, which as far as I knew, may or may not be green, but I didn't push Col. Harvey for her assurance. I'd come to trust her. Besides, if it got Derek on board with a security clearance, I'd be okay with a few colorful Canadian bucks.

Mam told Col. Harvey about the outcome of her conversation with Sad Sack about using a personal services contract and how, just maybe, she would be able to "facilitate efforts toward that end." Col. Harvey either wasn't aware of all that meant, or if she was, that wasn't her concern. Her concern was whether the Army Contracting Command here at Redstone Arsenal would go along with that. A legitimate point, considering the language would be that Congress "authorizes" a negotiated PSC. The wording wouldn't be that Congress "requires" a negotiated PSC. And for a seasoned bureaucrat like Chuck Bergen that was more than enough wiggle room.

We brought Sad Sack in via speakerphone.

"Well, I know most of those folks at ACC, and I'm pretty sure it won't be a problem. Usually, I just keep talking to them and I never shut up until they just get so tired of me that they do what I ask. But we won't have to do that in this case."

The conversation was only audio, but I could picture him winking at us, so I indulged him and asked: "Gee, Mr. Sanders, why do you say that?"

"Consider the two alternatives. If ACC were to approach this conventionally, they would have to do market research, prepare a detailed scope of work, advertise a solicitation, conduct a preproposal conference and answer questions, evaluate some high number of proposals, and then likely have to argue a protest. Alternatively, they could pretty much turn things over to you to negotiate a scope of work and a price and then write up a simple cost-reimbursable contract that both parties will sign without an issue."

Yep, a no-brainer. "And how long could that take?"

"Well, it could take a couple of days, but it will take six months because that's about the upper limit of reasonableness, the point beyond which they might be expected to actually work hard on it."

Surprisingly, both Mam and Col. Harvey thought that would work well for them, considering all the things they both had to coordinate. And that's when I started learning about the things I didn't know.

CHAPTER 14

The Attack Commences

IN RETROSPECT, I SHOULD HAVE ANTICIPATED a call. It's pretty common, once news of a contract award is announced, for the awarded company to get lots of calls from other businesses asking how they can "help." We hadn't obtained a contract yet, but being part of the team at the negotiation stage can earn a bigger stake.

I was surprised by the source of the call.

"Griff boy. How are they hanging?"

"Jim, to tell you the truth, they aren't hanging well at all. In fact, every time I swallow, I hurt myself."

That drew a laugh, convincingly real enough for me to figure out that Jim Strack wanted something from me. Why else would he go through the effort?

"Well, I'm here to help. Congratulations on whatever it is you guys have going on with Terrestrial Sensors. Pretty slick getting that piece of legislation stuck in WRDA. Good thing I keep my eyes on things like that."

I filled him in on some things, keeping the details out but leaving in just enough to keep him interested—up to the point where he would let me know what he had in mind. I might have implied that we already had a pretty strong team already working—you know, three PhDs and all—and that we had just a few positions left to fill.

"Well, Griff, just like always, I'm here to help. We've got some real studs here that are all over this kind of stuff. And frankly, you need a big brother company to help you through the details of working with the government and to foot some of the bills."

I didn't tell him he was only half right; apparently, just like me, he hadn't done his homework on Mamzelle Reynard. Still, half right was right enough, and I was about to invite him to come see us, except while I was thinking about it, he had already invited himself—this Friday. And his chief scientist, who could meet with ours and compare notes. And to show his good faith, he would prepare and forward a nondisclosure agreement, or NDA, so that we wouldn't have to worry about having anything less than frank and open discussions. That's how he put it. I was going to worry anyway.

I did feel pretty good about the compliment, intended or not, that he believed that all of this was something I could decide. What counts though is that I didn't believe it, so I laid things out for Mam.

She considered everything for a few minutes.

"Do you trust this guy?"

I wondered the same thing.

"Well, he'll always make sure that Number One comes out on top. But I don't think he'll screw us over to get there. And if he tries, I think I know him well enough to be able to see it coming."

"I suppose that's the most we can hope for. Give Derek the day off that day and have Mr. Sanders join us instead. And make sure he reviews the NDA—carefully."

For the next couple of days, Derek and I reviewed what all was contained in an operational requirements document. To his credit, he picked up on the most technical parts pretty quickly; that is, he picked up on what was required technically to be included in an ORD, but that isn't the same thing as knowing how we were going to satisfy those requirements. In fact, we didn't even have any *what ifs* or *should we considers*.

After pulling an all-nighter on Thursday, we were able to boil operational requirements down to four major functions:

- *Detect and identify explosive hazards.* Seems pretty straightforward, but it took us a while to get there, and it's why colleges make engineers and scientists attend English courses. We decided that *detect* meant that we had found something in the road that didn't seem like it belonged there. Derek liked the term *anomaly,* and so did I but only because I couldn't come up with anything better than "a big hunk of something that shouldn't be here." We decided that *identify* meant that there was a high probability that the anomaly contained explosives, which is only slightly more technically appropriate than my suggestion of "Oh, shit. It's a bomb."
- *Neutralize the explosive hazard.* We liked this term because it meant that we could either blow it up (hopefully without blowing up our guys) or go around it. Which took us off on the tangent of discussing the question of whether we should be able to go around it and did we have any requirement to eliminate the explosive hazard to protect the next guys coming down the road. Which is why colleges should make engineers and scientists take philosophy and ethics courses, and the course of study ought to be extended to at least five years, but they don't, so we spent a long time trying to figure that one out. We finally decided that it didn't make any difference because the same capability needed to neutralize the hazard if we were able to go around was the same one we would need if we couldn't go around.
- I wanted to call the next function *Clean up the mess,* but Derek suggested *Make a passable lane,* which was actually better than my idea, but I had already conceded the first two, so it was my turn. Which is why colleges should make engineers and scientists take at least one course in conflict resolution, but they don't, so we tried to find something we both could agree on and settled on the idea that undergraduate engineering and science students need about a six-year program before

they can graduate, only half of which are courses in their majors. This, at four o'clock in the morning, seemed like a perfect solution because if we had each undergone a six-year program, neither of us would have been here having to deal with this. Once that was settled, we again identified two different outcomes depending on whether we could go around the hazard or had ended up making a hole, a big hole, or a New York City pothole-sized hole.

- *Mark the lane.* By this time, neither Derek nor I had any energy left to debate what we called this function, so it's a good thing we both liked this title. Since we were going to alter the previous route, whether we made a detour or blew a big hole in the road, we should have the good manners to clearly mark the change. And since we both figured that out, we were okay with not requiring engineers and scientists to undergo a seven-year program that included etiquette courses. Thus dooming continuing generations of engineers and scientists to a life of social awkwardness.

And then we both passed out dreaming about BFTs—big freakin' trucks—and blowing things up.

That's how Sad Sack found us the next morning. I gave Derek his day off and had just enough time to go home, shower, change, and speed back to the office just as Jim Strack and his entourage were coming in the door. Maybe it was an entourage. Maybe it was only one person, and if there was an entourage, I wouldn't have noticed anyway. Wow! And if she really was Jim's chief scientist, her social awkwardness would be one of the last things I would notice. And it would be very forgivable.

I'm sure he introduced her around, but for the life of me, I can't remember her name. It wouldn't have made any difference anyway because about thirty seconds after Jim started his introduction, she started giggling and so then and forever after her name was Giggles.

At least to me. It got so bad that I figured that if Jim were to fart, she would be rolling on the floor hysterically. Come to think of it, the idea of Jim Strack farting in public would probably put me on the floor too. Needless to say, Giggles was the complete package, but chief scientist, my ass.

I ushered them both into Mam's office and introduced them to her and Sad Sack.

I could tell that Mam wasn't impressed, probably because Jim launched into one of his *Now that a few millennia have passed since I created the world, I'm here to help you out. No need to thank me; your worshipful adoration is all I need* spiels. She caught my eye and was throwing daggers, mostly figuratively, at me, so I tried to give her my *Have a little patience; this will all work out* look, but I haven't practiced that one in a while, so no telling what look I really gave her. But she settled down—a little.

When Jim got through describing how things were on top of Mount Olympus, Mam asked me to give him a rundown on our discussions with Col. Harvey and Chuck Bergen and an overview (meaning no details) on our plan to move forward. I have to admit I embellished my business development role, drawing some quizzical looks from Jim, but on the other hand, he wouldn't have believed how things had really happened, so no harm, no foul. Jim did sit up when I explained what Derek and I had come up with the night before.

Jim listened intently, threw in a few war stories, which I'm pretty sure weren't true, and at the end, actually said he was impressed—"Griff, I think you got it exactly right." But of course, that wasn't all as he added: "But I don't know why you went through all that effort before you got a contract. You know, you won't be paid for that effort until you have a contract in place."

I glanced at Mam and Sad Sack and figured out we were all thinking the same thing: how would the government know when we did the work? But instead we gave Jim an *aw, shucks* look, which just reinforced his ego.

We spent the next several hours sketching out roles and responsibilities, subcontract details, and a tentative schedule. Sad Sack had thought to bring in a whiteboard with a thick pad of chart paper, and by the time we finished, he had filled up the entire pad. In all fairness, Jim did contribute most of the thoughts, and Giggles had switched from giggling to cooing, which wasn't any less annoying, but at least it was different.

After Jim and Giggles left, following handshakes and broad smiles all around, Mam, Sad Sack, and I sat back down and exhaled. I couldn't resist a jab.

"You know, we didn't commit to a single thing, and Jim did most of the work today prior to us agreeing to pay a dime."

That sent Sad Sack into a laughing fit, but Mam just nodded. When Sad Sack composed himself enough, she asked us what we thought Jim was really after. After all, we couldn't tell that his company had any background in supporting military product development, so why now and why us?

Luckily, Sad Sack had a reasonable answer, and I certainly didn't, although I could definitely rule out that Jim was just doing me a favor.

"That's exactly why. They aren't in this business, but they have found what they think is a quick and easy way to gain access. A potential new business area and they didn't have to invest anything to develop it on their own. I don't know if you want to sign these guys up, but I'm pretty sure that I can write up an agreement that keeps us firmly in control"—he looked at Mam—"as long as we keep a firm hold of the reins." At that point he was looking at me.

Mam was deep in thought, but after a minute or two, looked up with what most people would call a grimace but what for her passed as a smile.

"I think you're right. As long as we know what motivates them, I am okay with including them on our team." And she emphasized the word *our*.

I had to admire her. This was David and Goliath again, and

she had discovered that she had a slingshot and pebbles. As long as there was a legitimate reason for Jim to want to participate, and his objective necessarily required him to play nice, she could stay in control. And she didn't have to like him because that would have been a certain deal-breaker.

On Monday morning, I had a few errands to run, so I got to the office a little late. Somebody was sitting in Della's chair and using her computer. I opened the door and she turned to me.

"Good morning. Welcome to Tiger Corporation. May I help you?"

"Maybe, but if Della comes back and sees you at her desk and using her computer, I won't be able to help you."

"You must be Mr. Finnegan. Ms. Reynard told me about you. I'm Ashley, Ms. Reynard's new executive assistant. Can I get you a cup of coffee?"

Ashley must have been one of the first of the generation of Ashleys that have been inflicted on the American public since the late '90s. In fact, she may have been the prototype. Still, she looked— what's the word I'm looking for?—efficient.

"Sure. Black, no sugar, no milk, nothing else unless you got something good and strong in that desk drawer."

"That's funny, Mr. Finnegan. Oh, not that you said it, but Ms. Reynard told me that's what you would say and that it was all I need to know about you."

She strode off after the coffee and I walked down the hallway. Something was off. The office doors were open. Clue two was that all the offices were inhabited by people other than the Jacksons. Wait, I take that back; we hadn't been introduced, so they might have been Jacksons. But not *the* Jacksons. Nope, no Jacksons on the nameplates. Clue three was that they all said good morning to me, and it sounded like they really meant it. Very unsettling.

Ashley showed up with the coffee and that saved me from having to talk to any of them as I grabbed the coffee, mumbled thanks, and did my own striding down the hall to Mam's office. She wasn't in, and neither was Derek, so I sat down and asked my poster muse, Heidi, what the hell was going on. She seemed to ponder the question for a bit, but the phone interrupted her.

It was Ashley, who told me that Mam was back and wanted to see me.

"So, are the Jacksons holding a family reunion and decided not to invite you?"

Snort.

"Stay away from the new people. I told them you were mentally limited but not dangerous. If you try talking to them, they'll become convinced of the first part but probably have serious doubts about the second. I don't want them all to quit after one day."

Ouch. Objectively, I have to admit her burn was far better than mine. I'd have to up my game.

"You're too late. I have already met Ashley and she is madly in love with me. Made coffee and brought me a cup. If she can do the same with martinis, we'll elope immediately. We'll go off forever and sail the world, or at least the parts with coffee and martinis. Besides, we have work to do, and if they can budget, prepare schedules, perform cost analyses, and probably a dozen or so more things I don't even know we have to do, I don't see any way around talking to them. And they may even be long conversations. Of course, that's why you brought them here in the first place."

Mam rolled her eyes. "Next subject. Col. Harvey wants to see us on Friday morning. Do you know why?"

"Probably something to do with the contract. That's the next step, as far as I can tell. They can't want something from us; the ball is in their court until they give us some direction. Do you want me to brief the four functions we presented to Strack?"

"Is what he said true? We won't get paid for anything we do prior to signing the contract?"

"Yep, that's the way it works. The government is very

uncomfortable with overachievers. That's why they don't hire any."

"I'll think about it. Be prepared, just in case."

So I met with all the new folks, who, despite having had all of Mam's warnings about me, turned out to be a pretty good bunch of folks. All were in their late twenties or early thirties, were mostly from the DC area, and initially called me "sir" before I disabused them of that silly notion. A couple of interesting things: they had all responded to recruiting announcements posted over a month ago and were attracted by, besides the promotions (hmm) to vice presidents, the higher pay (double hmm) and benefits (what!).

They were about to see the side of me that Mam had presumably warned them about when the vice president of administration showed me the memo, signed by Mam, announcing the health care, vacation, sick leave, and 401K benefits that were due to start at the beginning of the next pay period.

I fumed, I sputtered, I babbled incoherently, which was probably a good thing since what I had to say wasn't exactly suitable for mixed, or really any, company.

Sad Sack, attracted by the commotion, showed up and he and the vice president of finance calmed me down with a tutorial on how government rates are developed and how the government reimburses contractors for all these labor costs and adds profit on top of that. And also the three or four different types of labor-related taxes that the contractor has to pay, also with profit tacked on. So all of our benefits were costs that would be passed on to the government. It all sounded so reasonable.

Except I was past being reasonable and I stormed out, but Mam's door was now shut, so I continued my storming back to my office. I wasn't mad that she implemented these changes, but she went behind my back—after all, I was the program manager. I unloaded on Heidi about how I was through with that manipulative, scheming, two-faced, untrusting, and a bunch more adjectives Mamzelle Reynard and that I was going to stuff her into one of her own barbecue pits and cook her long and slow. Derek was rolling on the floor, and Sad Sack and the rest, who had followed me to my office and were skulking outside the door, were doing the same. It even looked like Heidi's smile was bigger, but she stayed calm, and eventually, I too calmed down. But, she didn't exactly try to talk me out of barbecuing Mam either.

I decided to take some of my new sick leave prematurely and headed to the driving range, where I hacked up about a half-acre and bent two clubs. And then went back to my apartment, where I turned a bottle of Jack Daniels Old No. 7 into about Old No. 1 and slept for sixteen hours.

Later, everybody said they were really impressed by the first impression I made and that Tiger Corp was going to be a really fun place to work. I just told them that—well, never mind what I told them.

I did my best to avoid Mam for the rest of the week, which wasn't that hard since she was "away on business," according to Ashley.

Meanwhile, the team kept giving me their work products and kept asking if they were all right and the way I wanted them, which since I didn't ask for them, didn't know what they were supposed to look like, and wasn't even sure what they were, I just checked the math. Which was always correct because it was done on a spreadsheet and spreadsheets are never wrong. So I gave them all a thumbs-up and said they were good, pending further review. Anyway, that made them happy.

But that doesn't mean that I didn't have any questions. Two things were very odd. First, the finance and accounting VP had given me a table that listed, in addition to those of us in the office, about a dozen or more other positions, from engineers and scientists to finance and accounting specialists, all with hourly labor rates listed. The other thing that struck me as odd was that the labor rates were more than twice what I knew them to actually be, even when I included all the newly gained benefits in our actual rates.

Sad Sack looked it over and said he thought it was right. The extra positions were the ones Mam evidently thought would be needed to do what we expected Col. Harvey would first assign us—write the ORD—whether we or a subcontractor provided the actual bodies.

"As far as the rate, remember that, so far, only you and Derek would be able to charge your time directly to the contract. The rest of us are all overhead, so we have to be paid from what you and Derek charge. And don't forget the overhead staff gets benefits too." He added the last with a very large grin.

"Col. Harvey will go apeshit over this."

"Are you kidding? These are bargain rates in her world. She'll sign off on it in ten minutes—before we have time to catch the mistakes she'll be sure we made."

Derek was happy. We ordered top-of-the-line design software for him, and I don't think he left his desk for the rest of the week. By the end of that time, he was posting YouTube videos on how to make the program sing, dance, and whistle. Well, not sing or dance, but literally whistle when a designer tried to do something that wasn't compatible with something else in the design. He was an internet sensation with a whole six views.

And I finally got a new desk and chair. Executive style, with a real leather seat. I think even Heidi was impressed. The reason I know that Derek didn't leave his desk was because I didn't either. The desk made me feel almost as good as spending Mam's money, so I ordered some teak in- and out-boxes too.

On Thursday evening I got a text from Mam saying she would meet me at Col. Harvey's office the next day.

I showed up a few minutes early, just in time to see Jim Strack exiting Chuck Bergen's office, and they were shaking hands like two old friends. They looked a little embarrassed, muttered a good morning, and ducked back into the office. The episode reminded me of a photo I had seen of Hitler and Mussolini shaking hands after deciding how they were going to conquer Europe; my guess is that Tiger Corp had just been selected to play Czechoslovakia in the sequel.

Mam was already in Col. Harvey's office. Both greeted me

warmly, Mam a little less so than Col. Harvey. A few moments later, Chuck Bergen came in with some stacks of paper and gave us a briefing on the contract structure and the first task we would be assigned. He asked if we had any questions.

Mam said no and made a move like she was ready to sign something right then and there.

"Wait just a moment. This is an awful lot of stuff to digest at once, and I think we ought to take it back and go over it. You know, just to make sure we understand," I said, leaning forward in my chair.

Bergen seemed uneasy. "To be clear, this isn't the contract. There are several things we need to get to first, and you'll owe us several things before we can even issue the contract. But you're right, take your time and make sure everything is clear, every step of the way."

Damn right, I'll take my time. Because I was going to find the "gotcha" that I knew was in there. Even if it took me all night.

It took me all night. But I didn't find it. That next morning I checked with Sad Sack.

"Griff, sorry to tell you this, but everything looks fine to me. A task order contract is just what we need—instead of giving us a contract to deliver a finished system, each task will build on the preceding ones; they'll be better able to define the requirements and we'll be better able to tell them how we'll do it and provide a price. As far as what we owe them—a description of what we'll do, an organization plan, bios of the top engineers and scientists, a schedule and pricing—that's pretty standard. They even gave us a whole month to turn it all in."

Oh, they were clever. Lull us into a false sense of complacency and then drop the hammer. Pure Strack.

There were three reasons I didn't tell Mam what I had seen. First, I had no proof, just my suspicions. Also, I was the one who had said we could trust Jim Strack, and I wasn't going to admit I was wrong, at least not so soon after having recommended him. But mostly, I was still PO'd at Mam and if she wasn't going to take me into her confidence, then I wasn't going to divulge things either. It would serve her right.

I contacted Strack and left a message to call me about preparing our response to Col. Harvey, and Sad Sack and I got to work on drafting a teaming agreement and a written set of requirements for Jim that matched what the government had given us, only with a due date a week before ours. I wanted to make it two weeks, but Sad Sack said that was unreasonable, so I said okay because everyone knows how reasonable I am. Sad Sack just rolled his eyes. And I threatened to punch him.

A guy named Peckham, or something like that, from Strack's company called and said that Jim was out visiting with customers and that he, Peckham, had been designated as project manager, would prepare their part of the response, and send on all the other information we requested. I kept calling him "Picklehead," and after correcting me several times, he just gave up. We'd get along just fine.

About half an hour later, Mam called and asked me to drop by. She seemed in a good mood—turns out that she had spent several days in Florida, relaxing.

"Yeah, I noticed the tan lines."

Snort.

"Griffin, you seem to be a little more on edge than normal. That's putting it nicely. The actual reports were: "unhinged," 'psycho," and "a bigger asshole than usual." Some people are worried that you may be working too hard, so I'd like you to take a couple of days off. Maybe even a week if you think you need it."

"Well, I don't need it. And if the pansies around here can't take it, maybe they need some time off, permanently."

Whoa. Now I heard it too. "Maybe you're right. How about I take a couple of days off?"

"Good idea. See you next week."

I headed to the golf course. A good round—or for that matter, a bad one—tires me out and sleep had been my only recreation lately.

I pulled into a full parking lot and saw the unmistakable signs of a large tournament in progress. I found a spot, grabbed my clubs out of the trunk, and headed to the clubhouse. It was past noon, so the tournament should have been winding down. Sure enough, a swarm was headed past me to the parking lot.

I headed to the clubhouse desk, signed up for eighteen and a cart, and headed to the bar to grab a beer to go. Most of the bar had cleared out, but sitting at one of the tables were Jim Strack and Chuck Bergen.

They looked surprised to see me.

"Griff, how did you hit 'em? How did your team do?"

"I wasn't part of the tournament. Going out to play now."

They looked a little embarrassed. Bergen more so than Strack, who quickly dropped the embarrassed look and started grinning.

"Griff, sorry, but when Jim dropped by to chat, I sort of just invited him to play with us."

"Besides, you suck at golf," Jim added.

If I had thought that a round of golf was going to relax me, it wasn't starting well.

"Oh, bullshit. We won the whole thing last time, with my putt as the winning stroke."

"We won the whole thing this time outright," Chuck countered.

Oh. Well, that hurt, but at least it explained why those two had been so secretive when I caught them on Friday. Wait.

"What do you two have going on? Picklehead said you were visiting customers. I didn't know you had business with Terrestrial Sensors."

That sent them both into convulsions of laughter.

"I don't. In fact, I don't even like this guy. But he is my brother-in-law and whenever I come to Huntsville to visit customers—you know, the ones I like—my wife comes along, so we end up staying with the Bergens."

Bergen didn't seem fazed.

"Yeah, well the feeling is mutual, and Griff may not be quite the golfer you are, but he is a whole hell of a lot better company, so next time, he's in and you're out."

And that sent them into another laughing fit, so I just walked away and hoped they had a stroke or fell off their chairs on their heads or something like that.

My round started off poorly, but as I was driving down the fairway on the fourth hole, I realized that if Strack and Bergen were not discussing business, then they weren't out to screw us, and the reason for my anxiety—well, there wasn't a reason. Except for the cracks about my golfing, which still pissed me off. But nowhere near as much. And the rest of the round was a lot better.

Even though I was feeling a whole lot better about things, I wasn't going to waste some free time off, so I finally made my long-anticipated pilgrimage to Lynchburg. What an amazing place. The guide had to ask me three times to move along with the rest of the tour group because I wouldn't leave the distilling vats and that heavenly smell. The guide explained that Jack Daniels, uniquely, mellows its sipping whiskey by dripping it through sugar maple charcoal filters, which seems to me to be very similar to the way I get mellow by dripping it down my throat. Obviously, this needs more study.

I bought a bunch of T-shirts for everyone but Sad Sack, who would have to settle for a hat, and headed home. I did some more studying.

CHAPTER 15

Did You Know That Blueprints Aren't Really Blue?

WE SUBMITTED OUR PRICING, schedule, and the other information to Col. Harvey and Chuck Bergen three weeks later. There were a few back-and-forths, nothing major, and three weeks after that, we were awarded the contract. In the interim, we had prepared a subcontract, and by the time we got our contract, we also had Jim's signature on the subcontract.

We pretty much followed the outline that Derek and I had developed to prepare the ORD. It was straightforward except for the part about defining the detection and identification performance requirements. The state of the art on that little task isn't too advanced, so we initially set the requirement to identify an explosive device at 50 percent probable, which means that the system would identify a bomb half the time. Which doesn't sound like much, except we weren't convinced we could do any better. And why establish a requirement we couldn't meet?

The other part that stumped us was the multiplatform part. We quickly shelved the idea of putting a system on a helicopter because pilots, besides objecting to a plow on the front of the helicopter, would not go for flying low and slow over a road to detect explosives. Can't say I blame them, but that left us with only big trucks as platforms for the MICLIC. Which would make it an ICLIC, and if there was ever an acronym that would kill a program immediately, ICLIC is the one.

We took both issues to Col. Harvey and Bergen at one of the In Progress Reviews we held every other month. We won one and lost one. The government said they wanted an 80 percent or better explosive identification rate, but they were okay with the capability of moving the system from one truck to another and calling it multiplatform and saving the program from certain death.

Oh, I almost forgot. It had to be green, Army green. That was my contribution.

We made these changes to our ORD draft, ran spell-check a couple of times, and submitted it to the government, who promptly approved it, to everyone's delight except Mam, who felt we should have taken several more months and run up the bill. I promised we would move more slowly in the next phase.

We submitted our plan, pricing, and schedule to engineer and design the MICLIC. As promised, if the schedule was accurate, we would be taking a lot more time on this phase, almost six months. We weren't sure if we were going to take that much time, but that depended solely on whether we could find, or develop, a reliable capability to identify a buried explosive device 80 percent of the time. Not everyone was optimistic.

I heard a lot of variations on the same theme: "The best minds in the world can't figure out how to improve on current systems, and you're betting that you can?" And by you, they meant me.

Ouch. That's not exactly how I would phrase our dilemma, being more of a *we* man than an *I* man, at least in this case, but on the other hand, Derek, who had to be numbered among the best minds in the business, hadn't yet taken his shot. Shoot away, Derek.

We had our first several team meetings via Zoom. At the first one we discussed our research—see, I'm a team player again—and showed that there are three approaches we could consider to detect explosives or explosive devices. Essentially, we can identify an IED or landmine by its physical characteristics, its chemical signature, or, specifically for IEDs that use an electrical trigger like a cellphone, an electrical signature. The rest of the discussion got very technical—or from my perspective, boring—but evidently, some people consider tying a German Shepherd to the front of a truck to sniff for explosives too cruel, even if it might work. Derek eased the tensions by saying detecting trace amounts of chemicals in the vapor around a device is a "sniffer" technology and that we could use an electronic "dog" instead.

By the way, did you know you can play solitaire while on a Zoom call and nobody will know? Here's a helpful hint though—don't press the screen share button accidentally.

The trouble is that the technologies used in these approaches aren't all that advanced. Certainly, they are not 80 percent reliable. So Derek's idea was to use two or more different technologies to raise our odds; for example, three independent technologies that are each right only half the time would collectively be 87.5 percent reliable and we would easily clear the bar set at 80 percent. At least in theory.

At this point it got even more technical, so I excused myself, claiming I had important program management stuff to do, which I did but I decided to hang out with Sad Sack instead.

He must have known I was coming because he was faking doing work, scrolling down the computer page and saying *uh-huh* into his phone a lot. Watching him, I saw him scroll back to the top and then continue his downward scroll again, and his *uh-huh*s changed to *but, but*s. Overall, a pretty good act.

But he wasn't acting.

"Griff, did you see what they sent?"

I hadn't and it didn't make any difference who *they* were or what it was they had sent. While looking at a Zoom screen for an hour and a half, and Derek set that up for me, I hadn't been paying attention to emails.

They turned out to be the Army Contracting Command and *what* was a modification to our contract. The Army had added a contract clause.

About half a federal contract consists of FAR-mandated contract clauses. And not just the ones in the FAR but all the ones in the Code of Federal Regulations. And if you think that the government spends all of its time spending your money, you're right, and sometimes they spend it on themselves by writing thousands of federal regulations. Luckily for the contracting officer, the FAR tells them what regulations to include for each type of contract. So the contracting officer doesn't really have to read them. The contractor doesn't read them. Nobody reads them.

Except Sad Sack. And apparently what he saw upset him. He was quivering, and that's a lot of flesh in motion.

"Griff, we are now required to perform most of the work on this program. That's 51 percent or more of the money that has to be earned directly by Tiger. In your engineering and design plan, how much of the work are we subcontracting to Strack and his engineers?"

"Oh, about 80 percent."

I could see why he was concerned. After the engineering and design, the bulk of the rest of the money would be for manufacturing and assembly tasks, so the percentage coming our way wasn't going to increase.

"Why would they do that? We never claimed that we would do half the work. What happens if we don't meet that number? And where did it come from in the first place?"

"The government does this frequently for contracts it sets aside exclusively for small businesses so that a small business doesn't win a contract and then just pass everything through to a large business. But this clause isn't mandatory and is rarely used where the government doesn't give specific or risk-free requirements. As far as the penalty, technically we would be in violation of the contract, and the government could force us to comply, and if we don't, or can't, we could be terminated."

"Can we refuse to accept that requirement? Just say no, thanks?"

"Nope, it's a unilateral modification. It doesn't even require our signature. Just an acknowledgment that we received it."

Strack! Everything about this screamed Strack! All he has to do is complete the lion's share of the design, and when Tiger can't demonstrate that it would self-perform more than half of the total work on the contract, he would just step in to complete the job. Even if the government couldn't directly award him the contract, realistically nobody else could compete against a company that had all of Strack's advantages.

The Army had taught me twenty-four ways to kill an enemy soldier. Numbers twelve, fifteen, twenty-one, and twenty-three were especially appealing right now. The rest would do just as well. Then again, a bunch of them came from Rambo movies instead of the Army, but that still left at least a dozen that would work.

Surprisingly, Mam remained pretty calm.

"Simmer down, boys. Let me think about this a little. Harland, you call that small business guy over there—McCarthy—and find out what's going on. Griffin, don't say a word about this to anyone else, especially Mr. Strack. Oh, and don't go killing anyone." I think she saw my disappointment because she added: "At least not yet."

She was too calm. But that was smart. If I were in her shoes, I wouldn't want anybody, if they were later called to testify, to say that I had been upset and made threats. I figured she was probably thinking of hiring professionals. But she'd have to pay. I might do it for free.

Of course, she could pay me. In fact, she should pay me. But I wouldn't haggle.

Sad Sack told me that the modification idea had come from the "front office." It wasn't something that Army Contracting Command had previously intended to include.

Meanwhile, back at what formerly had been his and my office, Derek was turning the place into a big design space. A round conference table with ten chairs, a projection screen, and whiteboards all over the place. Picklehead and his team would spend the next six weeks in town with Derek, hammering out a preliminary design.

Now, some of you may think that sitting around a bunch of desks working on engineering stuff and solving problems and making drawings and having breakthroughs is boring stuff. And of course, you'd be right. But if you have never done it before, and everything was new and challenging, well, you'd still be right. So naturally, I excused myself as often as possible, and after a week or so, nobody expected me to be there, so I wasn't.

I was having my own adventures.

One was really kind of pleasant. I got a phone call from one of the fellas from the VFW; I didn't recognize the name, but it turned out to be Grease Monkey, who, if he had only started with that, would have kept me from imitating a barnyard owl for five minutes. The VFW was going to honor Henry with a national award, and Grease Monkey wanted to know if I would like to attend and maybe say a few words. I suspected that he chose to ask me because all of those tough old vets were terrified of Mam, so when I said yes and heard a sigh of relief, I knew I was right.

So I invited her.

After a couple of snorts, she told me to quit wasting her time and that if she wanted to watch a bunch of old fools making even bigger fools of themselves she would just as soon . . ..

I told her I'd save a place for her.

It was a special night. There was a video message from the national head of the VFW and the presentation of a plaque, sash, and pin to put on his hat. I gave my little speech about an army marching on its stomach and how the mess sergeants were the backbone of the force, which went over just about like you think it would, but at the end I presented him a small bronze "V"—the army V-device for valor that he could put on his cap—and said something about how Henry had a courage that no man here could match. Well of course that sent everybody into howls of laughter, then applause and cheering, and finally a standing ovation, and I was about to take a bow when the post president hustled me off the stage and Henry came up. I didn't think his speech was any better than mine, but he got cheered after every sentence and received another standing ovation at the end. Maybe my timing was off.

I searched the audience and finally found the two dark eyes, about five feet up from the floor, way in the back among the shadows.

The doors behind her opened and I figured she was leaving and that there would be hell to pay on Monday, but instead an old Army deuce-and-a-half—a two-and-a-half ton truck—came rolling into the center of the floor and welded to the bed of the truck was custom-made stainless steel, with chrome highlights, giant barbecue smoker. Around the sides of the smoker were baskets and holders for everything a premier smoker would need, each with a chrome pig's head handle. There were large bins for the wood, refrigerated bins for the meat and sauces, containers for spices and rubs, and all the tools were strapped into the holders and baskets. The smoke vented through a pipe that was merged with the truck exhaust pipe, which on a deuce-and-a-half is a vertical pipe mounted in front of the passenger door. Fellow motorists would be able to drive by and inhale the heavenly southern aroma of smoked meat and diesel exhaust.

It was flawless. Every seam, weld, and piece was highly polished and fit perfectly with the next piece. I was the only one who saw the problem.

"You know, if that goes down the highway at sunup or sunset, it will blind every other driver for six hundred yards in all directions."

Grease Monkey grinned and pulled a handheld device from the cab of the truck. He pushed a button and hydraulically powered panels went up around the smoker, paused when they reached about a foot above, and jointed panels rose, articulated out and hinged to form a pitched roof, with a steeple and a cross on top. And it was all painted camouflage.

The crowd went wild.

He showed Henry and me the controller.

"See, this raises and lowers the enclosure. Because the smoke vents out through the exhaust pipe, you can smoke with the cover on. This button will make a tray slide into the stack of wood and bring a layer of wood into the smoker box, and this button will ignite it. You can control the vents with this knob, open and close to get the right temperature. This switch will raise, lower, or rotate the cooking grate. And if you come over here, when you are all done, this lever will open the bottom of the smoker and all the ash will fall out and then turn this handle and two brushes will come up through the bottom of the smoker and if you crank the handle, scrub out the smoker."

"What, no music?" I asked.

"Mr. Finnegan. Really?"

He didn't use my military rank because it was the kind of dumb question only a civilian would ask. He went into the cab, pushed a button, and from below each side of the bed, a mechanical arm holding an eight-foot speaker came out, rotated ninety degrees, and locked into position facing the rear of the truck.

"Mr. Finnegan, if I turn this up only halfway, it will knock the back wall of this building down. And that's playing Henry's gospel music. I backed this sucker up to my back field at home, cranked up my music, and it cleared the whole six acres of every rock, stump, and weed."

"Corporal Grease Monkey, this is the most outstanding piece of work I have ever seen."

"Now, there you go. Sir!"

My other adventure wasn't as much fun.

Strack called and said he would be in town the next day, and there was someone I had to meet. We went back and forth on that a little bit since I was pretty sure there wasn't anybody he knew that I wanted to meet, and he was just as adamant that there was. He must have been real sure because he called me back each time I hung up, so I finally relented and agreed to meet Mr. Smith the next night in the best suite of the best hotel in town. Seems like someone up there was trying to tell me something and next time you can be damn sure I will listen.

Mr. Smith, "You can call me Bob," was one of those people who were meant to rule the world and didn't waste any time making sure I knew that. Strack certainly knew that because the more deferential he became, the more condescending Smith became. He was a good number of years younger than me, which made him an even gooder number of years younger than Strack, and since that kind of pissed me off, I knew that Jim was even more pisseder.

"Jim tells me you are the brains behind this deal with Tactical Sensors. I'll tell you this also: Col. Harvey thinks very highly of you. So when Jim told me about you, well, I knew you were my kind of guy, and I wanted to meet you. Say, what about a little icebreaker here? Jim says you're a Jack man—I admire that—so I brought along a bottle that my friends in Lynchburg make especially for me. Jim, will you do the honors and pour a couple of sips for me and Griff?"

That's verbatim. Now I don't think for a moment that Mr. Bob Smith is linguistically clumsy, so I figured his ego wouldn't allow him to put me in the sentence before him, even subconsciously. Strack didn't seem to mind that he hadn't been included among those to receive pouree consideration, and after he portioned out quite a bit more than a few sips—more like five or six guzzles—into the two drink glasses in the room, he toddled off to the bathroom to retrieve another glass.

At which point, Bob pulled out a box of Opus X cigars, just about the best—and most expensive—cigars in the world and offered me one. He took one for himself, unwrapped it, clipped off the end, and started to light it. Now, I was pretty sure that the fire code didn't make exceptions, even for eighty-dollar cigars, but young Bob just smiled at me when I pointed that out like one of those medieval kings would at one of his unwashed peasants.

"Griff, I am going to invite you to join us. Not just for fine whiskey and exquisite cigars but to come into our corporate inner circle. And in the inner circle, we make our own rules. The world understands this. Hell, they expect it."

And he took a puff. One of those dainty little puffs, and he held the cigar daintily between his manicured thumb and forefinger and delicately waved away his dainty little cloud of smoke.

So as young Bob started to describe his inner circle, and all the entitlements they enjoyed, and how they were only the very best of the very best—because the simply best of the best just weren't good enough—I lighted up and started puffing away like an old-time steam locomotive climbing a 30 percent grade. Because what the very best of the very best hadn't noticed, but what I, as least of the least had, was that I was sitting just below the smoke detector, which was right next to the sprinkler. I couldn't resist and looked up at Strack, grinned, and then glanced upwards. He glanced up too, rolled his eyes, and then all hell broke loose.

The room alarm went off first, followed about a half second later by the sprinkler and then all the alarms in the hallway. I'll say this about the best rooms in the best hotels in town: they don't skimp on either the decibels or the gallons. Then the room phone went off and I figured it was about time that I let young Bob explain his set of rules to the hotel management.

"Smitty, you throw a hell of a party, but the peasants are revolting, so if you don't mind, I'm going to save the crown jewels and head to the old hovel," and I grabbed the bottle of whiskey and box of cigars, half-ass saluted Jim, left young Bob sputtering under a stream of water, and headed for the nearest stairwell, exiting the hotel just as Huntsville's finest were showing up.

Later that night I got a text from Strack. *I told him you were too dumb to go for that.* And then, *I enjoyed the hell out of that. But watch your back.*

I replied. Now that they have added the turd pile to the emoji set, you can get pretty digitally expressive. And then I went about forming my own inner circle of me, Jack Daniels, and Arturo Fuente.

I had just arrived at work the next morning when Ashley let me know that Mam was looking for me and that she wasn't in a good mood. I started to ask how she knew when the sound of my name blasted out of Mam's office. I say "sound," but thunder is a sound, artillery fire is a sound, someone sticking an air horn next to your ear is a sound—this wasn't just a sound; Mam apparently thought I had overnighted in New Jersey and didn't feel like using modern communications methods today.

"Guess who called me?"

"Ok, I guess the National Institute for the Deaf. They really think you are *the* cure."

"Someone named Robert Smith."

"That would be my second guess. Do you want to hear my side?"

"No. Is it true that you approached Strack and him for a job and then met with them last night and discussed working for their company?"

"In order: no, yes, and yes. Now, do you want to hear my side?"

"No—but go ahead anyway."

So I spilled all the details except the part that could result in her being charged as an accomplice to kidnapping if she knew about Jack and Arturo and didn't report me.

She didn't exactly smile, but the corners of her mouth went from pointing due south to a few degrees above the equator.

"You know, Strack is right. You are too dumb to ever put in with those guys."

Since that was the nicest thing she had ever said to me, I decided to not prolong the conversation, waved goodbye, and headed back to my office.

Which was filled to overflowing. Derek and the design team had pretty much wrapped up their work, and Strack had sent another team down to deliver a report on the design review they had conducted. And my furniture had been commandeered to help seat the congregation. Which I was about to make a significant point of contention when I saw that it was Giggles that had deposited her pretty butt into my chair and was delivering the homily to the faithful.

The review was a mixed bag. Overall, the independent reviewers didn't find anything too screwed up—a couple of minor things that could easily be fixed. Except for the detect and identify part. They bought into having to use several different technologies in order to be at least 80 percent reliable, but they concluded that detecting an electrical voltage in a device buried underground was beyond the reach of current technology. Sure, if the bad guys were using a couple of car batteries to keep the IED powered up—and a lot of them were—we could detect the voltage, but the bad guys would quickly adapt and start using a couple of AA batteries that we couldn't find. And they agreed that by relying on ground-penetrating radar and sniffer technologies, we couldn't consistently identify and detect at least 80 percent of the time.

Pure buzzkill. The room got real quiet for about five minutes. Not a single suggestion, no "How about . . ." or "What if . . .." So I figured it was up to me.

"Hey, what about this? If we can't detect the voltage because it's too small, why don't we juice it up? Kind of like what I did for the Wi-Fi in my apartment last weekend. I couldn't get Wi-Fi in the living room or kitchen, so I put in one of these gadgets that gooses up the signal, and now I'm good to go."

Well, that broke the tension all right. Not exactly the way I hoped for though as everybody started laughing at me and telling me that's not the way it works, and Wi-Fi and electricity aren't the same, and then Picklehead got personal and started asking things like where in the hell did I get my degree and stuff like that. Except for Derek and Giggles, who just were looking at each other.

Derek: "Holy shit."

Giggles: "Holy shit."

A duet: "Holy shit."

Kind of catchy, but the melody was a little flat and frankly, although the words initially grab you, they don't hold you through the whole song. A B-side at best.

But the rest of the room must have thought more about the song than I did because they were all looking at Giggles and Derek like they were rock stars.

Giggles: "What if we used an EM transmitter to excite the electromagnetic field . . ."

Derek: ". . . and then use magnetic sensors to detect the field . . ."

Both: ". . . so that we can measure the resulting electrical signal, and with some adaptive learning we would be able to identify an IED with very high reliability!"

And that kicked off another "Holy shit!" chorus, with several more of the audience joining in, and I have to admit the tune was getting better. I really think somebody like Beyonce could pull it off.

Well, that got the whole room excited and pretty soon ideas were flying around like bullets, so I decided it was time to find cover somewhere else.

On my way out I reaffirmed. "So, I guess I solved the problem."

That backstabbing bunch started booing and hissing and yelling, and Derek said I really wasn't close, and Giggles just shook her head.

I don't care what they think; I'm counting it for the kid. And if the song wins a Grammy, I'm counting that too.

After that, completing the design went pretty smoothly, and a couple of months later we had 214 pages of diagrams and specifications, signed and stamped by professional engineers, and neatly bound.

There was a big dish thingy that did all the detecting and had cables running to three analyzer modules that fed a synthesizer with a display screen that gave an operator the probability of an anomaly being an explosive device and the most likely type of device: drones that could drop a block of TNT with a thirty-second fuse on top of the location of the device; a big snowplow-type blade mounted on detachable arms in the front; a scissors-type bridge that a crane could pick up and place over a large hole; and a marking system that fired out a string of javelins with flashing strobe lights to identify a cleared lane.

The drones were an especially neat idea because they didn't need to be developed by the Army; when the Army buys commercially available technologies (COTS) directly from the manufacturer, they save all the developmental and manufacturing time and costs, and since that time is considerable, they can get a system into the field well before it becomes technically obsolete. And if the Army needs replacement drones in a hurry, there is something completely American about calling up Amazon and having their drones deliver our drones to the battlefield.

As a final check, I started thumbing through the pages when it occurred to me what was missing. "Derek, I know the thread count of every bolt, the thickness of every nut, and the prop wash coefficient of every wahoozit in this contraption. But I have no idea what it looks like."

Derek politely suggested that the 214 pages of diagrams and specifications quite possibly might give me a good idea, but I told him we needed something like an architectural rendering of what a fully assembled system would look like mounted on an Army truck.

Derek thought that was the worst idea in the world for a number of reasons, not the least of which is that architects have BA degrees, and their renderings have no place in engineering drawings, but Mam, with a little prompting, emailed him the same suggestion, at which point it became the best idea in the world. And soon we had a 215th page, in color, of the oddest-looking contraption ever devised by man—except for the helicopter and just about every American Motors Corporation car. It was as if Rube Goldberg had joined the Swiss Army knife design team and together they decided that Ripley needed a new entry for *Believe It or Not*. But just like the parents of ugly babies, we thought it was cute, or at least functional. Because every parent hopes their kid grows up to be functional. And supportive when we get too old to take care of ourselves.

CHAPTER 16

I Wear a White Hat 'Cause the Good Guys Always Win

IT TOOK THREE MONTHS for the Army to approve the design. A whole month was spent haggling over which of the Army branches would be the proponent for the system, and thus get to write all the operational and maintenance manuals, test the system, train the users, identify and manage replacement items, and a whole bunch of stuff the Army wouldn't staff or equip them for; the lucky branch would get to do all of this with resources already assigned. So Col. Harvey would have to use her powers of persuasion to get a branch to commit to being a proponent.

Which she did in a very, very direct way, getting the generals that were the commandants of the Engineer and Transportation schools on a conference call and telling them that they had better get off their blankety-blank blanks, pull their heads from their bleepity-bleeps, and do so ASAP or she was going to personally come down and kick their blankety-bleeps from here to next Sunday. Only she filled in the blanks and bleeps. So the two generals, who were generally very protective of their blanks and bleeps, agreed that the engineers would be the proponent but that the transportation folks would pick up several of the tasks.

And when nothing happened for another month, Col. Harvey dropped in on the commandant of the Engineer School, had a heart-to-heart-to-foot-to-blankety-bleep conversation with him, at which point the engineer general had a better understanding of what was expected of him, and when, and became very compliant. Especially after the soreness went away. And a week later, both generals got a personal thank-you note from the chief of staff of the Army, commending them for their outstanding support of a program that was vitally important to the Army and its soldiers. From that point, we received exceptional support from both branches. It was even better than outstanding.

So a month later the design was approved by Terrestrial Sensors, the Transportation Corps, and the Engineers, and Col. Harvey flew down to Huntsville and summoned Mam and me for our customary Friday afternoon meeting.

Col. Harvey was all smiles. And compliments. She especially appreciated the front-page rendering of what the mounted system would look like and called it "beautiful," which just goes to show that beauty is in the eye of the beholder.

She and Bergen laid out the next step. In the next month or so, we would receive an order to produce a prototype system, to be delivered to the Engineer School at Ft. Leonard Wood, accompanied by a subject matter expert that would explain how the system worked and would be mounted. And three pairs of eyes were looking at me.

I stayed pretty busy for the next month. I started getting calls from other government contractors asking if Tiger was interested in supporting them, as well as calls from big companies that asked us to join their teams as a principal subcontractor for their pursuits of new contracts. Sad Sack stayed busy negotiating teaming agreements and Mam couldn't help herself; she was smiling continuously. And they were real smiles, not the usual "I just ate a bad burrito" kind.

Part of the reason we were all smiling, myself included, was that we had an actual plan for producing the prototype.

"Grease Monkey, this is Griffin Finnegan. What are you up to these days?"

Turns out it wasn't much, so we issued him a vendor's contract. Derek and I showed him the plans, and when he stopped laughing, we explained that, yes, we were serious, so he studied the plans a little more, and when he asked again, we said we were still serious, so he became serious too and said it would be a "piece of cake" and asked if we wanted to add a barbecue smoker. Tempting, but we passed.

A week later, Grease Monkey provided a schedule, a bill of materials, and an estimate for his labor. I doubled the price and the schedule and then Mam doubled them both again. Predictably, Col. Harvey thought it was a bargain, so she doubled everything again in the task order she issued. Just so you know, I don't think this is the way it supposed to work, but this approach was working for us, and I guess Col. Harvey just wanted to make sure she had the funds available, just in case. By this time, her star was shining brightly in the Army acquisition community, so she could get all the funds she asked for, and bringing this program in under budget and early wouldn't hurt that luminosity at all.

Grease Monkey made steady progress, completing things basically on schedule, but we hadn't anticipated that he would want us to take delivery, because he had no room to store things, and pay for the items as he completed them. We solved the first issue by renting a storage unit, but Mam was reluctant to pay for something that the government might not reimburse her for right away.

So I took the matter to Col. Harvey and Chuck Bergen, who, as expected, were of two different minds. Chuck pointed out that: first, they had ordered the complete kit, and the task order didn't allow for partial delivery or payment, and second, by law, they couldn't pay for anything that they hadn't physically accepted and inspected. And if they accepted items, they couldn't very well give them back for the final assembly. Which, unfortunately, made sense to me.

But not to Col. Harvey. She directed Chuck to modify the task order accordingly and told me to turn over the storage unit key to Chuck, who could go over and accept and inspect to his heart's content, and when we submitted our invoices for each delivery, we could include the storage unit rent. Since Chuck was zero for everything in his arguments with Col. Harvey, he just nodded and held out his hand for the key. And that, fortunately, made even more sense to me.

So, six weeks—exactly on Grease Monkey's schedule—and three partial deliveries later, I asked Chuck for the key and invited him to observe the final assembly, which to my surprise he did, and at the end, inspected the prototype and, even more to my surprise, was very complimentary and said it was the best prototype he had ever seen. And he accepted the final delivery.

The trip to Fort Leonard Wood was noneventful. Sort of; if you don't count the drone incident. We crated up the prototype, shipped it off to FLW and flew on to St. Louis where we rented a car. By we, I mean Derek, Grease Monkey, and me, who were eager to come along after I described the breathtaking scenery of FLW and all the wonderful things there were to do. They were less eager when they googled it and found out that nothing I said was technically true. Or even nontechnically. So I just pulled rank and ordered them along. Col. Harvey had said that we didn't need to demonstrate the drone, since they were commercially available technologies, and we didn't need to demonstrate how they worked. But I decided that I would buy one and bring it along to complete the operational picture of how the system worked.

There was a pretty big crowd on hand to watch the demonstration. More than a throng, somewhat less than a multitude, to be precise. And a major constellation of generals—one-stars, two-stars, and even a three-star. Grease monkey and a platoon of able-bodied engineer basic trainees, along with an Army wrecker, laid out the components and assembled the system on an Army Heavy Expanded Mobility Tactical Truck (HEMTT) in about an hour. The Engineer School had laid out a demonstration route with some buried mines and an IED or two, along with cameras to record the demonstration, and the truck and crew (Derek, Grease Monkey, the Engineer School and Transportation School Commandants, the driver and me) took off down the road while the rest of the crowd moved on over to grandstands that were set up on the side of the demonstration area. Things went very well, as we were able to find and identify the first three devices and detour around, marking our path. The fourth device was easy to find as well, but the Engineer School had placed large rocks on each side of the road so we would have to neutralize the device in order to pass.

I was feeling pretty pleased with myself, and my foresight to bring along the drone to add some realism to the demonstration. It turned out to be a pretty fleeting feeling when I realized that I hadn't read the operating instructions and flying the damn thing wasn't exactly intuitive. And Derek, Grease Monkey, the generals, and the driver turned out to be no help at all. But, I was able to turn the thing on and get the drone airborne and headed more or less in the direction of the fourth device, which is about the same as saying less in the direction of the device and more in the direction of the grandstand at which point the joystick controller started jamming and I had to forcibly push and pull on joystick to keep the drone flying. Which it did, executing some pretty fancy maneuvers over the heads of the spectators. Maneuvers like strafing runs and dive bomb runs, which proved to be just a bit too disconcerting and sent the spectators dashing off in different directions.

Finally, Grease Monkey grabbed the controller from me, pushed the power button, and the drone fell harmlessly to the ground. Harmlessly, from the ground's perspective. From the drone's perspective, the fall turned out to be catastrophic. And for some reason, the crowd seemed to favor the drone's perspective even though no one was hurt, except for a colonel that pulled a muscle leaping out of the way. But the three-star general was gracious in his speech, saying the demonstration was overall very impressive, and once we ironed out a few kinks—and here he looked at me—

the system would be very valuable to the war effort. And that's how "Kinks" was added to the list of nicknames I've picked up over the years. And it's the only one I'll tell you about.

On the flight back, Grease Monkey and Derek kept retelling—and embellishing—the story, much to the delight of the nearby passengers and flight attendants, notwithstanding that I had warned them all that this was a classified program, and they were all subject to the most severe penalties our federal government could administer, up to and including a firing squad. This only set off another round of merriment and the overall consensus among 145 of 146 of the passengers was that they had never had so much fun on a flight.

The day after we got back, Col. Harvey was in town again, so Mam and I were called in to meet with her. I took Sad Sack along, and we arrived early to find that Mam and Col. Harvey were already meeting. Again, they were in a good mood and Col. Harvey kept calling me "Ace;" somebody should tell colonels that they really aren't all that funny.

Col. Harvey had been busy, coordinating with both the Transportation and Engineer Schools, and both of the Army's testing organizations: the Test and Evaluation Command (TEC) and the Operational Test Command. These latter two organizations would be responsible for ensuring, respectively, that the MICLIC satisfied the requirements of the ORD and that a typical Army crew could effectively employ the system. So she indicated that her office was preparing the next task order to manufacture a limited production run (low rate initial production, or LRIP) of six systems, or three for each testing command.

But that was only part of the news. She said that between the Army and the Marines, we could expect an order for three hundred systems. And that didn't include the Canadians, who had yet to submit their order. About half of the systems would be issued to units, while the other half would be stored in forward depots, prepositioned to be more readily available if needed.

I pushed Sad Sack's *on* button and he launched. He started with the origin of the FAR and the original authors' grand designs, and the intent to promote and foster small businesses, and the fundamental principle of fairness written in to all parts of the FAR, etc. About the middle of the second lap he finally got to the point that it was patently unfair of the government to demand that a small business like Tiger be more than 50 percent responsible for the production of such a large number of highly sophisticated systems, etc. At that point he paused for his first breath, giving Col. Harvey just enough of an opportunity to ask what we were talking about. I pushed Sad Sack's *off* button before he could relaunch into another Sadsackian monologue and replied that we were referring to the modification requiring Tiger to perform greater than 50 percent of the effort.

Col. Harvey looked at Mam.

Mam looked at us. "Boys, the Army didn't initiate that requirement, and neither did Jim Strack. I asked for it."

Sad Sack and I looked at each other just to make sure we had heard correctly. From the look on each other's face, we had. And it took a few seconds for that to register and to form an appropriate response. Which was a good thing, because what was cooking in my brain wouldn't have been appropriate for mixed and delicate company, like ladies and colonels. And whatever category Mam fell into.

"Let me explain. I didn't trust Strack from the start and I knew he had bigger ideas than just the engineering part. So to keep any other role off the table, and to remove any temptation to bugger us up, I just asked Col. Harvey to modify the contract. And that's that."

Sad Sack and I looked at each other just to make sure—well, just like above. Including my unspoken comments.

"Say, Mam. Have you just happened to consider how we are going to do fifty percent? Plus?"

"Boys, it's time for a little road trip. And the plan isn't fifty percent. It's all the rest."

So we all got into our cars and followed Mam. She headed out of Redstone Arsenal and west on the highway, signaling a right turn into the airport. Well, as the fellas at the sewer plant said when the tank wall burst, "This is going to get interesting."

But she didn't turn into the airport terminal area and headed instead to the industrial park adjacent to the airport and pulled up in front of a very large two-story building that looked something like a manufacturing facility. In fact, it looked exactly like a manufacturing facility because that's what the sign in front said it was. More precisely, it said that this was the Tiger Manufacturing Corp Huntsville Facility.

My first thought was that it was an amazing coincidence that there were two Tiger Corps in Huntsville, Alabama. My second thought was, *Please, let there be two different Tiger Corps in Huntsville, Alabama.* Unfortunately, Mam got out of her car, walked over to mine, and asked what I thought. I gave her a thumbs-up and a grin, all the while thinking about my only previous manufacturing experience: the wooden car I entered into the Boy Scout Pinewood Derby when I was eleven, only to have two wheels fall off in the first six feet. I had the uneasy feeling that it just might be the high point of my manufacturing experience.

The facility had previously belonged to Remington, the arms, electric razor, and typewriter manufacturer. Huntsville and Alabama had lured Remington to town (for a cool seventy million dollars in incentives) and Remington announced it would build an eight-hundred-square-foot facility (it did) and employ two thousand people (it didn't, topping out at around five hundred) and pay them above scale. And for a while you couldn't go anywhere in town without hearing country music legend Larry Gatlin sing "An American with a Remington," a song about blowing away foreign—presumably Muslim and not Yankee—fanatics with a Remington—presumably a rifle and not a typewriter. Anyway, it was a big hit until Remington went bankrupt, closed the plant, and skipped town with a bunch of good ole Alabama redneck fanatics, toting Smith & Wessons, on their tail. So the first order of business was clearly to write a song about Tiger Corp and a MICLIC. Didn't sound too melodic to me, but if anybody can write that song, ole Larry is the man.

Well, she tossed me the keys and sped off, so Sad Sack and I let ourselves in. The place was enormous, but since I didn't know anything about factories or what size we needed to manufacture MICLICs, it might have been way too small or maybe just right. And it was clean and shiny; the equipment, brand new forklifts, floors and windows all sparkled. There were three receiving bays that butted up to the loading dock, assembly lines, welding stations, a section for assembling the electronic components, and a bunch of other things that I assumed were important, but since I didn't know what they were, I couldn't be sure.

Sad Sack seemed similarly impressed. But he had a gleam in his eye.

"You know who Mam is going to have run this operation." It wasn't a question.

"Knowing her, she's already hired someone that knows how to do this stuff, and odds are that he or she is waiting for us in the office."

"Nope. Old buddy, I'm pretty sure it's you."

"Nope back at you. She knows what I can and can't do, and there is no way she would risk millions of dollars on me being able to figure out what to do here."

"Do you want to bet?"

"Are you kidding? That's easy money. No way would Mam make that mistake. You're on."

And that's how Sad Sack got the biggest steak and a whole bottle of very expensive wine at Conner's Steak House. I had a salad. And no wine. Wasn't even offered any.

I did have one good idea. I took Grease Monkey's bill of material for the prototype and multiplied everything by three hundred. Then added 50 percent more. And added six hundred gallons of Army green paint. And that's all I had. I had no clue where I would buy all that stuff, but I opened up an eBay account just in case. I said it was a good idea; I didn't say it would get me very far.

And then I had a second good idea, which may be a personal best two in a row.

"Grease Monkey, this is Griffin Finnegan. What are you up to these days?"

He said he was taking a self-defense course. That is, he was learning how to fly a drone so that I couldn't kill him. At least by drone.

So I decided to put the budding and untalented comedian out of business and hired a plant manager.

After that I got a string of good ideas. Not necessarily unaided but I'm still counting them. Soon I had several lists, including all the plant personnel we needed along with above average labor rates, a better bill of material (turns out that it wasn't just a multiplication drill), another list of the equipment we would need all the way from oxygen and acetylene cylinders to break-room furniture to OSHA posters. And I had a good idea how to get everything—I turned the personnel list over to our VP of personnel and all the other ones over to Grease Monkey.

And that broke the string because although Grease Monkey came through like a champ, our personnel VP crapped out. It wasn't exactly her fault; although we offered well above average salaries and benefits, there was too much new manufacturing going on in Huntsville, including a new Mazda-Toyota joint venture automobile manufacturing plant. So we had tough competition, and the added disadvantages of no one ever having heard of Tiger Manufacturing Corp before, and not being able to tell anyone what they would be working on. So after three weeks, our two-column list of positions and names was a one-column list and all blank spaces but one. I had tagged Derek to be the quality control manager, but soon the work we agreed to do for other companies piled up and Derek said he was scheduled for sixteen hours a day doing that. I reminded him that there would still be eight hours left over, and although he didn't disagree with the math, he did come down on the other side of the premise that those eight hours belonged to me. So after two weeks, not only had I not filled any position, I had lost the one I thought would be automatic.

Needless to say I started to become something other than my normally pleasant self, although everybody said they hadn't really noticed. Which, come to think of it, might not really have been the compliment I thought it was at the time.

So I started moping, until Grease Monkey, who got most of the grief, told me to hop in his car because he was taking me to lunch. He said that he didn't really expect me to snap out of my funk, but with my mouth full he could at least get a little reprieve. So he drove me up to Hazel Green to Henry's place. Henry wasn't there but Lefty, Henry's right-hand man, seated us and told us that they had just added hushpuppies to the menu, and the first order was on the house.

I had skipped breakfast, so I ordered the rib plate and the hushpuppy side and had just about completed it when Henry came in, greeted us, and sat down.

"Mister Griff, y'all look a bit down. What's the matter?"

I just sat there glumly, so Grease Monkey filled him in on my problem, although he was kind enough to call it *our* problem. Henry sat there calmly and nodded his head a couple of times.

"How many folks y'all lookin' to hire?"

Grease Monkey looked at me and when I didn't seem inclined to answer, he popped in with: "About forty."

"Woowhee. That's a passel of folks. What kind of jobs y'all lookin' to fill?"

And with that, Grease Monkey promptly pulled out the jobs listing from his pocket and handed it to Henry.

"Hmmm. Uh-huh. Uh-huh. Yep. Okay."

"Mister Griff, if y'all be ready tomorrow at nine o'clock, I jus' might be able to have some folks drop by to apply."

Well, that cheered me up a little. But I was just a bit dubious.

"Henry, just to be clear, this work might take a couple of years, so don't pack your servers, cooks, busboys, and Lefty into a van and send them my way thinking that a couple of days will work. Besides, I have to consider the good of mankind, and I'm not sure that you closing the restaurant for even a couple of days will put me on the right side of mankind's ledger."

"Shucks Mister Griff. Don't worry none. My folks can cook up lunch, but I don' claim they can build your clicky device. No sir, the folks that'll be comin' are first-rate clicky device builders."

So I paid the bill (because Grease Monkey's idea of taking me to lunch was exclusively coming up with the idea and driving) and headed for the door.

Around lunch time, on a clear day, the sun hits the glass door in just a way that the door reflects the images in the restaurant. So I saw Henry and Grease Monkey high-fiving behind me.

The next morning at eight thirty, there was a forty-person line outside the office door. The first thing I noticed when we started taking applications was that they were lined up in the order of the positions on the list. In fact, they each announced, "I'm here for position number one." Or two. Etc.

The second thing I noticed was that they were the vets from the VFW. They all looked somewhat familiar, and I remembered some of the nicknames like Grunt, DAT, Whirlybird, Lieutenant Dan, and both Docs. The whole process was very orderly, with a lot of "Yes, sir" and "Yes, ma'am," and we told them we would let them know in a couple of days. The whole thing only took about two hours; if there is one thing the military teaches you how to do well, it's to fill out forms.

I met with Grease Monkey that afternoon and we discussed the applicants, one by one. I told him it was his call, and he would have to live with his choices—for better or worse. I reminded him that not only were specific skills required, but these mostly Vietnam-era vets would have to be on their feet all day and remain focused on their work for that entire time. (We decided we would work four nine-hour days and then only half a day on Friday.) Grease Monkey assured me that they were the crew he wanted based on the logic that he and Henry had only invited the ones he wanted to show up. And that excluded a couple that had some very good precision manufacturing experience, but Grease Monkey thought that running a meth lab wasn't as good a fit as those aspirants thought it was.

So, we had our manufacturing crew. Grease Monkey ran the operation, Whirlybird and Grunt were foremen; the two Docs ran the safety program; DAT was the warehouseman; Lieutenant Dan maintained the equipment, and so on. And then there was Darlene "No Nickname," who had been in the finance corps and kept our books. Rumor had it that Darlene never made mistakes, but she had been married and divorced three times and had a "Puff Daddy" tattoo on her arm that had been altered so many times that most thought it was a Vietnamese cuss word. So by my count, Darlene had made at least four mistakes; but she kept our books perfectly.

The bright side of not being able to hire right away was that we were able to stockpile materials in one of the bays and Grease Monkey arranged and organized the assembly line for the MICLIC. So when the newly hired crew showed up on Monday morning, and after they held a morning formation and got their orientation briefing, they were efficiently marshalled off to their workstations, shown their jobs, and put to work.

Each morning started the same, with the morning formation, an updated orientation, and a safety briefing. The safety briefing never changed: "Keep your noses, fingers, toes, and peckers away from moving parts." Crude but effective; I'm pretty sure that everyone left everyday with everything they came in with.

We only had one incident. One of the youngest vets, an Afghanistan veteran, started agitating about unionizing and kept going until some started to take him seriously. And that was his mistake. Most vets, particularly in the South, and particularly those working on a system that would save military lives, aren't strong union enthusiasts. One of my classic understatements. So when it reached the point that the agitating turned aggravating, they tossed him into an empty fifty-five gallon drum and rolled him around the floor several times.

The first thing he did when they stopped and let him out of the drum—no, make that the second thing—nope, it was the third—the third thing he did, after puking all over the floor and then being forced to clean it up, was to denounce all unions, all union members, and everything else that wasn't 100 percent true-blue American. In fact, he started harassing the vending machine guy because he didn't tuck his shirt in, and everybody knows that's how union members dress. He kept that up until the vending machine guy gave him a free Mountain Dew and they entered into an uneasy truce.

We expected the first week to be slow, so when by Friday noon there were only three assembled MICLICs in the storage bay, we weren't disappointed. The first week we instituted our Friday lunchtime tradition with Henry backing his barbecue truck into the bay and serving ribs, pulled pork, and all the sides, including hushpuppies.

Then Lieutenant Dan showed how he got his nickname. He plugged his amplifier into Henry's speakers, pulled a Fender guitar from his work locker, and proceeded to raise the roof. Almost literally. He did blow out three windows and the assembly lines were knocked out of whack and had to be reset the following Monday morning. A keg appeared from somewhere, you're welcome, and our first week in the manufacturing business ended to everyone's satisfaction.

The next week was pretty much the same except we were able to get to eight completed assemblies, just short of the ten we had planned on. So we were pretty optimistic and feeling pretty good after our Friday bash, but part of that may have been because we turned Henry's speakers halfway down.

So with everything going so well, you just know that the bluebird of happiness is going to fly up and crap on you. And of course, you'd be right.

The news came in the form of a phone call on Friday evening.

Chuck Bergen told me that he was officially delivering a Stop Work notice and that on Monday we were to provide him our documented costs to date, as well as a projection of what it would cost to dismantle the manufacturing operation, satisfy any commitments or obligations we had made, and turn out the lights. And he wasn't permitted to comment further.

Mam, Sad Sack, and I met on Saturday morning to look at each other and wonder what the hell had just happened. We actually met to see if anybody had any answers, and since no one did, we resorted to Plan B and just looked and wondered. Sad Sack explained that the Stop Work notice was likely preliminary to a Termination notice, which might take some time to prepare. The good news, his air quotes added, was that we wouldn't be terminated for poor performance—the government would have had to establish a record of that, and of course there wasn't any—but instead we would be terminated for the convenience of the government. Which is another way of saying they didn't want the MICLIC anymore but since they were changing their mind, and it didn't reflect on us, the government would make us whole and reimburse us for all allowable costs. And pay us for the eleven MICLICs we did produce.

Small consolation. To her credit, Mam retained her composure. Certainly far better than Sad Sack and I did. So after impugning the parentage of everybody in the Terrestrial Sensors office, and then everybody in the Army, and then the rest of the government, we agreed that we were likely to hear more on Monday, at which point we would impugn everybody else that we hadn't already covered, and maybe some of those we had a second time.

Somehow, the weekend passed. There was a John Wayne marathon on cable TV that helped. I was able to keep my mind mostly off the Stop Work notice by reciting the Duke's lines along with him until I must have gotten a little carried away heading the herd north and the neighbors banged on the wall and told me to shut up. I did, but only because I fell asleep about then. I had decided to have a drink every time Duke went into a saloon. Do you know how many saloons John Wayne went into during his movie career? Me either; I lost count. But I had far more to drink in those saloons than he did.

On Monday morning we reconvened in Mam's office. We were expecting a call from Col. Harvey, but instead Mam got a text asking us to come to the Huntsville office—Col. Harvey had flown down over the weekend to talk with us personally. I joked that maybe we should give them our choices for a last meal, but nobody thought that was funny—and it wasn't.

Col. Harvey was waiting for us at the door and ushered us into her office and closed the door. It was just her—Chuck was absent.

"Mam, Griffin, Mr. Sanders, I'm afraid I have some good news."

That seemed oddly put. I don't know why she was afraid of good news, or why we should be, and her demeanor suggested something very different than good news.

"The White House has decided to wind down our almost twenty-year war in Afghanistan. They will be announcing a troop withdrawal schedule, and along with that, we'll be consolidating our forces onto a few key bases, and we'll shift from active operations throughout the country to preparing to hand over the war to the Afghan army."

Sure sounded like good news to me. But the mood hadn't changed so there was something more. And then Col. Harvey got real somber.

"I'm afraid that means we won't be ordering the rest of the MICLICs. Congress is overwhelmingly in favor of cutting military programs and diverting the money to local projects. Between you and me, we might have avoided that, but it's an election year and the White House just put another large serving of pork on the table."

I was outraged. I don't mean the normal kind of outraged that everybody says they are when they are just really mildly pissed off. I mean the vein-in-the-neck-throbbing, red-faced, spit-flying, incoherent, hopping-up-and-down outrage that some people practice when they want to get on TV. But mine was real.

"You may not think much of me as a program manager or

government contractor, but . . ." Here I paused to give them a chance to protest, but Col. Harvey just nodded, and Mam rolled her eyes. So I continued, more fired up than before. "But I spent twenty years in the Army, mostly in the tough places, and I know two things for sure. First, we'll be fighting again soon in some other shit-pot place, and those bad guys will have learned from the Taliban what was effective against us, and IEDs and roadside bombs are not only effective, they are cheap and easy to make and use. And when we finally develop a defense against them that will save soldiers' lives, we're going to piss it away so that some lard-ass congressman can build a senior center named after him and get himself reelected. They're wrong. Wrong, wrong, wrong!"

I didn't really expect the Army Band to come in and start playing the "Star Spangled Banner," or even a standing ovation. But I expected some reaction.

Nothing. Well, Sad Sack started to clap, but when he saw that no one else was, he stopped.

"Griffin. That was very moving. However, understand that just a few of the Army leaders have also served in those tough places and have also figured out exactly what you just said. And discussed it with the members of Congress. And got basically the same reaction you got. Two weeks ago. So let's talk about the reason I called you here to talk to you personally.

"Mam, this is completely unofficial and off the record. I'll deny having ever said anything. But do you suppose that some of your more influential friends might be persuaded to slip a few bucks our way to fund MICLIC? I have to tell you that we can't reimburse you for any persuasion you might have to come up with."

Mam just smiled. She later told me that the best way to make sure something was off the record is to make sure it's never said in the first place. But nobody had any doubts about what she would do.

A week later, congressmen and women started popping up all over declaring just how staunchly they supported "our" military men and women and how they wanted to ensure that blah, blah, blah and how unconscionable it was for the other party to abandon blah, blah, blah. And soon they were tripping over each other to climb onto the fund-the-military bandwagon, even though they didn't really mean it.

But they meant it enough to fund MICLIC for the full three hundred systems, so even though Canada bowed out, we were back in business.

It took a week to get back into full swing, but two weeks later we were cranking out twelve systems a week, and even set up another line for an order placed by Lockheed Martin's Theater High Altitude Air Defense Program, but I'm not allowed to tell you anything about that.

And then we were done. At least, with the MICLIC production.

Contract closeout is supposed to be anticlimactic, but we were sweating the audit and all the paperwork we had to submit. We even had OSHA stop by for an inspection, but Grease Monkey invited them on Friday afternoon and after a barbecue lunch and rocking with Lieutenant Dan, they forgot to inspect anything and gave us a 100 percent.

Mam had us include every last nickel in our final bill, up to and including every Friday barbecue lunch, and to our surprise, the government accepted all the costs. Except the barbecue; I figure that was because we never invited Chuck Bergen, so he couldn't verify those expenses. We even got a certificate from the secretary of the Army, with his personal challenge coin attached, which Mam framed with a gold frame and a purple matte and hung in her office.

And then we were really done. And in dozens of Army motor pools, and in several forward supply depots, are three hundred MICLICs that to this day haven't come out of their crates.

Epilogue

HERE'S WHAT HAPPENS TO ALL THE CHARACTERS you care about, and all the other ones too.

X1. X1's Mayan diet fad died out pretty quickly and she kind of disappeared from public view. A couple of years ago, she made some public appearances claiming to be the real inventor of Spanx and threatened all kinds of lawsuits, until the real inventor threatened countersuits. At that point, X1 made even more public appearances apologizing profusely and claiming that she had an alcohol and drug problem and was going to seek help right away. She checked into a facility, but when no one there had ever heard of her, and the press wasn't at all interested either, she promptly checked herself back out, went on a bender, and disappeared again. Her latest escapade is marketing green T-shirts with a picture of a beer mug and "Hey, it's St. Patrick's Day Somewhere" printed on the front, but neither the T-shirts nor the slogan seems to be catching on.

X2. X2 was appointed deputy district attorney for Kansas City, and a year later made a run to be elected district attorney. She campaigned viciously, bombarding TVs with commercials trumpeting that "under her leadership, criminal prosecutions had risen 300 percent," but lost badly when the incumbent's ads pointed out that this wasn't a good thing, especially when criminal convictions had dropped 50 percent.

The week after the election, the DA was found floating face down in one of the Kansas City fountains. That same day, X2 held a press conference assuring all citizens that she was outraged and would not rest until the perpetrators of this heinous crime had been brought to justice. Months later, no arrests had yet been made but presumably X2 is working comfortably in her new office as Kansas City DA.

On a completely unrelated note, buried in the same edition of the *Kansas City Star* that reported the murder, was a small item about a truck being pulled over on I-70 leaving Kansas City, with two "Middle Eastern-looking" men in the cab and "the oddest collection of plumbing supplies" in the back.

Mom and Dad. Mom's lottery winning streak continued and she became a minor celebrity, at least locally. She didn't hit any really big jackpots—a couple thousand here and there, but here and there proved to be pretty steady. Enough to get rid of the junk cars in the yard, plant some bushes, and remove most of the weeds. A grateful neighborhood placed a nice, permanent *Yard of the Month* sign in the front yard even though there wasn't a real competition.

As they started to buy nicer and nicer things, the Snake Pit had to get bigger and bigger, and at some point snakes found it inviting, including one particular copperhead, who having taken up residence, resented Dad's intrusion and bit him on the arm. Dad applied some external home remedy of mud, honey, and Tabasco, and an internal remedy of a half bottle of booze, neither of which is recommended by the American Medical Association for treatment of snakebites, so Mom got him to the hospital in time to save his life but not his arm. Once he was well enough, Dad would take a plastic chair and sit behind the yard sign, prop his good arm on the sign and with his pearl (plastic) handled Colt, blast away at anything that was moving in the grass, weeds, woods, and other people's lawns. Once the pet cat death count reached five, without a single known snake casualty, the neighborhood took the sign away and Mom took the Colt away.

So now they just travel a lot. They seem to enjoy it, almost as much as the neighbors.

Guy, the bartender. Guy made good on his plan to sell the Tampa bar and move to the islands. He quickly established himself as the most popular bartender in one of the trendiest bars on the island, took up with the owner's soon-to-be ex-wife, who—pending the divorce settlement—is also the soon-to-be owner. Guy's fame soon proved to be his undoing, as he entered one of those reality shows where bartenders around the world compete for the honor of being named the world's best, was spotted by some of his former Army buddies, and promptly arrested for about a dozen crimes he committed while serving in Vietnam. Fortunately, the statute of limitations had expired for all the crimes he was originally charged with, at which point he was charged with desertion, which has no statute of limitations. Not surprisingly, his real name isn't Guy.

He called me up. "Man, I really need a favor. My hearing is next week, and I need you to be a character witness."

"Well, from what I know of your character, you really don't need me. Besides, if I'm going to fudge that much in court, there is something I need from you."

He considered that for a while. "No. I will not do that. There are somethings worse than serving time at Leavenworth or even a firing squad."

But his new wife was apparently listening in, and after a muffled conversation, he came back on. "Yankees suck."

"That was beautiful. Okay, now uncross your fingers and say it again."

Muffled conversation. "Red Sox don't suck."

"Close enough. Where do I have to go and what do I have to do?"

Turns out it didn't matter because the Army dropped all charges the next day. I blocked his telephone number and reported his email as spam, but he sent me a half dozen telegrams before I called Western Union and told them he was a known terrorist, and they should forward all telegrams to the FBI.

Guy and I still exchange Christmas cards.

Jim Strack. Jim stayed on at that company for a few more years before all of the senior officer contacts that he knew retired and moved on, and he wasn't as close to the next cohort that took their place. And there was a new batch of more recently retired generals that were ready to take his place, for less money, so one day he got his pink slip and packed up. A few smaller companies were interested, but they weren't the heavy hitters that Jim wanted to work for, which is another way of saying that they weren't offering the money he had been making. So he got religion.

He became the Midwest Regional manager for the Gideons, the folks that put thousands of Bibles in hotel rooms, only thanks to Jim, they stopped that. He convinced the Gideons that they could just put a plastic card with a Bible app QR code in the nightstand and save hundreds of thousands of dollars. What he didn't figure on was that if someone wanted a digital bible on their phone, there were already plenty of free Bible apps available, and most of the people that read Bibles in hotel rooms think the Gideons are a cult and aren't about to download "that mumbo-jumbo," even if they knew how. So when that idea went bust, the Gideons went back to putting printed Bibles in hotels and Jim went back to the street, where I have kind of lost track of him.

Chuck Bergen. Of course, it turned out that Chuck isn't quite the evil schemer I imagined him to be, and all things considered, he isn't a bad guy. He represents the established, mostly successful, way of doing business and every business, including federal ones, need people like him to be their steady tiller in troubled waters. Of course, that doesn't necessarily mean they need them where they happen to be, especially if, as in Chuck's case, his established way of doing things became more and more at odds with the progressive elements of Army procurement who favored change over continuity. So Chuck was transferred to the Terrestrial Sensors station in Nome, Alaska where he keeps watch on something in the Bering Sea. I don't know if it watches back. Although it's true that you really can't fire a career civil servant if they are just two years away from full retirement with a pension and benefits, you can pretty much just send them to any hellhole you can imagine, and they'll likely agree to go. In the immortal words of Col. Harvey, "I own his heart, soul, and balls." Speaking of which, I sent him a box of orange colored golf balls and wished him well. He said he would let me know if he ever got a chance to use them.

Col. Harvey. This one turned out very strangely. Col. Harvey was certainly a rising star in the Army Acquisition community, guaranteed promotion to at least brigadier general—one star—and rumored to be fast-tracking to even greater rank. She was in line to become the program manager of one of the Army's biggest programs, when she just disappeared. She had cleaned out her office in Fort Belvoir and a search of her desk yielded nothing more than an old-fashioned coin purse and a piece of paper with the name *Dr. Chumley* and *Akron* written on it. Investigators were baffled because they couldn't even determine whether the note had been written by Col. Harvey; no one could find any examples of her handwriting to compare. The investigation found that the only Dr. Chumley in Akron had last been seen in 1950 but there had been reported sightings all over the country in the years since. After six months, the investigators still didn't have a clue, literally and figuratively, and filed Col. Harvey in the cold case missing person's file. After a while, people began to question whether she ever really existed.

Sad Sack. Sad Sack stayed on with Tiger Corp for a couple more years, and then decided to become a consultant instead. So Tiger went from his employer to his biggest customer, and since he is now charging three hundred bucks an hour, he didn't bother looking for other customers and turns down all those that look for him. Oh, and he married Giggles. Which was quite a surprise since everybody kind of assumed that Giggles was spending all her time with Derek, and they would eventually get together. Regardless, it turned out to be a good match, as Sad Sack lost about a hundred pounds and Giggles found them, so they kind of met in the middle. Sad Sack goes by Harlan now. He dropped the 'd' and said it stood for "dinero," so now he is just Harlan Sanders without the dinero, which considering what he charges is *mierda de toro*. And Giggles's name is really . . . damn, I can never remember her real name.

Derek. Derek has stayed on at Tiger as its chief scientist and has been responsible for many of our current successes. In fact, not much has changed with Derek over the last several years. He still works about seventy hours a week, and when not in the office, coaches youth basketball and hockey. Derek did market his mouse icon idea and when nobody was interested, he started up his own company. So now thousands of computer users have Star Wars spaceship mouse icons blasting other users' spaceship icons to smithereens. Coincidentally, national productivity in the service sector has dropped 3 percent over the last several years; each economist has a different theory. Actually, most have several different and contradictory theories because economists would rather be right than consistent. At least I presume so, but so far, they pretty much haven't been either.

Mamzelle Reynard. As Tiger's success soared, her interest in running the business seemed to wane. She seemed more and more distracted, and for a time, was spending more time running her barbecue empire. She was also more and more involved in politics, or at least, in supporting politicians, who kept beating a steady path to her door. Two months after the new president took office, Mam was nominated as the assistant secretary of the army for acquisition, logistics and technology. Her confirmation hearing lasted less than an hour; she read a prepared statement, and then glared at the senators who decided they didn't have any questions and limited their remarks to how pleased they were to confirm her.

So she and Henry moved to Washington, DC where Mam soon ingratiated herself with the Secretary of the Army, who encouraged her to "shake things up around here," and then promptly moved her office as far away from his as he could. This of course didn't deter Mam from striding down the Pentagon halls, sending generals scurrying for cover, to confer with the Secretary when she felt he needed her advice. Which made him wish he was more un-gratiated, but not to the point that he dared ask Mam to stay away.

Besides, Mam did shake things up, and Army procurement and acquisition became much more efficient, which may overstate it a bit because there is only so much that is humanly possible. So things became much less inefficient. She only got into trouble once, when her program to alter the weather to enhance friendly combat operations or hinder enemy operations proved to be technologically beyond our reach, principally because we couldn't predict the weather reliably enough to employ the right technology in a given situation. So Mam had to testify before the House Armed Services Committee, where she read a prepared statement and then glared at the representatives who decided they didn't have any questions; however, they all went on record praising her for her efforts. Notwithstanding the fact that altering the weather is against the Geneva Convention.

Henry's barbecue restaurant became *the* place to be seen in DC He alternated tables with red and blue tablecloths, which initially kept everybody pretty well segregated, until they figured out that the food was equally good at every table. So lunch became more of a bipartisan activity, and conversation remained civil, almost cordial. As long as the topic was barbecue. Henry had to impose that rule, with violators subject to excommunication. That concept had to be explained to several of the more liberal patrons, who quickly became converts. Or as Henry puts it: "See the light or see the exit."

Understandably, they became fixtures in the "Top Five Power Couples" lists generated annually by various national publications. Last year, they beat out the president and the first lady.

Finnegan. One of the things Mam hadn't counted on was a Department of the Army JAG determination that active ownership of a defense company was a conflict of interest with her new job. Consequently, she entrusted me with the direct management of Tiger Corp. Or as she more bluntly put it, "There are probably several dozen others that would do a better job than you, but I couldn't trust them as much as I trust you. I know you'll always do the right thing, even if half the time you can't figure out what that is. So I'm stuck with you."

It's a good thing my head doesn't inflate with praise. As it is, I'll have to go out and buy a smaller hat. The only instruction she gave me was that I had to report to Reginald, who she made the trustee of the company.

"A line or two in an annual Christmas card ought to do it."

And with that, she left, and I was in charge.

Well, it's turned out that I can figure out what the right thing is—most of the time—and Tiger continues its spectacular growth. We were the fastest growing small business in the country for three years in a row and continue to be the darling of the government and other businesses. We now have fifty full time employees in our main office and have set up branches in Colorado Springs, Sunnyvale, and Dallas. Our manufacturing plant is going full steam ahead and we periodically have to go to two shifts to meet demand. Most of the original vets have stayed on, and the new recruits are mostly vets too.

We have moved into our own building in the upscale part of Research Park; my office is about the same size as the one I shared with Derek, but fully paneled and decorated with awards, pictures of me with the high and mighty, and assorted other mementos of our successes. And behind my door, which I close when I need to think deep and ponderous thoughts, is a certain poster that I occasionally consult and think snow.

And I took the plunge again. She is a petite brunette, with a voice like honeyed magnolia—if that's a thing—and we got hitched. The preacher said, "Do you . . ." and I said, "I do" and she said, "I do," and the congregation said "Amen," and Della said, "Bless their hearts."

Last week she came home and said she had news, and then for about a half an hour, without stopping for breath, she told me all her plans for a nursery, and schools, and other stuff which was probably important, but I drifted off a bit.

And I told her about my Class VI Store College Education Fund plan.

Author's Notes, Excuses, and Alibis

I AM NOT FINNEGAN, but we sort of ran in the same circles, although he would have come along about twenty years after I did. I would recognize him, and he would recognize me, and I expect we would have gotten along well, even if I felt that he needed a periodic kick in the pants. Make that daily. So I wrote about him as if I would have liked to have a beer—or a martini—with him and swap stories. The less true, the better. And this book is what his story might have been.

So Finnegan is my everyman, the kind of guy that sometimes succeeds, sometimes fails, and more often just hangs with the pack and lets the Earth go round without touching him. I believe that at least once in everybody's life, on one of those earthly revolutions, fate reaches out and does touch a person. Sometimes the touch is so light it isn't even noticed. In Finnegan's case, fate reaches out and grabs him by the—we'll say ear—and forces him to go places where he isn't comfortable.

That's how I have tried to present Finnegan. He grows up (you can't see me, but I'm making air quotes here) in a system in which he is comfortable; a wise-cracking smart-ass who pushes only as hard as he needs to, has experiences that test him (he passes, a solid C), drives on, and when the dust settles, tells a funny story about it.

And then fate puts him in a place where there are bottom lines, not missions; spreadsheets, not bayonets; production schedules, not training schedules; and strangers with whom he doesn't share common experiences, or even a common language. The experiences still test him, but he can't tell if he passes. And he can't find that many things that are funny, and if he once in a while does, it's a dark humor.

Yet Finnegan, and all those like him, does succeed after transition. It's kind of hard to explain why, but it has something to do with being mission-oriented; using the tools issued, and at times improvising; developing and following plans and schedules and getting everyone he is responsible for to do the same; bonding with strangers and forming cohesive groups; being self-disciplined; being tested and overcoming adversity; and maintaining the proper perspective, which when appropriate includes humor because things aren't all that bad when you can smile about them.

Keep that in mind, Ms. or Mr. Business Owner.

There is such a thing as a MICLIC, and the Army has it. In fact, they've had it since 1988. The M58 Mine Clearing Line Charge is a trailer-mounted system that features a launch arm from which a rocket-propelled string of C-4 explosive-filled pouches plays out and is then detonated to create an approximately 100-yard long, ten-yard wide lane through a minefield.

There are just a few tiny problems:

A. The MICLIC doesn't detect a minefield. That is done the old-fashioned and painful way.
B. The C-4 pouches don't always detonate. So combat engineers get to run out into the minefield and place blocks of explosive with time fuses to detonate the C-4 pouches that don't explode. While they are at it, they string a line of white tape down the middle of the lane so the following forces can see where the lane is, especially at night.
C. If everything works, there is a cleared and marked ten yard wide lane. This means that the mines just to the outside of that lane have become very sensitive. (I think the technical

term is "pissed off.") And those mines will let everyone know just how pissed off they are when heavy vehicles like tanks come rumbling by.

D. It's not like the enemy is going to let you know how long or wide their minefield is, and since our system capabilities are not classified, we don't really expect him to make this easy for us. So this little ballet takes place again when a second MICLIC has to drive to the end of the cleared lane and do this all over again. And consider our method of determining whether or not we have passed through the minefield.

E. All this is happening while the good guys are under intense fire. The thinking is that if the enemy has gone to the effort to put in a large minefield to block our advance, there are a bunch of little guys with big guns showing their appreciation for our reenactment of *Swan Lake*.

So yeah, there is room for improvement.

That improvement came in the form of the Grizzly Combat Mobility Vehicle, or CMV. The Army Engineer School began development in the 1980s, working with a concept vehicle, and after almost twenty years, cancelled that program in 2001 after having produced exactly one prototype.

Meanwhile, the Marines were developing their own system, M1150 Assault Breacher Vehicle, or ABV, or just Breacher, which they finally fielded in 2009 and sent to Afghanistan. It must have worked well enough because the Army decided to buy some for themselves and began fielding it, which it is still doing to this day.

If you think that my ideas for the design of my fictitious MICLIC is whacky, the Breacher has a dozer blade, and a large steel-tined plow to plow up mines, with a high lift adapter that allows the crew to change back and forth between the plow and the dozer blade, a MICLIC, and two lane marking systems. And a machine gun. All mounted on a M1 Abrams tank chassis. Now admit it, you thought my Rube Goldberg-Swiss Army Knife design was whacky; Rube and his team established their bona fides on the Breacher.

So why do we need another system? Because tanks don't go where trucks go, and vice versa. We don't have any capabilities for wheeled vehicles similar to what the Breacher provides for tracked vehicles. By the way, don't put any stock in my concept. I can think of a dozen reasons why it wouldn't work. Unless of course it does. Which would be a real trick because I made up some of the science.

After nearly eighteen years in Huntsville (actually, Madison), I've become thoroughly Southern. Having lived all over, including big cities, I appreciate the pace of life; the consideration people give to one another; the way people speak—both the manner and the accent; the overall quality of life; and the fewer stressors than one finds in the great Northern cities. This year, *US News & World Report* named Huntsville the best place to live in the whole country. They got it right.

So stay away! That's right, stay away. Over these eighteen years, things have changed too much. All the cotton fields are gone, replaced by housing communities, you can't get into a restaurant without waiting for an hour, and traffic has gotten significantly worse. It used to take me fifteen minutes to be able to drive clear across town. Now it takes eighteen, and sometimes as much as twenty. I'm warning you.

Since you aren't going to pay attention to my warning anyway, you are liable to see me all over. When you are driving, I'll be the guy in the white SUV yelling at you to go home. And I'll make fun of your accent and your inability to understand the way we speak. Which is the proper way.

✩ ✩ ✩

And speaking of the way we speak, clearly Della's favorite expression is about blessing people's hearts. And not just her, but just about every little white- or silver-haired old lady in Alabama has the same favorite. But nobody else uses it. It's like there is a little old lady debutante ball, where upon reaching seventy, little old ladies have a soiree or cotillion or whatever is popular here and are then bestowed the honor of being able to use the expression. And if you have frequent conversations with little old Southern ladies, you probably have heard it so often that you don't even notice it anymore. But I do, and it always sounds kind of nice, and after a while, I was able to form some conclusions.

It's a remarkably versatile expression, and depending on context, can mean one of three things:

1. It's an elaborate thank you, honey-dipped and magnolia-scented. The non-Southern translation is, well, "thank you."
2. It's an appreciation for a well-intentioned effort made, even though the outcome wasn't all that successful. The non-Southern translation is "Nice try, chump. Better luck next time."
3. And then there's the use that translates roughly as: "Since God didn't see fit to bless your looks, your brains, or your personality, maybe He will bless your heart, but I very much doubt it." You don't hear this version as often because it is usually reserved for atheists, union members, socialists, and liberal politicians, and from the little old lady perspective, there are thankfully not a lot of those around. And Yankees. Don't forget Yankees.

Only, it's not, "bless your heart," as if it were a three-syllable single word: blessyourheart. Instead, it's a seven syllable amble—

"Buh-lay-yes yo-aah hah-aht." And is always said with a smile, no matter the context.

The point is:

If you bought this book, especially if you paid full price: Bless your heart.

If you borrowed this book, or checked it out of the library, or chose to wait for the movie: Bless your heart.

If you didn't buy this book, and don't ever intend to, I don't know how you are reading this, but: Bless your heart.

And if you hire a vet or donate to Army Emergency Relief: Bless your heart.

About the Author

BRIAN OSTERNDORF (Colonel, US Army, Ret.) is a class of 1976 US Military Academy at West Point graduate. During his twenty-eight-year career, he served as a combat engineer officer in the 1st, 2nd, 3rd, and 7th Infantry and in the 1st and 3rd Armored Divisions. He also built railroads in Brazil, was an assistant professor of mathematics at West Point, obtained two master's degrees, commanded the Army Corps of Engineers in New England, and led the Corps response team in New York City following the 9/11 attacks.

After retiring from the Army, he had a number of other jobs, retired again, and got bored. So he wrote a book. Visit his website at osterndorf2.wixsite.com/author

www.ingramcontent.com/pod-product-compliance
Lightning Source LLC
LaVergne TN
LVHW041758060526
838201LV00046B/1042